A Bram Stoker Mystery

A Mistake Through the Heart

Raymond Buckland

Bram Stoker Mysteries

CURSED IN THE ACT

DEAD FOR A SPELL

A MISTAKE THROUGH THE HEART

A MISTAKE THROUGH THE HEART

Copyright © 2015 Raymond Buckland

ISBN 978-0-9794560-3-9

Queen Victoria Press

P.O. Box 892, Wooster, OH 44691-0892

www.raymondbucklandbooks.com

To Tara and in loving memory of "Tish"

A MISTAKE

THROUGH THE HEART

London, 1881

Chapter One

Sam Green, foreman of the Lyceum stagehands, came out of Mr. Bram Stoker's office with a hangdog look on his face. I passed him as I went in.

"Cheer up, Sam. Things can't be as bad as all that," I said.

He gave me a strained smile but said nothing and hurried away. I looked after him, gave a shrug, and went in to see my boss. We were now more than two weeks into the production of *Othello* and all had gone well. Any early missteps had been overcome and we had settled into a smooth run not due to end until Saturday 2nd of July. At that time the American actor Mr. Edwin Booth would bid

1

farewell to our Lyceum Theatre and continue his tour of England.

Mr. Booth and "the Guv'nor" – Mr. Henry Irving – were alternating the roles of Othello and Iago. The first week Mr. Irving had played Othello; the second week Mr. Booth had taken that part, and so on. This week the Guv'nor was playing Iago. I had learned that Iago, as the villain of the play, was by far the most desired role for any actor and was, in fact, a particular favorite of the Guv'nor's.

My name is Harry Rivers and I am the Lyceum Theatre's stage manager. I am also personal assistant to the theatre manager, Mr. Abraham "Bram" Stoker. My boss is the oil that ensures the smooth running of the Lyceum. With over 300 employees, he has his work cut out managing everything from payroll, actors, stagehands, front-of-house personnel, plus dealing with publicity, programs, advertising, and everything else. I would say that Mr. Stoker is married to the theatre, despite the fact that he has a wife and son sharing his home in Chelsea. Rumor has it that the family union is not a happy one but I have seen no evidence of that myself.

At twenty-two years of age I am a relative newcomer to the theatre. I was orphaned at fourteen and roughly pushed out into the world to earn my bread as best I might. After a variety of employment – crossing sweeper, errand boy, newspaper seller, cab driver – I found myself as theatre doorman for a small novelty theatre on Great Queen Street, Lincoln's Inn Fields. When Mr. Irving took over the Lyceum Theatre in 1878, I applied for a position there and managed to secure it. I have been part of the Lyceum family ever since, managing to work my way up to my present position.

"Close the door, Harry."

I did so and took my usual seat in front of Mr. Stoker's desk. It was, as always, covered with playbills, invoices, notes scribbled on odd pieces of paper, newspaper cuttings and various other theatre paperwork. I thought my boss looked tired. As if to confirm my thoughts he removed his gold-rimmed spectacles, rubbed his gray green eyes and then pinched the bridge of his nose. He gave a long sigh.

"Problems, sir?"

He ran a hand through his dark auburn hair and resettled the glasses on his face. Sitting back in his chair, he forced a smile. "No more than usual, Harry. No more than usual."

"I saw Sam Green leaving," I ventured. "He didn't look happy."

He gave a shrug. "The Guv'nor was a trifle miffed with Sam. Claimed that he missed a cue last night. Asked me to have a word."

"That's not like Sam."

"No, it's not. And that's what I told the Guv'nor. Still, I had to speak to Sam about it." Mr. Stoker did not make a habit of sharing employees' grievances with me but on occasion he would ask for my opinion on something. "It was a minor infraction. Apparently Sam has got his head into a book that will not release him except under the strongest duress."

"A book?" I was surprised. Sam did not strike me as the reading type. I knew that many of the stagehands in fact were not able to read, though Sam didn't have that problem. "Whatever book could have caught Sam's attention to the point of causing him to fall down on his job?"

Stoker chuckled. One of his deep, rumbling chuckles. I saw the humor restored to his eyes as he looked at me and smiled.

"*Varney the Vampire*," he said.

Varney the Vampire: or The Feast of Blood first appeared in a series of Penny Dreadfuls nearly forty years ago. As with all such offerings, it was a very cheaply-produced publication of about ten pages, selling for one penny. Surprisingly – considering its poor writing and shabby manufacture – it ran for 237 on-going chapters, being put out two or three chapters a week. Such was its popularity that eventually all of the episodes were put together and published in book form . . . over 800 pages! Apparently Sam Green discovered the lurid tale, which has recently seen rebirth as a book, and has been drawn into it to the point where it is affecting his work.

"I know of the work, of course," I said, nodding at my boss. "But I've never read it."

"You haven't missed a great deal, Harry, though it is perhaps notable in that it seemed to stir up quite an interest in the subject of vampires."

"Haven't there been other such books?" I asked.

He leaned back in his chair and stretched out his long legs under the desk. "Byron, of course, wrote a short story on the subject in 1819 titled *A Fragment* and, that same year, John Polidori penned *The Vampyre*, but both were short stories with no great depth to them. The adventures of Sir Francis Varney, in contrast, actually has a plot of sorts and well-developed characters. But I really don't think the public is yet ready for a solid work of fiction on the subject."

I thought for a moment. "You say fiction, sir," I said. "Are vampires purely fiction, or is there some basis of fact regarding them?"

I recalled Mr. Stoker briefly talking about vampires two or three months ago, when he and I somehow found ourselves in a cemetery at midnight digging up a coffin, but I didn't remember any of the details of what he told me. The event was not a memory I often dwelt upon.

"Oh yes, Harry. There is a wealth of material about vampires. You would be surprised at how many people believe in them."

"I seem to recall you once saying something about Gypsies?" I offered, hoping he might retell the tale. My boss has a love of the occult and – perhaps through his Irish birth and upbringing – seems to relish the old folktales of ghosts and goblins, fairies and fays. He frequently refers to his old grandmother's second sight and stories of blessings and curses. His education at Trinity College has led to him developing an encyclopedic knowledge of metaphysics.

"The Roma? Oh, yes. The gypsies of Transylvania, for instance, are great believers in the living dead. They firmly believe that aggrieved

5

spirits murdered by an enemy will rise from the grave to seek vengeance in the form of vampires. Such beings may strike solely at the ones who brought about their death or might, on a whim, go on a killing rampage striking indiscriminately. They are found in Hungary, Romania and elsewhere. But going much farther back than the Roma, the Persians, in ancient Mesopotamia, had tales of blood-drinking creatures, as did the Babylonians. In ancient Greece Homer himself speaks of them in his *Odyssey*. Even the Roman striges, as suckers of blood, are related."

"But you don't believe in vampires do you, sir?" For some reason I felt uneasy.

Stoker ran his hands through his hair and gazed up at the ceiling. He was silent for a moment. Then he put his hands down flat on the desk and seemed to study his fingers.

"In Sumer there was a beautiful maiden named Lilitu, who was both a harlot and a vampire, so legends tells us. The Hebrews speak of Lilith, possibly a corruption of Lilitu."

"But do you believe in them sir?" I persisted.

He looked up at me, his face serious. Then, after a moment, he smiled. "Whether or not I believe in them, Harry, will make not a jot of difference to whether or not they are real," he said cryptically. He got to his feet. "Come! Let's get about our business and leave all paranormal creatures to be or not to be, as the Bard might put it. I want to have a word with Herbert Gardner. He claims that recently there have been a number of

6

thefts from the commissariat. Pork pies and oranges, would you believe? And you might chase after Sam Green. He mentioned that he thought the seaport set in Act Two was unstable and might need another scenery anchor."

Bram Stoker was the third of seven children born to Abraham Stoker and Charlotte Thornley. He was born in a suburb of Dublin and for the first seven years of his life was afflicted with an unknown disease that rendered him unable to walk. Yet after being bedridden for so long, he recovered and went on to excel at school both academically and in sports. He continued to Trinity College where he again did well and then, to please his father, took up a position as a civil servant at Dublin Castle. Long an enthusiast of the theatre, Mr. Stoker took to writing theatrical reviews. As my boss tells it, theatre critics were not well regarded but he managed to draw attention to himself by the quality of his own reviews. One such lauded the performance of Henry Irving, when that gentleman visited Dublin and played *Hamlet* at the Theatre Royal. Mr. Irving was impressed with the evaluation and invited my boss to dine with him at the Shelbourne Hotel. The upshot of this encounter was that Mr. Irving invited Mr. Stoker to London to become manager of the Lyceum.

My boss greatly admired Mr. Irving and I, in turn, had admiration for Mr. Stoker. He and I were a strange contrast. He was over six feet tall – the same height as Mr. Irving – while I was a scant five feet and five inches. I would like to say that we were both red-headed but in truth Mr. Stoker's grey-flecked, thick auburn crown put my own carrot-red "ginger" mop to shame. Added to that, Mr. Stoker has a fine, almost military bearing and sports a luxuriant mustache and beard, while my ears protruded and I can produce nothing more than a straggly mustache no matter how hard I try! I must also own to having freckles.

Yet we seem to work well together and, in a relatively short space of time, have endured a number of extraordinary exploits, not least being lost in a London sewer while rescuing Miss Ellen Terry's young son from kidnappers.

But I digress.

I made my way backstage and tracked down Sam Green. Sam is a taciturn individual who, though working best when working alone, commands the attention and respect of all the Lyceum backstage workers. He is not much taller than myself but far stockier, though that may be a too polite way of saying it. To be blunt, his stomach has grown tremendously in the time I have known him, almost certainly due to a fondness for porter stout. I cannot truly fault him since I enjoy the black beer myself but I venture to say that I am not so apt to overindulge.

Sam's dark hair is thin and plastered down across the top of his head so that it looks as though it's painted on. He now sat perched on a stool in the Opposite Prompt corner with his head buried in a book. I made a silent bet with myself as to the title of that volume.

"'Arry!" he cried, when he finally looked up and saw me. "What's to do then?"

I pointed at the book as he came to his feet and slid it behind himself onto the stool.

"*Varney*?" I asked.

He paused before nodding and grinning. "You read it, 'Arry? Right bit o' never mind, eh? I didn't realize there was such books about."

I tried to be stern. "Sam, didn't Mr. Stoker just reprimand you for reading that book and forgetting your job?"

He waved a hand. "Nar! 'E did say as 'ow I 'ad missed a cue last night – and 'e was right there, no doubt about it. But I ain't working right now, am I? Truth be known, it's comin' up to me lunch break."

"Aren't you supposed to be anchoring a flat, or something? Mr. Stoker said you thought part of the seaport set was unstable."

"Act Two, Scene One. Right. But I can fix it, no sweat 'Arry. Don't you be afrettin'."

I looked hard at him. Sam was a good man. I indicated the book on the stool. "Best give Varney a rest, eh, Sam?"

"'Ere, 'Arry. What do you think about these vampires then?"

"What do you mean? I haven't read the book, Sam."

"No. I mean, what about 'em in general? I've 'eard there's a whole bunch of 'em in the East End. Don't you think the bluebottles should do somethin' about 'em?"

"Vampires in the East End?" I was surprised.

"Round about Mile End Old Town, so I 'ear. Fella last week was chased all down Whitehorse Lane."

"From where?"

"Eh?"

"Where did the chase start, Sam?"

"I dunno. 'E'd just come out of the Rose and Crown and . . ."

"Ah!" I cried. "That's exactly what I mean. He'd just come out of a pub, after a full night of drinking, I'd wager."

Sam tugged on an ear and sniffed. "You think?"

"I do," I said.

"But there's lots of other stories of vampires in that part of the East End," he protested.

"I don't doubt it," I said. "And lots of pubs throughout. One on just about every street corner, as I recall." But I could see that I hadn't dissuaded Sam. His heart was set on there being vampires. And the more I thought about it, I really knew nothing to say that he wasn't right. It just didn't seem possible though, I thought.

I had a few moments to myself in the early afternoon and retired to my own office to relax. "Office" is perhaps a pretentious word. I have an area with walls on three sides but the fourth side open to anyone walking by. My desk is squeezed in and the space around it peppered with scripts, programs, notes, and newspaper cuttings. Not unlike my boss's domain but with the added dimension of assorted props, broken and unbroken. A stack of spears and banners leans in one corner, a cracked cuirass and a solitary greave sit on top of a cabinet close by, a royal crown missing half its jewels rests on the corner of my desk.

With a sigh I sank down into my chair and pulled the morning newspaper to me. Earlier I had glanced at it briefly, to see if there were recent theatre reviews, but hadn't had time to look at any news. Not that I found much of interest. Leastwise, not until I turned to the penultimate page. Halfway down my eye was caught by the headline

*ANOTHER CLAIMED VAMPIRE ATTACK
IN WHITECHAPEL.*
Victualler attacked in his own tavern.

The story did not live up to the promise of the headline, I'm afraid. It seemed that a late evening customer, on being told he had drunk too much and should leave, grabbed the tavern owner – one Simon Pucker - and threw him to the ground. Kneeling astride him, the man thrust his face up close to Pucker's and bared his teeth. Pucker claimed that the man "had glowing red eyes and great fangs. I was afeared for my very life. Any minute I expected 'im to sink 'is teeth into my throat." But apparently the man did not. His breath, according to Pucker, "smelled of the sulphur and brimstone of 'ell". After slapping the tavern owner soundly across the face, the man got up and ran away.

11

I was left wondering which of the two individuals had drunk the most. I'm sure the innkeeper had sampled plenty of his own ale throughout the evening. It would be a rare such man who hadn't. That, and the need to show himself as brave in front of his regular customers, would more than explain his charge that it was a vampire who attacked. But reporting such stories was designed to sell newspapers. Thus was the rumor of vampires in Whitechapel fueled. Leastwise, that was my own theory. I hoped I was correct.

Chapter Two

I was coming back from an early dinner, and looking forward to the Monday evening performance, when I bumped into Herbert Gardner. Mr. Gardner ran the Lyceum Theatre commissariat and it was he whom my boss had gone to talk with earlier that day. Something about missing supplies, if I recalled correctly.

"Mr. Rivers!" he hailed me. "Soon be time for curtain up, I believe."

Herbert is a dour gentleman and I always thought he should have been a funeral director. I don't think I have ever seen him smile. Tall and painfully thin, he always dresses in a black frock coat with a dark green waistcoat sporting a heavy silver watch chain from which dangles an emblem of the Freemason fraternity. Completely bald, he wears a trim beard and mustache with similarly trimmed sideboards. His eyes are striking in that they appear grey and lifeless. He takes things very seriously, does Mr. Gardner.

"The inevitable first night of the week," I responded. "Mr. Irving is playing Iago tonight."

"I believe so."

"The Guv'nor is by far the better of the two in that role, I think."

He nodded but did not speak. We fell into step with one another. I don't know where he had dined but it certainly hadn't been at the *Druid's Head*, where most of the cast and crew broke bread.

"I understand that you have been having food thefts," I said. There was little small talk one could engage in with Mr. Gardner but his viands and their variety were always of interest to him.

"That is so. Mr. Stoker examined the storage pantry but could find no sign of forced entry. The amount of stolen provisions is minimal but it is nonetheless distressing. I endeavor to maintain my books without blemish."

"I'm sure you do, Mr. Gardner. Would it help if I took a look? I'm sure Mr. Stoker has been thorough but in cases like this I know that two heads can often be better than one."

The commissariat was, in effect, a refreshment saloon where audience members of the stalls, boxes, and the dress circle might purchase anything from a pint or half pint bottle of Moët's champagne to a pork pie or even an orange. Ginger beer, lemonade, and stout were the generally preferred drinks of the gods. The saloon saw much business during the intervals and slow trade during the actual performance. Gone were the days when the audience, in what was then the extended pit, brought all variety of foods into the theatre with them, some of it cooked on the pavement outside as they queued up and waited for the doors to open. The aroma had frequently risen to taunt the actors on stage.

We checked in with Bill Thomas and then made our way around to the front-of-house and to Mr. Gardner's territory. He unlocked the door into the main selling area and then took me through to the rear where stood the pantry that held the supplies.

"Here you are, Mr. Rivers," he said, indicating the plain, solid door. He pointed to the lock. "As you can see, and as Mr. Stoker was quick to point out, there is no indication of attempted forcing of the lock. No scratches or marks of any sort around it."

"On the face of it, that would then indicate that the burglar had a key," I said, leaning down to look closely at the lock.

"Impossible. Only myself and Mr. Stoker have keys. His is kept in his office – safely in his desk, he assures me – while mine is on my watch chain and never leaves my person."

I stood back and looked at the door and its surround. I had a sudden thought and stepped forward again to examine the hinges.

"Why are you studying that area, if I may ask, Mr. Rivers?"

"Look! Here, Mr. Gardner. Would you not say that these pivots are marked? See! Scratches around the upper edges."

He withdrew a pair of ancient pince-nez spectacles and, clipping them on his nose, bent to examine where I indicated. Slowly he nodded his head. He looked up at me, removing the glasses. "So what does this indicate, Mr. Rivers. I am at a loss, I must admit."

"To me, it hints at the removal of the hinges. Someone has taken a tool of some sort and pried up the hinge pins so that they may be removed; slid up and out of the main body of the hinge."

"I still don't . . . "

"Taking out the hinge pins frees the door," I cried, somewhat pleased with myself. "With the hinges gone, the door can be opened by lifting it out and away, simply sliding out of the lock, which would then be ineffectual."

"Well bless my soul! I do believe you are correct, Mr. Rivers."

There was no time before curtain-up to speak with my boss and little enough time during the intervals. It was therefore not until after the final curtain, when actors and crew were hurrying to leave the theatre and head for home, that I had a chance to tell Mr. Stoker of my theory.

"Well done, Harry! I do believe you have hit on it."

"Do you want to go and have a look, sir?" I asked.

He shook his head as he struggled into his surtout. "What you have said makes perfect sense. There is just one question that remains however."

"Sir?"

"I believe Mr. Gardner not only locks the larder door but also the outer door to the saloon itself. How did our burglar get into the saloon? Did you examine the hinges on that door?"

I shook my head. I felt a little as though the rug had been pulled out from under me. I felt like rushing around to the saloon right away to check on it.

"Don't bother checking, Harry," said Mr. Stoker, as though he could read my thoughts. "I happen to know that the outer door opens inwards so the hinges would be hidden inside when the door is closed. There is no way those hinge pins can be removed on that door while it is closed."

"Damnation!" I couldn't help myself. "I'm sorry, sir. I was just so . . ."

My boss chuckled. "No need to apologize, Harry. You did a good job with your thought on the pantry door but we will have to think further about this outer one. Now, I have to hurry home. We'll examine this tomorrow morning. Good night, Harry."

After he left, I closed up his office and then wandered around to the front-of-house and on to the saloon. There was no way I could simply go home – besides, Mrs. Bell's rooms in Chancery Lane were hardly a draw – so I had to satisfy myself with at least a cursory examination of the door in question.

Mr. Stoker was right (of course!). Mr. Gardner had long since locked up and gone home but it was obvious that the hinges to the outer door were completely hidden when closed. I stood studying it and gnawing on my lower lip.

Timothy Bidwell, front-of-house manager, was having a final walk through the stalls before leaving and saw me standing there.

"Can I help you, Mr. Rivers? I do believe Mr. Gardner has already departed."

"No. No, it's quite all right, Mr. Bidwell," I said. "I was just looking at the saloon door." Even as I said it, I thought it sounded strange. I was about to elaborate but he came over and stood beside me. "If you need to get into the saloon, I can unlock the door for you. Mr. Gardner keeps his supply larder strictly to himself, of course, but I do have a key to this outer door. It's in my office, if you . . ."

I was elated. "No! Thank you, Mr. Bidwell, that won't be necessary. But it's certainly good to know that you do have access here in case of emergency. Thank you. And good night, Mr. Bidwell."

"You seem to have solved the 'how', Harry. That only leaves the 'who?'"

Tuesday morning I told Mr. Stoker that there was a second key to the outer door of the saloon. Obviously someone had managed to take that – it seems Mr. Bidwell had not treated it with any special care – and entered the saloon, where he had removed the hinge pins to get into the larder.

"What puzzles me, sir," I said, "is why anyone would go to all that trouble just to steal a small amount of food. Mr. Gardner says that nothing else is amiss."

"I have been thinking about that, Harry," said Stoker, sipping his early morning cup of tea, brought in by old Bill Thomas. I had eschewed a cup myself since Bill tended to make it so strong that you could stand up the spoon in it. "I need to give it a little further thought but basically there is a third question – Why? If we can answer that then I think it will lead to the Who?"

"Perhaps I should spend a night lying in wait for the perpetrator, sir?" I said. I didn't fancy such a task but thought it might be worth suggesting it myself before my boss came up with the idea.

"Thank you, Harry. A good thought and I appreciate your offer, but it's not as though the thefts take place every night. Just once every few days, it would appear, and we don't know which days they will be. No, I don't think we need to make this a priority. Now that we know the means of ingress we can take precautions and secure those hinges. This might cause the person to try another tactic that, in turn, may bring about his downfall. No. Let us return our focus to the stage." He took a long drink of tea and set down the cup. "Speaking of which, Harry, I hear that those two old rascals Guy Purdy and John Saxon are at each other's throats again. I don't know what it is with those two."

"I think it started when the Guv'nor gave Mr. Purdy the role of Cassio and John Saxon the part of Roderigo. Apparently Mr. Saxon coveted the Cassio role and tried to pressure Guy into changing with him."

"The Guv'nor wouldn't go for that."

"No, sir. I know. And that's what I told the pair of them. And as it's turned out Guy Purdy has done a creditable part with Cassio. I don't know whether or not that has increased any possible bad blood between them."

19

"Both men are seasoned actors and have been with the Lyceum a goodly while," said Stoker. "They should be past such nonsense. Have another word with them, Harry, if you would? The Guv'nor likes his theatre to be a happy theatre, you know that. Tension off-stage leads to tension on-stage. He's said it a thousand times."

"Yes, sir. I'll get on to it right away."

Chapter Three

I did speak with Guy Purdy that afternoon, about the spat between himself and John Saxon but he pooh-poohed the whole idea.

"Why, John and I are the very best of friends, dear boy. You must surely know that, after all our years together."

"You had complained to me, back during the run of *Hamlet*, that Mr. Saxon was seeking to have the Guv'nor switch the *Othello* roles assigned to the pair of you," I said.

"But that was only a rumor started by that other young lad, what was his name?"

I nodded, remembering the incident. "Seth Hartzman, who turned out to be a thoroughly bad egg. But that's the point, Guy. If there really was no good reason for you and Mr. Saxon to quarrel in the first place, then why are you ...?"

"We are not, dear boy." He waved a flabby hand at me and pursed his lips. "Pshaw, Harold! Let it go. I really don't know why you hold on to these things."

"But Mr. Stoker . . ." I started to say.

"Our King of Worry, Harold. You know how Mr. Stoker takes everything to heart. A dear, sweet man whom we all love, but he embraces the cares and woes of the whole theatre. He really needs to let some of us work out our own problems."

There was a certain amount of truth in what Guy Purdy said. My boss did worry about everyone and everything, or so it seemed to me. But that was because he cared so much for the Lyceum and the Lyceum family. Perhaps I could reassure him that all was well between Guy Purdy and John Saxon. I would certainly try.

"Many thanks, Mr. Purdy. I'm glad to hear that all is well."

Again a wave of the hand from him as I left and made my way back to my office.

I had plenty of time before the evening's performance and, on a whim, decided that it might be fun to take a cab into the East End and sup at one of the local public houses where I might be able to get a first hand feeling for the locals' thoughts on vampires. I was sure that Sam Green had the wrong idea and that only an odd individual might truly believe in them, but it wouldn't hurt to make sure.

The hansom dropped me off at Whitehorse Lane and I went into the Rose and Crown public house on that corner. It was an old tavern with a low ceiling and smoke-blackened oak beams. Sawdust on the floor absorbed the many spills of beer that occurred. A small fire crackled in the fireplace. It wasn't needed for warmth at this time of the year but the patrons always seemed drawn to that area. I found a table close to the fire nook yet far enough back to not intrude on the locals' habitual seating.

A young girl, no more than twelve, in a grubby apron and far-from-clean cap, took my order and hurried away. I looked about me. A group of three old men sat closest to me, puffing on their pipes, nursing their drinks, and staring vacantly into the fireplace. Next to them were two younger men, with a pork pie and a hunk of cheese apiece, concentrating on their food and washing it down with ale. The girl brought me sliced roast beef, potatoes, peas, a half-loaf of surprisingly good hot bread, together with a tankard of porter. I settled back to enjoy the meal.

"You not from around 'ere, then," said one of the old men. It was a statement not a question and it took me a moment to realize that he was addressing me.

"No," I said. "No. I was in the area and thought I'd drop in for a bite."

He hadn't turned to look at me but continued staring into the embers of the fire and puffing on his pipe. "What you up to then?"

"Up to?" I asked.

"Why you 'ere?" demanded the man sitting next to him.

"As I said, I was in the area . . ."

"For what?" snorted the same man. "'In the area.' What's that supposed to mean?"

I hadn't prepared to be interrogated. Of course, I thought! Locals are always inquisitive about strangers. The room was not yet crowded but did have a goodly number of patrons. Those closest to the fire nook seemed to sense that something might be brewing and turned their attention in my direction. I should have thought out a story ahead of time. I decided to stick as close to the facts as I could.

"To tell you the truth," I said, smiling and hoping to give the impression of friendliness, "I heard from a friend that there are vampires in the area." Why not get it out in the open, I thought? I didn't have a lot of time so I didn't want to waste any of it. I chuckled to let them know that I didn't really take the subject seriously. They did not join me in laughter.

All three of the old men turned to look at me. The two younger men stopped eating and looked up. The young serving girl, who was passing by, stopped and stared at me. Had I said the wrong thing?

"Where you 'ear that, then?" demanded the man who had first addressed me.

"Oh. Just . . . from a friend. I think he saw something in the newspaper . . ." My voice trailed off.

The two younger men went back to eating and the serving girl moved on. The old men remained staring at me.

"Jus' what – *exactly* – was it you 'eard? This ain't no little thing to be a-joking at, you know."

"No. No, of course. Please don't think I take it lightly." I laid down my knife and fork and edged my chair a little closer to them. "May I get you fresh drinks?" I waved to the girl, who came forward and stood wiping her nose on the sleeve of her dress. "Drinks for the gentlemen," I told her. She hurried away.

"What's your name?" asked the third man of the three, who hadn't previously spoken.

I stood and extended my hand. "Harry Rivers. Pleased to make your acquaintance."

He ignored my hand so I let it drop and sat back down again.

"Well, Mr. Rivers – if that really is your name – we don't make a 'abit of talking to strangers." At that moment the drinks arrived. The man looked down at them and then continued. "But seeing as 'ow you come all this way . . ." All three of them laughed, and drank deeply of their ale.

"What you know about vampires, Mr. Rivers?" asked the man who had first addressed me.

"Not a great deal," I admitted. "That's why I came here. Hoping to learn more."

"You best get your victuals down you and get off 'ome." It was one of the young men with the pork pies who spoke. "This ain't no place for a stranger to be wandering about after dark."

"What do you mean?" I asked.

"Ain't you noticed? Why, even the bobbies go around in pairs 'ere."

"Take no notice of Tom," said his companion.

"You afraid o' vampires?" asked the first old man.

I paused. I hadn't really thought about it. "No," I said, uncertainly. "I don't think so. Why, I don't even know if I believe in them."

Once again they all – the whole room, it seemed – stopped what they were doing and stared at me.

"Sorry," I said. "I didn't mean to offend anyone."

"Show 'im your marks, George," said the old man nearest to me.

His closest companion twisted around on his seat and tugged at the dirty kerchief tied around his neck. There was no collar to his shirt. As he pulled on the kerchief it slipped down enough for me to see two red spots on his scraggy neck.

"What am I looking at?" I asked.

"Why, vampire bites o' course!" said George.

I leaned closer. "Aren't they kind of wide apart?" I started to say.

George twisted away and dragged up the kerchief. "What the 'ell do you know anyway?"

"No, seriously," I said. "They don't look like bite marks to me."

"You ever seen a vampire bite afore?" demanded his friend.

"No. But . . ."

"Then 'ow'd you know?"

There was no refuting that logic. I decided to change the focus of the subject. "How did you come by the bites?" I asked.

George now seemed to be sulking because I'd questioned the authenticity of the marks on his neck. The third old man spoke up again. "'E got 'em late one night when 'e was going 'ome from 'ere. When was it, George?"

"Saturday," came the mumbled response.

"Last Saturday?"

"Right."

I thought about it. I decide to push for a little more information. Trying to sound more interested – and believing – I asked "Was it close by here, George?"

He nodded. "Just down the street."

"Tell 'im, George," said his neighbor.

"I 'ave to cut through a alley by St. Dunstan's Church, to get to Old Manor Road," he said, slowly warming to his story. "I been going that way for years. And wouldn't you know, just this one time – last Saturday night, as Bill 'ere told you – just last Saturday, I'd no sooner turned the corner into the alley than this creature jumped on me . . ."

"Creature?" I couldn't help interrupting him.

"That's the only way I knows to describe 'im."

"Or 'er!' said Bill darkly.

George continued. "Afore I knew it, this creature had grabbed me by the 'air and forced my 'ead back so's 'e could get to my neck. That's when 'e bit me." He sat back, satisfied that he'd told his story.

I absorbed that. It certainly sounded authentic, though from the brief glimpse I had of the bite marks they just didn't look as though they were made by my image of what a vampire was. But, as the men had pointed out, what did I know? Perhaps I needed to have a talk with Sam Green and see if he had become any sort of vampire expert through absorbing the tale of Sir Francis Varney.

The men settled into their pipe smoking and ale drinking and I digested food and story. Perhaps I now had enough material to present to Mr. Stoker and to ask his advice. The whole subject of vampires fascinated me, as it seemed to do many people. Were there really such things? And if so, did they exist in London, not far from the Lyceum Theatre? And, again if so, was there any likelihood of them intruding on the life of the theatre? It was indeed food for thought. But for now, I needed to get back to the Lyceum and prepare for curtain-up.

Chapter Four

What I had to report to Mr. Stoker Wednesday morning really didn't amount to a great deal, I realized. But my boss listened quietly when I told him of my visit to the Rose and Crown and merely nodded from time to time, as though already familiar with the story.

"You say the supposed bite marks did not look genuine?" he asked.

I shook my head. "Not that I know anything of vampire bites, sir, but I got the impression that they were two individual punctures rather than a set of two, or a pair, if you know what I mean?"

Again he nodded. "What I find of interest, Harry, is the mere fact of there being so many such reports, and more surfacing every day it seems. Whether or not there is truly a vampire problem in the East End is beside the point. There is obviously *something* happening there."

"So what should we do, sir?"

"Do? Why nothing, Harry. This is not our problem. Unless, or until, it directly affects the Lyceum we must leave this to the Metropolitan Police to deal with. We have both, you and I, spoken to Sam Green so we must assume that his work will no longer be affected by these rumors. Let us then continue with our daily round. Food disappearing from Mr. Gardner's commissariat is far more tangible, though even that is not exactly a high priority. The show must go on, as the Guv'nor constantly reminds us. That, Harry, is our watch word."

And so it went. My focus returned to the theatre and its environs.

The auditorium was always well lit. Even during a performance there was a considerable amount of light playing upon the audience. People came to the theatre as much to be seen as to see. Formal dress was de rigueur in the Dress Circle – which holds a little over 100 persons – and, of course, in the boxes. The auditorium was still lit by gas though the stage area and all its lights was now electric. The Lyceum's generator was, happily, located outside the building, unlike some of the other London theatres where the hum of their generators reverberated throughout the theatre for the entire production of the play.

A large gas chandelier hung down in the center of the auditorium. If not properly adjusted, the light from it interfered with the stage lighting during the performance. The stage lighting had a lot of illumination coming up from the floor level while the chandelier's light came down from above. Mr. Irving was very particular about the lighting effects and could become quite irate if the balance was in any way incorrect. Mr. Stoker had advised me that the new Savoy Theatre, being built in the Strand, was due to open in October and was to be lit entirely by electricity; the first public building in the world to be so illuminated. He was certain that it would be only a matter of a few years before we were all so lit. I find it difficult to keep up with the rapid progress of science and technology but I think the Guv'nor will be delighted to see this advancement.

My thoughts wandered to Jenny, my inamorata. She is a housemaid at the residence of the Guv'nor and I had first met her when sent on an errand to Mr. Irving's rooms. She and I have been walking out together for three or four months now. Recently she underwent a harrowing ordeal when kidnapped by a crazed American bent on destroying Mr. Henry Irving, and she has only recently returned to her employ after recuperating at her aunt's home in Bermondsey. This past Sunday she and I spent a quiet and enjoyable few hours strolling in Hyde Park. Thinking of her now, I can hardly wait for this coming Sunday, her day off, to meet with her again.

"Have you seen Guy, Harry?"

I brought my mind back to the Lyceum. It was Arthur Swindon who addressed me. Mr. Swindon had played the Ghost of Hamlet's Father in *Hamlet* and was playing Gratiano in *Othello*. Although more often inebriated than sober, he was one of the Lyceum stalwarts. Mr. Stoker had once said of him that "he came with the theatre", inferring that he was here even before the Guv'nor took over from Mrs. Bateman three years ago. Arthur was tall and thin, with salt-and-pepper hair, a straggly mustache and thin beard.

"Not recently, Mr. Swindon," I said. "Have you tried the Druid's Head? He usually pops in there for lunch."

"No. I mean yes! Oh dear. No, he wasn't in the Druid's Head. I just thought you might have seen him about the theatre."

"Sorry. No."

He wandered away. It was unusual to see Arthur Swindon, or any of the actors, about the theatre at that time in the morning. Being Wednesday there was a matinée performance but even so most of the actors didn't appear until after lunch. Thinking about the meal, I decided to have an early one myself.

I thought to have a quick look in on Sam Green first, just to make sure that Varney was safely put away. I found Sam with two of the newer stagehands, Lonnie Plimpton and Davey Llewellyn. They had joined the Lyceum family at the same time, being taken on at the start of *Othello*. They were quite a contrast. Lonnie Plimpton was a great bear of a man, six feet and six inches in height – even taller than the Guv'nor and Mr. Stoker – and built like an oak tree. He was bald and beardless and struck me as being a little slow in his grasp of things, though his friend Davey seemed to keep an eye on him. In fact they kept an eye on one another in their own way. Davey Llewellyn was a little Welshman even shorter than myself, with black hair, dark brown eyes, and clean-shaven. When I came upon them I found the hulking Plimpton holding the Welshman up in the air, above his head, so that Davey could reach to fasten a scenery flat where it had come loose. Sam Green stood by, a great grin on his face.

"See that, 'Arry? No need to go looking for a ladder. Lonnie just picks up 'is mate and 'olds 'im up."

I wasn't quite sure if it was appropriate, but Sam was in charge of the stagehands so if he was happy then it was fine with me. I set off for the Druid's Head. As I passed Bill Thomas's cubbyhole I slowed. Bill was the theatre doorman and seemed to know the movements of everyone.

"Have you seen Guy Purdy, Bill?" I asked. "Mr. Swindon is looking for him."

"Not in yet, Harry," he said. "Don't expect to see him afore two of the clock."

"But curtain-up is at two-thirty," I said.

He nodded. "Like I said, I don't expect to see him afore two of the clock."

So Guy Purdy always cut things close, did he? Well, so long as he wasn't in any of the opening scenes that was fine, but I knew that Cassio – the part that Guy was playing – was in Act One, Scene Two and so should be made up, in costume, and ready by the start of the play. The Guv'nor hated tardiness. I made a mental note to have a word with Guy on that score.

"I was just making the acquaintance of Lonnie Plimpton and Davey Llewellyn," I said.

"Ah! Now there's an interesting couple." Bill peered at me over the tops of his steel-rimmed half-glasses. "Little 'uns sharp enough, though I hear he has a fierce Welsh temper. And the big 'uns a bit dim-witted, I'm thinking. One or two make fun of him, though there's no harm in it, I suppose."

The Druid's Head was busy when I arrived and I noticed many Lyceum players there, but no sign of Mr. Purdy. I ordered my lunch and, true to form, Penny the serving girl saw that I had a tankard of porter at my elbow almost before I seated myself.

"Busy," commented a shabbily dressed man sitting at the next table. His coat sleeves were short and the cuffs frayed and his trousers similarly brief. I presumed they were hand-me-downs of some sort. His hair was dirty, long, and untidy.

"Not unusual for this time of day," I said. "You've not been here before?"

He shook his head and indicated an old hurdy-gurdy resting at his feet. "Just stopped in for a quick bite. Not my usual bailiwick. Do better up on Waterloo Bridge."

"So what brought you over here?" I asked, as my platter of roast beef, potatoes, and Brussel sprouts arrived. I saw his eyes fix on it and his tongue run over his thin lips. I noticed that he nursed a small cheese sandwich and a half pint of ale.

He shrugged. "Looking for new territory. There's a bit of a shift, if you like. Lot o' street pitchers, patterers, screevers, musicians and the like don't care much for the East End any more. Leastwise not after dark. Some of the piemen and 'ot potato sellers don't like to 'ang about. Affects their business something awful."

"Why is that?" I asked, tucking into my lunch.

Again he shrugged. "Dunno. Some say it's 'cause of the . . . you know."

"No," I said. "I don't know. What?"

He leaned towards me. I could smell the cheese on his breath. "Vampires," he mumbled.

"Vampires?"

"Ssh!" He looked about him to see who might have heard me. "No need to go inviting 'em in!" He lifted his mug but, finding it empty, set it down again. His eyes fixed on my repast.

"Have you had any encounters yourself?" I asked.

"No, and no more do I want to," he said.

"Just stories, then?"

"There ain't no smoke without fire, they says." He sat back, his eyes squinting and his head nodding knowingly.

I got on with my meal, dismissing his suggestion of a vampire invasion. Rumors can grow and easily get out of hand. But it was interesting that they were now affecting the street performers. They were the people found on just about every street corner and outside every tavern throughout the city, begging for money under the pretense of providing entertainment. Most people gave them a coin or two to go away rather than in gratitude for what they provided. I pulled out my half-hunter and looked at the time. I must get back to the theatre, I thought. I pushed away my plate and started to get to my feet.

"You not going to finish that then?"

My neighbor pointed at the half-eaten baked potato and small section of roast beef I had left on the plate. I smiled. "Go ahead," I said.

As I re-entered the Lyceum I again paused by Bill Thomas's cubicle.

"What have you heard about vampires in the area, Bill?" I asked.

His eyes came up from the *Sporting Times*, his regular reading material.

"Vampires, Mr. Rivers? Aren't you a bit old to be believing in them things?"

I chuckled and nodded my head. "Thank you, Bill. That's what I needed." I continued on into the theatre.

Arthur Swindon continued to seem upset, even after he had managed to meet with Guy Purdy. I didn't know what the problem was though Bill Thomas had vouchsafed that he had all the details and it involved Mr. Swindon's brother. I hadn't even been aware that Arthur had a brother and asked Mr. Stoker about it.

"Younger brother, yes," he said. "Apparently the man is very sick and has been for some time. I am not privy to the particulars but it does seem to be serious enough to affect Mr. Swindon. We must hope it does not encroach on his performances. Keep an eye on him, Harry, if you would be so kind."

"Yes, sir. Of course."

Arthur Swindon's role of Gratiano was not a demanding one so I was not too concerned but I did remain watchful. He seemed to keep to himself a lot and I thought that he did not smile as much as I remembered him doing. In my opinion he seemed very nervous, though I could see no reason for it. The only person he seemed to have time for was Guy Purdy. I did notice that he seemed sober for far longer periods than in the past. Something especially noteworthy, I thought.

There was a minor emergency during the Wednesday evening performance when the electricity suddenly failed. All of the stage lights went out at the beginning of Act Three, Scene One. Guy Purdy, as Cassio, was on stage with the musicians and Toby Merryfield, as the Clown. Mr. Purdy's years of experience came through as he continued with the scene without pausing, merely raising his voice a little. Sam Green was quick off the mark and brought up the house lights to their maximum. Mario Pinasco, the theatre electrician, quickly had the stage lights up and running again and it was doubtful that many of the patrons were even aware of the problem but Mr. Irving was very much aware and complained to Mr. Stoker and myself.

"See to it, Abraham, will you, that this does not happen again? It is disconcerting to both the actors and the audience. And we do not want another Surrey incident."

"What did he mean by 'another Surrey incident', sir?" I asked my boss later.

"He was referring to the destruction of the old Surrey Theatre in '65," said Mr. Stoker. "Before the present one. Terrible tragedy. They were playing a pantomime, *Richard Coeur de Lion*, and had a transformation scene; needed to go from a near dark stage to a sudden bright Harlequinade. Apparently the gas was turned up too rapidly and it set fire to the ceiling. Of course the whole theatre was gas in those days."

"What happened?" I asked.

"Happily there was a small house that night so the audience got out very quickly. But it was a close call, as the Americans have it, for the performers. The gas superintendent of the theatre, a Mr. Hinkley, turned off the gas in the back portion of the theatre to avoid an explosion and this plunged everything into darkness so there was panic for a while. Eventually all were able to escape, with actors and crew pulling each other out of the back windows of the theatre."

I felt grateful that we were gradually moving over to the modern electricity, even if it did mean we had to put up with an occasional blackout. That was very much preferable to the burning down of the theatre.

I had a chance to speak to Guy Purdy for a while, in the greenroom during the performance, and asked him about Arthur Swindon.

"I know that you and Mr. Swindon are good friends," I said. "I can't help but notice that Arthur is not his usual self these days. I wondered if you could throw any light on the reason?"

"'Good friends', dear boy? I don't know what you mean by that, I'm sure," he said.

"Don't you agree that he seems upset about something?"

He took his time answering. "Arthur has a lot on his mind."

"Mr. Purdy. You know that we are all friends here. All part of what Mr. Irving likes to call the Lyceum family. If one of us is in trouble then, as you know, the others are concerned. A play is a group presentation. It depends on us all working together. You know that; I don't have to lecture you."

He seemed to relax a little. "Of course, dear boy. Of course. We *are* all family, we who tread the boards together."

I waited.

He sighed. "Arthur has a lot on his mind."

"I understand he has a brother."

He nodded. "Yes, he has. And the boy is not doing well. Arthur, of course, is very concerned."

"What is the problem? Perhaps we can help. I know that Mr. Stoker would want . . ."

"It's all right!" he snapped, and then calmed and smiled. "It's all right," he repeated quietly. "Arthur can handle it. It's just . . . a little disconcerting for the poor boy right now. But he'll pull through."

"Arthur, or his brother?" I asked.

Guy's mouth set in a firm line. "Arthur will be fine. Just give him some space, please Harry. I'm keeping an eye on him."

"I know you are, Guy, and I appreciate it as I'm sure he does. I just wondered if there was anything we can do, that's all."

He gave a quick smile. "Not at the moment. Oh, I think I hear my cue! I must get back up to the stage."

He hurried out leaving me standing in the greenroom, but still not happy. I needed to find out more. And why was Guy Purdy being so secretive? I determined to do some digging.

Chapter Five

"Another break-in," said my boss, next morning. "Herbert Gardner is most put out."

"What was taken?" I asked.

"Much the same as previously. Some of our staple pork pies, apples, some bottles of ginger beer."

"Had those hinges been reversed?" I asked. "To hide the hinge pins?"

"That was my first question to Mr. Gardner. No, Harry, they hadn't yet been fixed, so obviously the same means of ingress was utilized. Herbert said that he hadn't expected another raid on his supplies quite so quickly, which was why he hadn't yet changed the pantry door opening. He has Sam Green working on the hinges now; even as we speak."

"Good. Anything else, sir?"

"Yes, Harry." Mr. Stoker shuffled some papers on his desk and pulled out a folder that he opened and turned around so that I could see what was in it. "Look at these figures, Harry."

"What am I looking at?"

"It's the figures for the past week or so showing occupation of the upper balcony."

The upper balcony was commonly referred to as "the gods", since it is the highest of the balconies and, because of this, has the cheapest seats in the theatre. Impecunious patrons would queue up outside for well over an hour prior to the doors opening, so that they might make the long climb up the winding passage and innumerable stairs, to the roof of the theatre. Until a year or so ago the seats in the gods were simple backless hard wooden benches but last year the Guv'nor had seen to it that they now have some sort of padding on the seats, albeit thin. Yet the view remains the same: looking almost straight down the very steep incline onto the stage far below, and enduring the smoke and fumes that came up from the rest of the house. But at sixpence a seat, the upper balcony was always popular.

I tried to make sense of the figures, not being familiar with that side of the theatre's operations.

"You can see that starting about a week ago sales started to fall off."

I nodded, trying to get the financial picture into focus.

"The Gods have always been popular," continued Mr. Stoker. "No matter how sparse the bookings in the rest of the house, you could always count on a healthy following up there. But look, Harry! By last night's performance the upper balcony was less than half full; a fortnight ago it was packed."

"And the rest of the theatre was full last night. So why is this, sir?" I asked. "There have been no price increases. No changes of any sort, so far as I know."

"None at all. It's a mystery, Harry."

"Something must be keeping the people away," I said.

"Something . . . or someone," agreed my boss. He was silent for a moment then, with a brief shake of his head, he continued. "Now, Harry, I have to see some young lady who is looking for employment, it seems. She claims to be an actress – once in the employ of the Charles Keane company, no less – but we have a full complement at present so I must refuse her. I do hate to turn away talent yet we cannot employ them all."

I decided to spend most of Friday doing a little investigating. From Mr. Stoker's filing cabinet I obtained Arthur Swindon's address. He resided at a boarding house on Carlisle Street, off Drury Lane. A tidy walk to and from the theatre, it seemed to me.

The morning was overcast with no sign of the sun visible through the fog coming off the river. I turned up my coat collar, pulled down my bowler hat, and hurried along Great Queen Street. I really didn't have a plan. I thought that I would simply look over the house and see if I could ascertain whether or not the old actor was home. If, as I hoped, he was not, then I would approach his landlady and see what information I might acquire.

Things started out well. Just as I turned the corner off Drury Lane I spotted Mr. Swindon himself, leaving a house partway down Carlisle Street. He seemed intent on going somewhere in the opposite direction from where I stood so I simply slowed my pace enough for him to draw away and, eventually, to disappear around the far corner.

The boarding house was respectable looking, with a recently whitewashed front step and a gleaming brass doorknocker, showing pride on the part of the owner. As I stood appraising the home, a housemaid came up the area steps. She was bundled up and carrying a large shopping bag. I presumed she was off to do some errands for the housekeeper.

"Good morning." I raised my hat and smiled. She looked at me askance and said nothing. "I wonder if I might have a word or two?"

"'ere! What you want?" She held up her shopping bag in front of her, as though to protect herself from any advance I might make.

I smiled even more, as friendly as I could. "Oh, have no fear, miss. I am Mr. Rivers from the Lyceum Theatre. I believe you have one of our number in residence here? Mr. Swindon?"

Her eyes narrowed and she lowered the shopping bag a fraction, though not completely.

"What about 'im?"

"Nothing, really. I just wondered if I might enquire . . . you are familiar with the gentleman then?"

"I knows of 'im, yes. What's it to you?"

This was not starting off as well as I had hoped. I really should have thought it through a little better.

"I – we – that is to say . . . do you happen to know if Mr. Swindon has a brother? Does he, perhaps, also reside here?" The words rushed out.

I heard a noise from below, in the area. Looking down, we both saw the figure of a large woman glaring out of the kitchen window and tapping on the pane.

"Lor' that's Mrs. Ramsbotham, the 'ousekeeper. I gotta run!"

The girl turned and made off at a fast rate down the road. I followed after her.

"'ere! You following arter me? I can call a Bobby you know."

I kept pace with her. "No, please miss. I just need a quick answer and then I'll leave you alone. Are you familiar with Mr. Swindon's brother? Does he also live at that residence?"

"No, 'e don't. And never did, to my mind. 'E used to live around the corner somewhere, so far as I know. Now leave me alone."

"You don't know the address, I suppose?" I called desperately, coming to a stop and watching her hurry away.

"No I don't!" she threw over her shoulder. "Don't know where 'e's gone."

So I had confirmation of there actually being a brother but now no lead on where he might be. Had he moved? Gone into hospital, perhaps? Maybe even died? I stood mentally scratching my head. I very much doubted that the brother had died, since Arthur Swindon was still concerned about him. Hospital seemed more likely, I thought. I would have to enquire more of Bill Thomas. I was sure he had more information, if I could only pry it out of him. I headed back towards the Lyceum.

Bill Thomas was of little help, however.

"Yes, Harry, I did hear that the brother had recently moved. Something about the landlady not liking the looks of him, or something. I don't know. Why don't you ask Mr. Swindon himself?"

"I don't like to, Bill. You know how some people like to keep family matters private. And Arthur is not the most communicative at the best of times."

"If you can even catch him sober," muttered Bill.

"Well, that's true too. Though in that respect he seems to have been behaving himself better more recently. No, I'll see what I can come up with myself. Mr. Stoker might even have some of the answers I'm looking for."

I was kept busy the rest of the day and since my boss was out somewhere with the Guv'nor, I didn't get a chance to talk to him about things. However, shortly before that evening's performance I did overhear some theatre tittle-tattle that I found of interest. Not to do with Arthur Swindon or his brother, but pertaining to John Saxon.

I was in a corner of the greenroom. William Hammermind had asked me if I'd go over his lines with him. I didn't have anything else pressing so I agreed to. Bill Hammermind was playing the Duke of Venice and, as was always the case it seemed to me, he was feeling insecure in the part and afraid of forgetting his lines, although we had been doing the play for a fortnight now and he'd had no problems. Mr. Hammermind was in his mid-forties and, as Margery Connolly the Wardrobe Mistress liked to put it, was "a very close friend" of the older Anthony Sampson.

In another corner of the room were Edwina Price the Prompt, Miss Meg Grey, who had done such a fine job as the Queen in *Hamlet* and was now playing Emilia, and Margery Connolly herself. They had started to talk between themselves in quiet voices but as time went on their voices rose. Although I was trying to concentrate on the dialogue with Mr. Hammermind, I couldn't help but overhear much of what the ladies were saying. It had started out with them criticizing the eating habits of some of their fellow actors but quickly descended into frequently unkind comments on looks, mannerisms, and other idiosyncrasies. It quickly became obvious to me – half-listening as I was – that there was real animosity on Meg Grey's part toward John Saxon. I was surprised, never having been aware of any arguments or disputes of any sort between the two. If anything, now that I thought about it, they seemed to go out of their way to avoid each other. Edwina Price, on the other hand, had nothing but good things to say about Mr. Saxon.

"Now that Mr. Swindon," put in Margery Connolly. "If that man is ever sober . . ."

"Harry! Harry!"

"What? Oh, sorry Mr. Hammermind." I brought my attention back to the script in front of me. I had missed a cue in the exchange between the Duke and the gentlemen of the court and left Mr. Hammermind floundering. "Sorry. I guess my mind was wandering."

"Ah, never mind, Harry. I suppose I'm worrying over nothing. I should let you get back to your own work. I'm sure you've got plenty to do. Many thanks for your help anyway."

I left him and the ladies, still deep in discussion, and went back to my office. It would not be long till curtain up. But as I moved around making my final checks on properties I kept thinking back to the ladies and their criticisms of their fellows. I had been surprised at the vehemence in some of the remarks by Miss Grey. She had always struck me as a level-minded person who saw the best in everyone. But I finally decided that all was fairly typical of a group of over-worked thespians and their views on their fellows and the backstage staff.

Chapter Six

I try to get to the theatre early on Wednesday and Saturday mornings, since we have matinée performances on those days. I like plenty of time to check on the condition and placement of the many properties used in the play. Some of the actors have a bad habit of taking a prop back to the dressing room with them – especially if it's a small hand prop – instead of handing it in so that it can be placed correctly for the start of the next performance. I can't begin to count the number of times I have had to spend endless hours searching for a fan, a book, a dagger, or even a sword, which has been mislaid through the unthinking action of an actor.

This Saturday morning was no exception. Mr. Booth – who should most certainly have known better – had left a note to me saying that he "seemed to have mislaid the handkerchief". The all-important handkerchief around which so much of the plot hung, and he had "mislaid it"! Happily I did have more than one of this particular prop, just in case of such an eventuality, but I still had to search for it. It wouldn't do to have two such items suddenly turn up on stage. I eventually located the piece of linen carelessly tucked into Mr. Booth's discarded costume on the floor of his dressing room. I sighed and carried it through to Wardrobe, to be ironed.

I decided to take a brief respite and wandered through one of the two ground-level pass doors into the empty auditorium. In the theatre, front of house is a completely different world from backstage and the pass doors are the only connection between the two. The light was low in there, since the front-of-house staff had not yet come in. I sat down in the front row, center, and admired the decorative proscenium arch across the orchestra pit. The whole interior of the Lyceum was beautiful, to my mind. There had been a theatre on this site since 1765 though the present one was less than fifty years old, designed by Samuel Beazley. It is unique in that it has a balcony overhanging the circle. When Mr. Irving took over the theatre in 1878 he had the entire auditorium redecorated at a cost of 5,000 pounds. The theme is myrtle green and cream, with purple backgrounds for the gilt moldings, frescoes, and medallions. The gas-lit chandeliers burn in wine-colored shades. It has an atmosphere of great luxury and is a pleasant contrast to the prior stark scarlet and gold. I looked about me, feeling warm and confortable.

I heard the doors to the vestibule, behind me, open as the front-of-house staff filtered in. It was time for me to get back to my own domain. But suddenly there came a scream.

I jumped to my feet and spun around. A woman, one of the staff, stood in the aisle to my left, her hands up to her face, screaming and sobbing. Others – I saw Mr. Timothy Bidwell among them – came rushing in from the foyer. I noticed what looked to be a greatcoat or bundle of clothes resting on the backs of the seats close by the screaming woman. As I hurried forward, I saw that in fact it was a body. A man's body draped over the seat backs.

"What the . . . ?" Mr. Bidwell started to say.

"Stay!" I held up my hand as I moved forward. "See to this woman, someone," I added, indicating the screamer. Two other people moved forward and took charge of her, assisting her out of the auditorium. I advanced on the figure on the seats.

"What is it?" asked Mr. Bidwell, slowly moving to join me.

As I drew level I saw the head of the man, hanging back over the seats. It was John Saxon. I looked upward. It seemed that he had fallen from the Gods, from the upper balcony far above us. He must have broken his back when he hit the seats.

Inspector Samuel Charles Bellamy of Scotland Yard was a middle-aged man with dark brown hair sprinkled with grey, mutton-chop sideboards but no mustache or beard. I was all too familiar with his little beady brown eyes. He had visited the Lyceum on more than one occasion in the past and, for whatever reason, he seemed to hold me in disdain. He preferred to speak directly to my boss and to completely ignore me. This was the pattern in the present situation. Mr. Stoker stood, a good five or six inches taller than the inspector, and listened while the policeman walked around the body of John Saxon.

"Nasty fall. Nasty! Must have broken his back when he hit the seats. We don't see that a lot." He had his notebook in his hand and, after checking to see that his stub of a pencil was sharp, made a notation. He eased past Mr. Saxon's head and came around the rows to stand close to the front of the body. He looked upward to the balconies above. "Nasty fall," he repeated.

"From the gods," said Mr. Stoker.

"Beg your pardon, sir?"

"From the gods." Mr. Stoker pointed. "The top gallery. We refer to it as the gods."

The inspector came around again and forward another row, to get a better view, craning his head to look upward. "You think he came all the way from the top then, do you, sir?"

"Isn't it obvious?"

"No, sir, it is not obvious. And anyway, why don't you have some sort of barrier or something to prevent such a mishap as we now find ourselves with?"

My boss was always patient. "Indeed we do have such barriers, inspector. If you look you will see that at the foot of each aisle there is a horizontal brass rail. Not enough to interfere with the audience's view of the stage but sufficient to prevent such an accident as we seem to have now experienced."

"One step at a time, sir, if you please. First off, what makes you think that the body fell from the top and not just from the, what d'you call it? Dress Circle, is it, just above us?"

"Look at those rails I just told you about, inspector. Do you not see that the lower two are bent. It seems to me that if the body fell from the top it must have hit the Upper Circle rail directly below it, with force enough to bend it, and then continued on down to hit the similar rail of the Dress Circle, similarly bending that before bouncing off and landing on these seats in the Stalls. Poor Mr. Saxon might well have been dead long before he reached the bottom."

The inspector moved backwards and forwards a row or two, looking up, and made several notations in his book. "Your little barriers, as you call them, would not seem to be sufficient for their job, wouldn't you say sir?"

I thought the inspector looked pleased with himself.

"They have saved patrons in the past," I said. "It's extremely unusual for anyone to slip and fall down the aisle steps but no one has ever gone over the top before."

As in times past, he ignored me.

"We will say that the bending of these bars does seem to indicate the fall commenced higher up. At what hour did this accident occur?" He looked expectantly at my boss.

"Who can say? Presumably it happened either last night or early this morning. Mr. Rivers here discovered the body not an hour ago. Can you not determine the time of death, inspector?" Mr. Stoker looked down at the policeman and frowned.

"All in good time, sir. All in good time. Please allow us to assess this accident and to ask our own questions." He licked the tip of his pencil. "Now, we notice that the deceased . . ." He turned back a page in his notebook, obviously looking for something.

"Mr. John Saxon," I volunteered.

He looked hard at me but said nothing, turning the pages forward again. "We notice that Mr. Saxon is not wearing one of your theatrical costumes. What does that tell us?"

"That it was either last night, after the performance, or early this morning, as Mr. Stoker just said," I burst out.

"Harry! Please. Just let the inspector take his time . . . he obviously needs it." We had both suffered through the inspector's questioning on previous occasions. It could be very frustrating. I stepped back a pace and bit my tongue.

"Who was the last person to see Mr. Saxon?" Bellamy looked about him as though expecting someone to step forward, but there were only the three of us there, Mr. Bidwell having cleared the auditorium and kept his staff out in the vestibule.

"I think you'll need to do some questioning to determine that," said Mr. Stoker. "Mr. Bidwell's people are already awaiting you."

The inspector still stood silently studying the body, with occasional glances above.

"I understand that this all takes time, inspector," my boss continued, "but I know that Mr. Irving would want me to point out that we are due to open for a matinée performance at two-thirty. Do you think we might have poor Mr. Saxon's body removed by then?"

The inspector's head jerked up. "We will be taking all the time that this accident deserves, Mr. Stoker. We will see to it that the body is removed when we see fit. It may well be that you will have to cancel your performance this afternoon."

Mr. Stoker's expression darkened, though he said nothing. It would indeed take a most serious incident to bring about the cancellation of a Lyceum performance. "Harry," said my boss to me, "The Guv'nor is aware of what has happened. I sent word to his home. He is on his way to the theatre even as we speak. As soon as he gets here, let him know the current situation. Alert Mr. Saxon's understudy. If necessary we can delay curtain-up for half an hour but no longer. We do have an evening performance to follow."

"Yes, sir."

Without looking to the inspector for any sort of permission, I turned and hurried away. He could question people at any time, I was sure. No need to delay the matinée for that. As I reached the stage and crossed it, I wondered if Guy Purdy might now take the role of Roderigo, that he had coveted. Someone else could take over his Cassio part, but then, none of that was up to me. The Guv'nor would decide when he got here.

I found that Bill Thomas knew almost as much as I did. I was constantly amazed at how he came to know everything about everyone although he never seemed to leave his post by the stage door.

"Accident, Harry, or suicide?" he asked, squinting at me through his steel-rimmed spectacles.

"Suicide?" I hadn't thought of that. I had assumed that Mr. Saxon's tumble from the gods was nothing more than an accident. But the moment Bill Thomas said the word my mind started racing. What was Saxon doing up in the gods anyway? Especially if it was at night or even early in the morning. There was no reason for him to be in the auditorium at all, certainly not in the Upper Gallery. If this were indeed a suicide, then that would explain his presence there.

"Thanks, Bill," I said. "Thanks a lot. That is certainly food for thought."

By noon the body had been taken away to Scotland Yard's morgue. I caught up with Inspector Bellamy and Mr. Stoker near the roof of the auditorium. The inspector was standing at the top of the steep steps leading down to the front of the gods. I noticed that the safety railing here was straight and intact and commented on the fact.

"Yes, Harry," said my boss. "I was just pointing out that very fact to the inspector. Obviously poor Mr. Saxon tumbled over the rail here and hit first on the brass rail at the next level, the Upper Circle."

We slowly descended the steps to the bottom. I noticed that the inspector allowed both Mr. Stoker and myself to precede him. I held on to the brass bar and peered over the edge, thinking of John Saxon falling. The heavy brass seemed solid enough but John must have weighed all of eleven stone. I imagined a one hundred and fifty pound bag of potatoes making that fall. It would most certainly have bent the bar below it, and then the one below that as it fell on down to the theatre floor. I was sure the seat backs, where the body had finally landed, were also badly damaged.

"Have you considered that this might be suicide, inspector?" asked Mr. Stoker.

I gasped. I had said nothing of that possibility. Had my boss been talking with Bill Thomas, I wondered? No, he had been with the inspector all this time. I mentally shrugged. I suppose it was an obvious thought to someone with as questioning a mind as Mr. Stoker. I turned to see what Bellamy had to say.

Rather than continue standing on the steep steps he had sat down on the aisle seat of the second row. "Of course," he said, pulling out his notebook and scribbling in it. "Suicide. Yes, we think it's a possibility."

"So what would have prompted it?" I asked.

He graced me with a long, hard look. "We will determine that when we question your people," he said, and loudly sniffed as he looked about him. "Yes, we think that might be a very possible . . . possibility."

"Unless, of course," said Mr. Stoker, "he was *pushed* over the safety rail."

Chapter Seven

"It would seem to me that there are two questions we must address," said Mr. Stoker, when he and I were ensconced in his office later that day.

We had bid farewell to Inspector Bellamy less than half an hour before curtain-up for the matinée. The Guv'nor had swept in and immediately designated that Guy Purdy take over the role of Roderigo, which pleased Mr. Purdy tremendously, and that John Whitby should take on the part of Cassio. Despite the sudden changes, the matinée went off very well, with a responsive house. We had then all dispersed to our various favorite dinner venues where, I am sure, much gossip regarding Mr. Saxon took place. My boss and I now met for a discussion before the preparations for the evening performance.

"What questions would they be, sir?" I asked.

"I think we can almost certainly rule out accident as the cause of death, Harry. So firstly, why would Mr. Saxon commit suicide, if suicide was in fact the reason? Secondly, should it actually be a case of murder rather than suicide, then who would want to kill him and why?" He sat a moment and then added, "I suppose if I add the 'why?' then it makes it three questions."

"I can think of no good reason for him to commit suicide," I said, "but then, I certainly don't know all the facts of Mr. Saxon's life."

"That might be a good starting point for our investigations, Harry."

I blinked. "*Our* investigations, sir? You are not, then, content to leave this to the Metropolitan Police?"

He looked at me. "With Inspector Bellamy in charge?"

There was a moment of silence and then I nodded my head. "You are right, of course, sir. Where would you like me to start? Do I follow the suicide road and exhaust that before looking at the murder possibility, or do I work on both at the same time?"

"I think we need to entertain both possibilities. See just what you can learn about John Saxon, Harry. Was there anything in particular worrying him? Did he owe money to anyone? We have something of a grasp on his life here in the Lyceum, but what about his private life? Find out all that you can, Harry. Talk to his fellow thespians. Speak to his landlady. See if he had any particular friends outside of his theatre life."

"Yes,   sir."

"Meanwhile, I will be having a word or two with the Guv'nor and see if he can throw any light on matters."

"Was John Saxon married, sir?"

"I'm not sure, Harry. That's a good question and I should know the answer to it but I don't. I will check on that. Perhaps the Guv'nor knows."

"What is Inspector Bellamy doing?"

My boss gave a wry grin. "I would not attempt to follow the good inspector's reasoning on any of this but I must assume that he is taking much the same tack as ourselves. We must try not to run afoul of the good policeman."

"Time is getting on and I must get ready for tonight's performance," I said, getting to my feet. "I'll get started on this first thing in the morning, sir."

"Good man, Harry. Thank you."

Well, I thought, I should now give up worrying about Arthur Swindon's brother. There were far more important things calling for my attention.

I admitted to myself that it was also a good change of focus to leave behind the vague possibilities of vampires and to now concentrate on something as concrete as John Saxon's death. First thing Sunday morning I was knocking on the door of the rooming house on Dickson Street, where Mr. Saxon had stayed. I didn't have to meet with Jenny until after lunch so I had time to do a lot of investigating.

"Mr. Saxon? Yes, the police was 'ere yesterday and told me of his tragic haccident."

Mrs. Stone did not look especially sad about his passing and I noticed that there was already a hand-written sign pasted up in the front-room window, advertising the availability of

Third floor back room to let to a professional gentleman of sober habit. Three shillings and sixpence a week.
No pets; no lady callers.

She certainly lost no time in mourning, I thought. "I wonder if I might have a look in Mr. Saxon's room?" I asked.

"T'ain't Mr. Saxon's room no more then, is it? That hinspector policeman said as 'ow 'e was dead."

"That is correct," I said. "But it might be of help to us if I could just have a quick look at what used to be his room?" I smiled and let Mrs. Stone catch a glimpse of a half-crown in my hand.

Her eyes fastened on the coin but she remained standing blocking the doorway.

"Policeman already done that."

I added a second half-crown.

"I was just about to pack up all 'is things in a tea chest and put it down in the cellar," she said. She seemed to think for a moment and then she stepped back and held open the door. As I stepped forward, she made sure that her hand was on a level with mine holding the two coins. I dropped the five shillings into her palm and entered.

"Third floor back," she said. "I hain't climbing up there again. Gonna 'ave me a cup o' Rosy. You mind you don't go takin' nothing' and be down 'ere again in 'alf an hour. No more."

I nodded and started climbing the stairs. The bannister rail was loose and so I kept pressed against the wall as I climbed. The smeared wallpaper seemed to indicate that most stair climbers did the same. At the third floor I saw two closed doors with a third standing open. Peering into the open one, it seemed to be the newly vacated room. A bed frame, freshly stripped of its bedclothes but still bearing an old, soiled mattress, stood in the center of the room. Assorted shirts, socks, and underwear were stuffed in a cardboard box sitting on top of a three-drawer chest. This stood in front of the single tiny window. The drawers of the chest had been pulled out and left half open. All were empty. The wardrobe door was wide open displaying two suits, one of which I recognized as Mr. Saxon's "Sunday best". I had seen him wearing it at the funeral of a fellow thespian some months before.

I looked about me. There were two small pictures hanging on the walls; one a watercolor of Kew Gardens and the other what looked to be a framed Christmas card of a snow-covered thatched cottage at the side of a country road.

Behind the open door to the room I noticed a small writing desk with a bookshelf hanging on the wall above it. The shelf contained worn copies of several of Mr. Shakespeare's plays side by side with one or two cheap novels. I turned my attention to the writing desk. On the top rested an inkwell and a pen with a broken nib. There were many old spills of ink ornamenting the top writing surface.

I pulled open the top one of the two desk drawers and found it contained some clean writing paper and envelopes. The second drawer had more of interest. Old bills, invoices, and correspondence, together with another pen and some pencils, all of which seemed to have been thrown in there in no particular order. I was sure that Inspector Bellamy had already gone through it but I settled to examining the contents anyway.

My attention was quickly drawn to a small bundle of letters at the back of the drawer and I pulled them out and scanned them. There were three or four, tied with an old, soiled, blue ribbon and addressed to John Saxon at a previous address in Manchester. They were undated, and from the brief endearments that I read I presumed that they were from a past lady friend. They didn't tell me a great deal, though I got the impression that the young lady had also been on the stage. There was no address nor signature on any of them; just the initial J, done in an elaborate feminine hand.

There were a number of rent receipts, a clipping from an out of town newspaper praising Mr. Saxon's role in Ben Jonson's *The Alchemist* at some theatre in the Midlands, a second demand from a tailor in the East End, and an old empty envelope that had come from a lawyer though the letter itself was long gone. There seemed to be no recent correspondence. No invitations to visit friends or to go to any entertainments. It seemed that John Saxon had very little life outside of the Lyceum. But, on reflection, I realized that that was true for many of us.

That reminded me that I had to see Jenny after lunch. I had better wind up my investigation. I started to turn away from the desk and bumped into

Inspector Bellamy. He stood in the doorway with Mrs. Stone, tight-lipped, close behind him. I had the lawyer's envelope in my hand and quickly thrust it into my pocket, pushing the desk drawer closed.

"Mr. Rivers. Why are we not surprised to find you here, we wonder?"

"Ah, inspector!" There was really no reason I should not be there but I knew how touchy the inspector could be about his investigations. I had assumed that he had already been through the room but perhaps I was wrong. Whether or not I actually needed an excuse for being there, I quickly thought up one. "I – we – were concerned that Mr. Saxon might have taken home one of the props from *Othello*, and I just needed to make sure it wasn't here. Can't be too careful, you know."

"No, Mr. Rivers, we can't be too careful, can we?" He shook his head in despair and moved back to allow me to pass out of the room.

"I'm surprised to find you working on a Sunday, Inspector," I said as I eased past him.

"A policeman's work is never done, sir. Especially when we have a suicide, or possibly even a murder, to investigate."

"You do agree, then, that it could be murder?"

"We are open to all possibilities, sir. All possibilities."

"I thought you had been here already, inspector?"

"Oh? And what would lead you to believe that, might we ask?" He raised his eyebrows.

"Mrs. Stone said that you had been here to give her the news. Presumably that is why she is in the process of clearing out the room in order to let it."

"Ah. Yes," he said, enigmatically. He then stood there silently.

I mumbled something and ducked out past him and the landlady. There was just time to get some lunch before I met Jenny.

It turned out to be a beautiful afternoon. The sun had some very real warmth to it and Jenny and I ended up relaxing on the grass alongside the waters of the Serpentine in Hyde Park. Jenny was wearing a pale yellow and white organdie dress trimmed with tiny flowers and I thought she looked as pretty as a picture, reclining with her back against a weeping willow tree. Her matching parasol kept the sun from her eyes, where it reflected off the sparkling water. The man-made lake was a popular spot on such beautiful summer days. The surface of the water is always dotted with rowing boats, available for hire at the south end of the lake. We laughed as we watched a family of four in one of the boats, the father trying to teach his young son how to row, cheered on by wife and daughter. They twice lost an oar and had to call upon another boat to retrieve it for them.

I purchased lemonade and some ham and cucumber sandwiches from the refreshment stand. It felt good to relax with Jenny and to try to forget the horror of John Saxon's death. I had told Jenny a little of it though, of course, without the details.

"Do you really think it was murder, Harry?" she asked, unexpectedly. I suppose, like myself, she had the question buzzing about her head. I took my time answering.

"Isn't it too beautiful a day to be thinking about such matters?" I asked.

She smiled . . . her dimples melting my heart. "The day helps put such matters into perspective. It would not be a suitable matter to contemplate on a dull, dreary day."

I smiled. "You have a lot of wisdom, young lady," I said. She smiled in return. "The problem is, we – both myself and Mr. Stoker – don't know of anyone who would want to harm Mr. Saxon. He is not . . . was not, I suppose I must say . . . he was not especially disliked by anyone."

"Someone must have disliked him if he was, indeed, murdered."

"That's true. But there was no one who *obviously* disliked him. Not to that extent anyway."

"'Not to that extent'? So from what you are saying, there was someone who was not happy with him?"

"Oh, there are always disagreements in the theatre. Petty squabbles. Arguments over costumes, or lines, or pacing. One actor up-stages another, whether deliberately or unintentionally, and they won't speak to one another for a couple of performances. But there's never any real animosity."

Jenny sipped on her lemonade for a while. "I'm sure you're right, Harry. So where does this leave things?"

"We think it must be something to do with someone outside the theatre. Perhaps someone from Mr. Saxon's past. But then again, the question is who? We can find no clue to such a person."

I refreshed our drinks and then we took a stroll around the edge of the lake. Before we knew it, it was time for me to return Jenny to Mr. Irving's residence. We both knew that Mrs. Cooke, the housekeeper, didn't tolerate tardiness. Jenny gave me a quick kiss on the cheek, under the cover of her parasol, and I set off back to my own rooms with my heart flying high.

Chapter Eight

Anthony Sampson had taken it upon himself to clean out John Saxon's corner of the men's dressing room. It was only the Guv'nor and Miss Ellen Terry who had their own private dressing rooms. All the other actors and actresses were divided between four rooms: two larger rooms for the principal men and women and two smaller rooms for the extras. John Saxon had long been established in the back corner of the principal men's dressing room and had amassed an assortment of nick-knacks on his makeup table. Old programs, cue sheets, hand-written notes, and the all important makeup box. This box contained the various greasepaint sticks manufactured by Mr. Ludwig Leichner, together with fake hair and the gum for applying it. Over the years the box had lost any semblance of order it may have had originally and become a hodgepodge of makeup bits and pieces known only to John Saxon.

Mr. Sampson appeared at my office Monday afternoon. I was surprised to see him. He didn't normally arrive at the theatre until a couple of hours before curtain up.

"Do you have a minute, Mr. Rivers?"

"Why yes, Anthony. Come on in. What can I do for you?"

He sat down on the only available chair in front of my desk and deposited a small key on the desktop.

"You're in early," I said.

He nodded. He was an older man of medium height, about 60 years of age. He had spent most of his adult life on the stage. He had grey hair, worn long, and matching grey eyes. He was clean-shaven. "I was cleaning up John's corner of the dressing room," he said. "Just thought it needed to be done . . . and I didn't see anyone else offering to do it."

"Yes. Thank you, Anthony. It was on my list of things to do. Just hadn't got to it yet."

"Oh, no criticism, Mr. Rivers. I know how busy you are. It's just that I can't stand to see things get too untidy." He gave a rueful laugh. "Probably comes from my mother always on at me to clean my room, as a child."

We both laughed.

"So what can I do for you, Anthony?" I asked.

He tapped the key that he had on the desktop. "Found this. Was in his makeup box, of all places. Stuck against a stick of number 5. I think John must have dropped it in the box some time and then the makeup stick got put down on top of it. Thought it might be important."

I reached out my hand and he put the key into it. I examined it.

"Probably to his suitcase," I said. "I was just around at his rooms yesterday." I thought for a moment. "But now that I think back, I don't remember seeing any case there."

"So shall I leave it with you then, Mr. Rivers?"

"Yes. Yes, you do that, Anthony. I'll check with Mr. Stoker and see if he thinks it's important. Thank you for bringing it to my attention."

He got up and went off back to the dressing rooms. I got involved in a number of small jobs and didn't remember the key until I came back from dinner. I saw it lying on my desk and, picking it up, went along to my boss's office to show it to him.

"Did you see a suitcase in his room, Harry?" Stoker asked, examining the item.

"I've thought about that, sir, and I'm almost certain there was nothing there that looked as though it would need a key like that. There was a battered suitcase of sorts, in the bottom of the wardrobe, but I distinctly remember that it had only one latch to it – without a lock and with the other latch broken off – and it looked as though it had been fastened up with string."

Mr. Stoker put on his spectacles and held the key close to his eyes, slowly turning it first one way and then the other. "Have you had a good look at this, Harry?"

"No, sir. I didn't think it was especially important. Why? Is there more to it?"

"Indeed there is, Harry." He held it even closer to his eyes for a moment. "See here. It has letters stamped on it. Let me see . . . NPB37."

"NPB37? What does that mean?"

He sat back in his chair and looked up at the ceiling, squinting his eyes as he did when thinking. "NPB. Isn't that the National Provincial Bank? They're over on Bishopsgate. Just past the end of Threadneedle Street and along from the Bank of England."

I had to think but slowly recalled the bank there. A large, ornate building. "Yes, sir. I think you're right. So what does this mean? And what about the number 37?"

Bram Stoker sat with a satisfied look on his face and tapped the key on the desk in front of him. "Harry, I think this may be a key to a safe deposit box at that bank. Did our Mr. Saxon have any assets that you are aware of?"

"John Saxon?" I almost laughed. "Not so far as I know. He always seemed to be living hand to mouth, like so many actors."

"Hmm. Then here's a job for you, Harry, when you can fit it in. I'd like you to get over to Bishopsgate and visit the National Provincial Bank. See if they do in fact hold safe deposit boxes and see if there is one numbered 37."

"Do you want me to open it, sir?"

He was silent for a while, and then said, "I think we need to, Harry. We need to find out all we can about our late thespian friend. We owe it to him, I think. There is no need for you to remove anything from the box – not at the moment, anyway – just to make note of what is there. Can you fit that in, Harry, do you think?"

Tuesday morning found me at the doors to the National Provincial Bank on Bishopsgate. It was a very impressive building, architect-designed, with a set of elaborate wrought-iron gates opening to a pair of tall, solid oak doors. I seldom went into the City and felt somewhat out of place with all the big financial institutions there. But Mr. Stoker had given me a job to do so I boldly went forward, up the stone steps of the bank. A commissionaire held open the door for me and I went inside. I walked all around the imposing lobby, rapidly reading the various signs indicating the different areas. I spotted *Safe Deposits* and presented myself at the counter.

"Good morning, sir. How may I help you?"

It was a young man dressed in the typical uniform of the City: black frock coat, striped trousers, spats, grey waistcoat with silver half-Albert watch chain, black cravat. His dark hair was smoothed back with Rowland's Macassar Oil; so popular with many young men. He didn't smile but looked to be all business, though with that blank stare that one seems to find in bank clerks throughout London.

I tried to give the impression that I was thoroughly familiar with the working of banks. "I would like access to this safe deposit box, if you would be so kind?" I waved the key in front of him.

"Certainly, sir. And your number?"

"Thirty-seven." I held the key steady for him to verify it.

"If you would care to take a seat, sir, I will return immediately with your box." He waved a hand in the general direction of a chair and, turning briskly, disappeared through a door. I sat down and waited.

After a few minutes the bank clerk returned carrying a flat metal box. He went around behind a counter, put it down, and produced a ledger, which he opened and spun around for me to see.

"If you would just sign here, sir?"

I got up and moved to the book. It was open to today's date and it was obvious where I needed to sign. My slight hesitation was as to whether I should sign with my own name or with John Saxon's. I quickly made the decision. We needed to find out what was in that box. I boldly wrote *John Saxon* on the line alongside the number 37.

I found that I had broken out in a sweat. Suppose they had some way of immediately checking the signature? Did this clerk know John Saxon by sight? What if they thought I was a bank robber? Suppose I was arrested? I was about to blurt out the whole story to the young clerk when he turned away to acknowledge an older gentleman who had just arrived in the area.

"Good morning, Sir Jeffrey," he said, with the slightest of bows. "I will be right with you, sir."

He whisked me and the box across to a line of private cubicles, opened the door to the first of these, placed the box on the table within, and then hurried back to Sir Jeffrey. I closed the door and mopped my face.

The key fitted the box and I opened the lid. It was not a large box . . . I imagine they had various sizes available. Inside was a mishmash of papers. There were several betting slips signed to horseracing bookies and marked *Paid*. It looked as though John Saxon had been in the habit of paying off his bets far more than he did of collecting any winnings. There were also slips from two or three of the gambling clubs, similarly marked as paid. Other than the horse racing at Ascot and Epsom, the days of open public gambling were long over. In 1845, under pressure from the reformers, Parliament had passed an act to amend the laws concerning games and wagers. Anyone with an urge to gamble had to seek out the private establishments, where various games of chance were played with bets anywhere from half-a-crown to five pounds or more. I had learned from Bill Thomas that these places included the popular Berkeley in Albemarle Street, Lyley's, Morris's in Jermyn Street, and "Goody" Levy's in Panton Street. Obviously John Saxon had been familiar with all of these.

There were a lot of cancelled checks made out to a person named Summerfield. They seemed to have been paid on a regular basis over a long period. Interestingly there were also a couple of threatening letters, both from an anonymous female. At least, I presumed that they were from a female since they were on scented letter paper. There was no address nor signature on either of them. The threats were vague and it didn't seem possible to determine the reason for them, though perhaps Mr. Stoker would be able to tell.

In a plain envelope was what, after glancing inside, I presumed to be John Saxon's birth certificate. I didn't examine it closely but pushed it off to the side with the cancelled checks. I was more interested in an old theatre program from the Charles Kean Company, playing at the Manchester Theatre Royal in 1861. The play was *Romeo and Juliet.* A quick glance showed me that John Saxon played Romeo. I was not surprised that he had held on to that program.

My boss had asked me to use my own discretion as to what, if anything, might bear closer investigation . . . in other words, what needed to be "borrowed" from the box and taken back to the Lyceum. I opted for a selection of the cancelled checks, since there were so many of them and they were paid out on such a regular basis. I also took the threatening letters.

Chapter Nine

"Good work on the safe deposit box, Harry," said Mr. Stoker. "These cancelled checks are most interesting. All made out to a 'Summerfield' but with no first name given. Paid regularly on the first of the month. A sizable sum, too. Close to half of what Mr. Saxon was earning here at the Lyceum."

"No wonder he lived in such a cramped little room," I said. I had reported to Mr. Stoker as soon as I returned from the National Provincial Bank. "Is there any clue as to whom the money was being paid?"

"The checks were deposited in a bank in Manchester. I will write to the bank manager there and see what I can find, but it may well necessitate a trip north, to speak to the gentleman face to face. Bank managers can be very protective of their customers, you know."

I knew who would be delegated to make that trip, if it became necessary. Then I had an idea. "Do you think these might be payments to a bookmaker, sir? There were a number of chits in the box showing a history of payments for lost bets at a variety of gambling establishments. Could it be that Mr. Saxon owed a very large sum and was paying it off piecemeal?"

"An excellent thought, Harry, but again I would venture no. These payments have been going on for too long . . . a number of years. I cannot conceive of a gambling bet of such magnitude."

He was right, I knew. "No other clues, sir?" I asked.

"Not unless the recipient of the checks is the same person who wrote the threatening letters, Harry."

"Blackmail?"

"I had wondered about that. But on reflection I doubt it. I think that the payments were probably being made before the letters started and were continuing, uninterrupted, long after. Right up until Mr. Saxon's demise, in fact." He picked up one of the letters and looked at it. "No envelopes with these letters, as you saw, Harry, so it doesn't help us there. I think you are correct in that they were from a woman. We don't know whether they were posted to him or hand delivered. No dates on the letters either. I do have a strong feeling however . . . what my old granny would call a 'glimpse'."

"A glimpse?"

"A glimpse with the third eye, Harry. A brief look beyond."

I said nothing. When my boss got onto the subject of his old grandmother, I found it safest to say nothing and simply smile and nod my head. A hunch or gut feeling to me was a glimpse into another world for Stoker's granny. I waited for him to continue.

"Yes, Harry. I believe that these letters have nothing to do with the monetary payments. They seem to be from a disillusioned young lady. Not to imply that Mr. Saxon had been playing fast and loose with a lady's affections, but certainly there had been a not inconsiderable schism." He looked again at the letter in his hand. "The lady does threaten that 'no one goes free', as she puts it, though she does not say in what manner this retribution will come about." He lay down the letter.

I picked it up and read it.

John: Your little actress friend will pay even if you don't. No one goes free!

I turned to the second one.

John: You cannot make a fool of me and get away with it. Wait for the final curtain. Beware!

"Just a lovers' quarrel, do you think, sir?"

He nodded. "Yes, I think so, Harry. Basically empty threats, although the emotion that I sense in these few brief sentences does rather concern me."

"Do you think they are recent letters, sir?"

"It's difficult to say, Harry, though I rather doubt it." He sniffed the letter. "As you so smartly observed, the paper is perfumed and so we must assume it is from a lady, yet the redolence is but slight, as though it has faded over time. I think these two letters may not be as recent as we might have thought."

"Strange, then, that he would hold on to them."

Stoker shrugged. "It may simply be that he hadn't yet got around to discarding them. No, I think we'll put those aside for now. I will, as I said, follow up on the cancelled checks. You say there was nothing else of relevance in the box?"

I shook my head. "Not to my mind, sir. But I can always go back there at any time, if you think it necessary?"

He shook his own head. "No, I don't think so. Not now, at any rate." He sat back in his chair, put down the letter, and stroked his beard. "Meanwhile – setting this aside for the moment – I don't want to neglect the concern I have for the sudden lack of attendance up in the gods. You remember I had spoken of this before this terrible business with John Saxon? Have you given that any thought, Harry?"

I had to admit that I had not. I didn't like to say that I just hadn't had time to think about it. After all, Mr. Stoker seemed able to do a dozen things at a time. "Have you spoken to anyone else about it, sir?"

Again he shook his head. "I thought you might keep your ears open, in the Druid's Head and whatever other watering holes you frequent. People talk, as well you know, Harry. Just see if you can pick up on any concerns that people have about the Lyceum's top gallery. It's a mystery why they should suddenly stay away. The gods have always been packed, as long as I have been here."

"One thought does occur to me, sir," I said. "What about Sadler's Wells?"

The Sadler's Wells Theatre had been taken over by Mrs. Bateman when she handed over the Lyceum to Mr. Irving, three years ago. She and the Guv'nor had not got along and there had developed bad feeling and rivalry between the two theatres. Mrs. Bateman had died shortly after moving to Sadler's Wells but her place had been filled by her daughter Kate, now Mrs. Kate Crow, who perpetuated the animosity. A few months ago we had suffered a number of incidents – apparent accidents that were designed to affect our play production – that were finally traced to Mrs. Crowe's younger brother Ralph.

"Ralph Bateman?" My boss raised an eyebrow. "I thought he was out of town?"

"So did I, sir, but it won't hurt to double-check. It's possible that Ralph, or one of his cronies, has been spreading lies about the Lyceum."

"Even if it was him, I'd be surprised if he had managed to make such an impact on the very backbone of the Lyceum's audience."

"I'm sure you're right, sir, but I will see what I can find out. As you say, I can keep my ears open at all the local taverns." I chuckled. "Perhaps there's a vampire loose and he's been seen up in our gods?" Mr. Stoker did not laugh.

I made a point of dining at the Druid's Head, before the evening performance. I waved to big John Martin, the tavern keeper, and settled down with a tankard of porter and a huge helping of steak and kidney pudding, mashed potatoes, carrots, and peas. A hunk of still hot, freshly-baked bread and a wedge of Cheddar cheese, completed my repast.

The inn was crowded, as it always was at that hour, and I had no difficulty overhearing more than one conversation at neighboring tables. However, no one seemed to be talking about the Lyceum so I thought I would throw out a comment. As John passed nearby I called out to him. "Haven't seen you up in the gods at the Lyceum lately, John."

He stopped short and turned to look at me. The conversations died in the immediate vicinity of where I sat.

"I'm 'earing as 'ow it mayn't be the best place to be sittin'," he said.

"What do you mean? You've always loved the gods and you know it."

He slowly nodded. "No denying that, 'arry."

"So what's changed?" I pressed him. I looked around, to see if anyone else wanted to speak. I didn't have to wait long.

"John's right." It was a young man I'd seen in the tavern on a number of occasions. He came to his feet. He was tall and thin with hooded eyes and a hooked nose. I believe he worked for a lawyer in Lincoln's Inn Fields. "I used to go up in the gods every week, but I started hearing rumors of . . . I don't know. Strange happenings? Appearances? Ghosts? Vampires? I don't hold with such but I tell you, I wasn't going to take any chances!" He sat down again.

"How long has this been going on?" I asked.

He shrugged. "Only a week or so I suppose. Seems longer."

"That's ridiculous!" I cried, looking around and daring anyone to contradict me. "There's nothing up in the gods at the Lyceum! You said yourself that you've been going there for a time. Have you actually seen anything?"

"I 'eard as 'ow one of the main actors was murdered up there and 'is body thrown down into the pit!" A   short, bald-headed man with no neck and a red face spoke up. He wiped the froth of his beer from his mouth with the back of his hand. "I ain't been there for more'n a week. Used to go all the time. Could watch that 'enry Irving over an' over. 'e's a right one an' no mistake."

I was gratified to learn that we had patrons who did not tire of the same play, but it was disconcerting to hear that some wild rumor could turn them away. "I don't deny that one of our actors fell from the top balcony. Not a 'main actor', I would add. But that doesn't mean there are ghosts up there . . . or vampires!"

"P'raps it was a vampire what pushed 'im off the balcony," said someone a few tables away. I couldn't make out who it was.

I laughed, though even to my ears the laugh sounded hollow. "Vampires don't go pushing people off balconies."

"No! Worserer than that," said the bald man.

John Martin spoke up. "There's a lot of people come in 'ere, 'Arry. A lot who feel the same way. I 'ear what they say, though I don't say anything m'self. I 'ear 'em talk about vampires, or what they think are vampires. Strange, frightening creatures. Pale skin and red eyes, they say. I 'aven't 'eard tell of anyone being bitten by a vampire, but I'm thinking lots of folks is playing it safe and staying away from your Lyceum for that very reason, so that they *won't* get bitten."

"What do you suggest I do, John?" I asked.

He shrugged. "That's something you must decide." He went back behind his counter and resumed carving the roast beef.

I sat and thought about it. Around me the conversation settled back into talk of the weather, the increase of four-wheeler traffic, the surliness of the bobbies, and the cheekiness of crossing sweepers. I finished my meal and drained my porter. I really hadn't learned a great deal, just that fear of vampires was at the bottom of the fall-off of attendance in the gods. Nothing of value to carry back to Mr. Stoker. I paid my bill and left.

All through that evening's performance I went over, in my head, what John Martin and his customers had said. What had started this sudden rebellion against the Lyceum upper gallery, I wondered? What, or who? I could understand how such stories of horror can spread, like a wild fire. Such was the nature of rumor. People seemed to love to be frightened especially when, in their heart of hearts, they knew that they were safe. How many truly believed in vampires, I pondered? How many truly believed that they were risking their life by sitting up in the gods to watch a stage performance? And yet the news of John Saxon's death now added fuel to the flames. Until we discovered the exact cause of his fall we could not dispel the rumors with any conviction. I determined to find out that truth. To find out whether it had been accident, suicide, or murder.

Murder? That was something I really did not want to find. It would certainly be one thing to know definitely that Mr. Saxon had been murdered but that, in turn, would then open a whole new investigation as to who had murdered him and why. Answering one question led to asking a new one. It was never ending, it seemed.

The newspapers did us no favors. Rumors were reported as though they were facts. One man imagining that he had been pursued by a vampire rapidly became "proof" that vampires existed. The slightest mention of these creatures of the night was invariably followed by neighbor telling neighbor "It must be true, I saw it in the newspaper." By the time of the final curtain that night my head was spinning. We could, perhaps, leave it to Inspector Bellamy to probe the suicide or murder question, but it was up to me to expose the fallibility of the belief that a vampire haunted our upper gallery.

Chapter Ten

I determined it was time to make another expedition into the East End. Somehow I always seemed to do this on a matinée day. Today was no exception: it was a Wednesday. This meant that I had to be back at the Lyceum by two of the clock at the latest. I may well have to forego lunch, I thought ruefully.

I left Mrs. Bell's lodging house right after I had broken my fast. Burned porridge, watery eggs, and weak tea were not my preferred fortification but I had little choice. I had originally thought to hop onto an omnibus but none of them started operating before eight of the clock in the morning and I wanted to be well on my way by then. Also, most were pulled by two slow-moving shire horses and none went deep into the East End. One of the light green suburban ones went as far as the Old Kent Road but if I was to get to Whitechapel and Mile End Old Town, as was my intent, then I would have to spring for a hansom or a growler. The fares on the omnibuses ranged from a ha'penny to sixpence, though if you were going out to Richmond, for example, it would cost you a shilling. By contrast, the four-wheeler would cost me at least a florin and a hansom more likely half-a-crown. But beggars can't be choosers so I hailed a hansom and was on my way.

I knew that many of the regular theatre-goers who frequented the gods came from Aldgate, a Jewish sector of the East End. Houndsditch and the Minories were the main Jewish quarters. The worst part of Whitechapel abutted them on the east and Spitalfields on the west. When I say "the worst part of Whitechapel" I'm talking about that area marked to be demolished because of its poverty and filth; insanitary dwellings breeding disease and crime. It was an area of the foulest rookeries. Some of the houses were three stories tall, leaning inwards and built close one on another so that the light of the sun never did reach through to the ground. Privies, if they could be so called, were pits in the cellars of the slums and the only running water available was from a standing pipe at the end of the street. I determined to avoid that area altogether.

The Jewish tailoring workshops were mostly in Whitechapel. Spitalfields and part of Shoreditch formed the manufacturing district, once occupied largely by silk-weavers descended from the Huguenots of two centuries ago, though today the chief industries are furniture and boot making. I knew when I had arrived at my destination by the plethora of shop signs in Hebrew. I had no real idea of where I was going so I had the cab set me down at the junction of Whitechapel High Street and Commercial Road, where I stood for some considerable time gazing about me.

"You lost, young fella?"

It was a man of my own height, with black hair, beard and mustache. He wore a black bowler hat and a faded grey suit that had obviously seen many seasons. His shoes were scuffed and down at the heel. In contrast, his brown eyes were bright and sparkling, the lines around them crinkling as though he smiled a lot.

"Not lost, exactly," I said. "More like, getting my bearings."

"What are you looking for?"

"That's just the problem. I'm not sure." His black eyebrows rose in question. I laughed and he smiled. I introduced myself and told him of my quest. "I know we get a number of patrons from this area who come to the Lyceum on a regular basis," I said. "But where do I find them? I'd just like a chance to talk to one or two; to get their thoughts on what is going on up in the gods."

"Perhaps I can help you," said my newfound friend. He tipped his hat and then put out his hand. I shook it. "My name is Matityahu Max Meisel. You can call me Max. I am Latvian. Come! I'll take you to where you can sit and talk."

Latvians were one of many Jews who had found sanctuary in England's capital and now called home this area around Aldgate. Pogroms in many Russian towns, in Poland, Latvia, Estonia, and elsewhere, had driven them here. I recalled reading in the newspapers of the Odessa pogroms in recent years. I felt for these people, cast out of their homelands.

After traveling through a number of narrow, winding streets and alleyways, we soon found ourselves in a small café, sipping cups of strong black coffee. I studied a dish of what Max called moussaka. It featured lamb, aubergines and tomatoes. I was suspicious of it at first but quickly found it to be delicious. Max ordered himself some of the same thanking me as he did so, I think to ensure that I picked up the bill. But that was all right. I was there to meet people and Max was the one who could introduce them.

Max waved a hand to a young couple as they came into the café and they crossed to join us. He introduced me and told them why I was there. They were Mihhail Lotman and his wife Zara, both Estonians. Mihhail was tall and painfully thin, clean-shaven with fair hair rapidly receding. His pale blue eyes locked onto mine as he gave me a firm handshake.

"*Tere,*" he said. "Hello."

Zara was equally tall and thin, though the slimness seemed to suit her. She was strikingly beautiful and I found myself fascinated by her high cheekbones and flashing brown eyes. She wore her long black hair loose, to her shoulders; not a style approved by the gentry of the West End.

They both sat and I ordered coffee for them. I asked if they'd care to eat anything and they both called for goulash. When we were all settled I started my questions.

"Yes, we love the theatre," said Mihhail, his wife nodding in agreement. "We go as often as we can afford it, though we can only afford to go up in the gods even then."

"Have you heard the stories?" I asked.

They did not answer immediately but glanced at one another. Zara sipped her coffee while Mihhail quietly murmured "We have. Yes."

"Can you give me any idea of what is being said, and by whom? Do you think there is any truth to these stories about vampires?" I sat forward on the edge of the hard wooden seat.

"It is said that there is a vampire that lives in your gods." I started to respond but Mihhail held up his hand to stop me, and continued. "All who attend the theatres in this city know of the Drury Lane Theatre's Man in Grey. A ghost who is supposed to haunt that venue and to appear, from time to time, in various parts of the auditorium. Some have suggested that your Lyceum is trying to create its own ghost, to attract people to it." He chuckled, mirthlessly. "After all, many go to Drury Lane more in the hopes of seeing the ghost than with any true desire to see the offered play."

I laughed. "If that were true, the idea has certainly rebounded for the Lyceum, for our audience is staying away, not increasing."

He nodded. "And if true, then a vampire was a poor choice of phantom."

"It is one thing to view a spectral gentleman seated in one of the boxes but quite another to come face to face with a vampire," said Zara.

"But are there not other theories?" asked Max.

"Oh, yes." Zara nodded and then deferred to her husband.

"There is a faction that truly believes in vampires and, consequently, will never return to your gods until the theatre has been exorcized," said Mihhail. "But the larger group are those who have previously had no strong feelings for or against the living dead, but are easily swayed by the *possibility*, backed by waves of gossip, fear, newspaper reports, and the pure love of being frightened."

"Does anyone claim to have actually seen a vampire at the Lyceum?" I asked.

"Oh, yes." Mihhail looked at his wife.

Zara – reluctantly, it seemed to me – said, "I have."

Max almost spilled the coffee he was on the point of raising to his lips. I must admit that I was unprepared for that answer. We all waited for the young lady to explain.

"I was in the front row of the gods. A good seat over to the right. I think you call it 'stage left', which I always find confusing. Anyway, I forget which scene was playing, I think it might have been where Emilia gives the 'kerchief to Iago. For some reason I happened to glance up to my left. The top box on that side of the stage is seldom used, it seems to me . . ."

"There is a very poor view of the stage," I explained. "Most people take the boxes more to be seen than to see, but they do still want to take in the performance. Those top boxes are not the best for either reason, and so are often empty."

Zara nodded agreement. "So I believe."

"Go on, Zara!" urged Max.

"Oh, sorry. Yes. I happened to glance up towards the box and I saw this face looking out. The box curtains were still pulled closed but the face was thrust out between them, looking not at the play but all around at the audience. It was the face of a vampire, I swear!"

"How can you be so certain?" I asked.

"It was deathly pale. White. I thought I caught a glint of red in the eyes, as they turned on me."

I immediately thought of the stories from both Sadler's Wells theatre and the Theatre Royal Drury Lane that state that the old clown Joseph Grimaldi's face, eerily painted in his white make-up, has been seen to appear in those theatres' boxes. Reportedly Grimaldi's pale face gazes down on the stage watching the performance, as the audience members sit in the dark unaware of the apparition silently floating just behind them.

"The eyes turned on you?" Max was incredulous, as was I.

"He – I presume it was a he – looked all around the auditorium, down towards the circles. And then, suddenly it seemed, he looked across into the gods. He saw me looking at him!" Her own face had turned pale and she clutched her coffee cup to her and drank deeply. No one said anything for a long moment and then she continued. "His eyes locked on mine and I found it difficult to look away. Then, just as quickly as he had appeared, he withdrew his head inside the box and I sat back in my seat. I found it hard to breathe."

"I remember that," said Mihhail. "I wondered what was wrong. Zara is always so full of life. It was quite unlike her to feel faint."

"We left in the middle of the performance," said his wife. "Something we had never done before. I couldn't wait to get outside, into the cool evening air. We have not been back since."

"But – but . . ." I searched for a rational explanation. "There is still no proof that it was a vampire."

"What about the white face?" asked Max.

"If true, that is certainly unsettling," I said. "But it could just have been a trick of the light. The gas chandelier is so much closer to you up in the gods, and to that top box. It can drain color from you. That's why the actors wear stage make-up . . . because they need to compensate for that lighting."

Max nodded his head. "You may be right."

"I know what I saw . . . and what I felt," said Zara quietly.

We spent an hour or more talking and then the Lotmans excused themselves and left. Max was able to bring one or two others to our table but they had nothing new to impart. Very much aware of the time, I thanked Max for his help and prepared to return to the Lyceum. As soon as I could, I vowed I would search the upper boxes in the auditorium.

"Before you leave, Harry," said Max as I stood up, "I was wondering if you knew of the *Aluka*?"

"Aluka?"

"Yes. It is an ancient female creature that is found in old traditional stories among the European Jews of the Rhineland. It is referred to in the Testament of Solomon and is much like the vampire."

"I have an idea that Mr. Stoker mentioned it," I said. "Though I wouldn't swear to it. He tells me so many tales of legend and folklore."

"Well I just thought I'd mention it," said Max. "It might be why your theatre goers from this area are prone to believe in vampires. More so, perhaps, than others."

"A good thought, Max. Thank you."

Chapter Eleven

Between houses I determined to have a good look at the boxes up at the level of the gods. A number of theatres, including the Lyceum, only sell those seats as a last offering when there is a packed house. As I mentioned to Max and the Lotmans, anyone in the top box, unlike the lower ones, cannot be seen well by others in the audience and has a very poor view of the stage. But if there is nothing else available, then people will sit up there.

As soon as the audience had dispersed after the afternoon performance, I started up the stairs. It's quite a climb to the top level and I was breathing heavily by the time I got there. I moved along the narrow passageway behind the top row of the gods and came to the door of the box. For some reason I stood for a moment and listened, with my ear to the door. I don't know what I expected to hear . . . sounds of vampire activity? There was, in fact, silence. I opened the door and looked in. It was dark so I moved forward and opened the curtains that were drawn across the front of the box. Although we were between houses the main chandelier was alight in the auditorium, to allow the front-of-house personnel to do any necessary cleaning before the evening performance. I looked over the edge of the box and saw the crews moving through the circles below.

Turning back to the inside of the box, I noted that the ornate, gilt, upholstered chairs had been lined up against the left side of the box, leaving the center area empty and I was able to move about freely. There was really nothing to see. I felt slightly disappointed. I don't know what I was expecting. What sort of evidence does one find, to confirm vampire activity? There were no blood-drained corpses (thank the heavens!) nor empty coffins.

Such thoughts brought a smile to my lips and I turned away and left the box, closing the door behind me. I walked across to the box on the opposite side of the proscenium but it was the same story, though there the chairs were still set out in two lines, facing to the front and the box itself appeared slightly larger than its counterpart. I wondered what the explanation might be for the face that Zara Lotman had seen. I did believe that she had seen something, she was not the sort of woman to have imagined such a thing, but whether or not the face she saw belonged to a vampire was another question.

Closing that door, I turned away and almost bumped into my boss.

"Mr. Stoker! What are you doing up here?"

"I thought to take another look at the spot from which our Mr. Saxon fell, Harry. And yourself?"

"I just wanted to have a closer look at the top boxes, sir. Make quite sure there was nothing . . . unusual there."

He nodded understandingly, and then beckoned me to follow him. We went into the gods and down the steep stairs to the railing over which Mr. Saxon had toppled.

"I've been turning over in my mind that question of suicide or murder, Harry."

"You've reached a conclusion?"

"I think so." He waved me forward to stand beside him looking over the rail. "Now, if you were going to kill yourself by jumping over the edge here, to land on the floor of the stalls far below, how would you do it?"

I looked at him blankly.

"Would you just climb over and jump?" he persisted.

"Well, yes. I suppose so."

He shook his head. "No, you wouldn't."

"I wouldn't?"

"No! Look over, Harry. If you just jumped off you would do precisely what the body of Mr. Saxon did . . . you would strike the edge of the balcony below and then, from there, hit the one below that, and eventually land in the stalls. That's not a clean way to kill yourself, now is it?"

I began to see what he was saying. "You're right, sir. If you wanted to kill yourself then you'd want a quick death, by falling the whole way without interruption and hitting the floor far below"

"Exactly." He looked pleased with himself. "And to do that you would need to jump as far out and away from this top edge as possible, not drop straight down."

"Jump out far enough to be sure of missing the lower two balconies."

"Exactly. But the bent guard rails on those balconies, not to mention the bone-breaking they must have caused – presumably we'll learn the extent of that when Inspector Bellamy gets the autopsy report – indicate it was a fall that started straight over the edge. The sort of thing that could result from being pushed over."

We were both silent for a moment, as the implications sank in. Mr. Stoker was right, I was sure. We were certain it was not an accident so, if John Saxon had not committed suicide then he must have been murdered. Satisfied, we both returned to the lower level of the theatre and, with an agreeable grunt, my boss went off to his office.

Guy Purdy was waiting for me when I got back to my own office. His face had its usual worried look.

"Harold, dear boy, I really must ask you to speak to Mr. Stoker."

"What's the problem? Perhaps it's something I can take care of?"

He shook his head. "No, Harold. I think this calls for action from our theatre manager. No offence, dear boy."

"None taken. So what is it, Mr. Purdy?"

"It's that wretched policeman. What's his name . . . Bellamy?"

I sighed. "Inspector Bellamy. Yes, he's in charge of the investigation of John Saxon's death. What's the problem?"

"The problem, Harold, is that he thinks I did it! He thinks I killed John!"

I was surprised. Guy Purdy was the most inoffensive gentleman you could imagine. I have seen him stepping to one side so as not to disturb the theatre cat. To even think of him harming anyone was inconceivable. But then, we were talking about Inspector Bellamy.

"Where does he get that idea?" I asked.

He shook his head. "I cannot imagine. Yes, John and I had our differences on occasion. Of course we did. But John was a sweet man. I would never have harmed the hair of his head."

I could see that the old actor was getting emotional. This was definitely something for my boss to manage.

"Don't worry, Guy. I'll speak to Mr. Stoker right away. Why don't you come with me to his office now. We should have plenty of time before this evening's performance. I don't think he has gone to dinner yet."

Mr. Stoker seemed to agree with me that Guy Purdy was probably incapable of harming anyone, least of all John Saxon. He said a few soothing words to the old actor and Mr. Purdy departed to dine before the evening performance. I was beginning to feel peckish myself.

"Oh, by the way, Harry, now that Inspector Bellamy's name has been brought up again, would you do me a favor?"

Being asked to do a favor for my boss really meant that he was giving me a job to do. There was no question of declining.

"Of course, sir."

"Get hold of the inspector and find out his views on vampires. I'm not sure whether or not he believes in them but with all the rumors circulating, it may influence how he views our troubles here at the Lyceum."

"You want me to go around to Scotland Yard?" That would not be a favorite destination of mine.

"You needn't do that, Harry. He'll turn up here at the theatre again before long. John Saxon's death is an ongoing investigation, after all. I'm sure you can wait until you encounter him here, but I would like to get some sort of an idea as to where he stands on the subject. As you know, he can be extremely biased on occasion. We need to be aware of where he may be heading in his enquiries." He ran his hands through his hair. "Slanting the guilt for Saxon's death towards Guy Purdy, for example, is something we should definitely try to turn aside. I am now certain that it was murder – apparently Bellamy is following that line of thought – I just don't believe that Guy Purdy was the one who committed it. Meanwhile, I would be interested to learn whether or not the good inspector might be deciding to tie it in with vampires, or some such nonsense."

"I don't think he has mentioned them so far."

"No, I don't think he has. But I'd be surprised if our good inspector doesn't do so before long. Forewarned is forearmed, Harry."

"Yes, sir. Oh, by the way. My friend Max Meisel spoke of a vampire called Aluka."

"The aluka, or aluga. That's the ancient Hebrew word for a leech. A blood-sucker. You'll find it in the Jewish Bible in Proverbs 30:15, Harry."

"And you believe in those, sir?"

He waved a hand. "Whether or not there might be credence to the ancient vampire, Harry, I withhold judgement. But this modern influx, these supposed vampire attacks in the East End and elsewhere? No, I do not believe that there is such a creature loose among us."

I felt somewhat relieved to hear him say that. I didn't believe in vampires myself, but when you hear so many stories, and they strike so close to home, you cannot help but wonder. I was encouraged by my boss's words.

"Are you going to share your thoughts on suicide versus murder with Inspector Bellamy?" I asked.

He smiled as he shook his head. "No, Harry. I think we'll wait awhile and see what line of thought he's following."

"If he's accusing Mr. Purdy then presumably he has settled on murder."

"We both know that the good inspector likes to cover all eventualities. He may be pointing the finger at poor Guy but I'm sure he's still juggling the possibility of suicide. Meanwhile, it's up to you and me to examine the murder scenario."

"Where do you suggest I start, sir?"

He thought for a moment. "You might see what friends John Saxon might have had outside of the Lyceum."

"Outside the theatre?" It was a novel idea, I thought. I was always so involved in the productions myself that I never really considered anyone having a life beyond the Lyceum walls. But of course! I mentally slapped myself. "I'll get right on it, sir."

"Now I must be on my way," Stoker continued, getting to his feet. "I'm supposed to be partaking of refreshments with the Guv'nor before the second house." He picked up his top hat, gloves, and cane and left his office.

I had better get over to the Druid's Head myself, I thought.

"Vampires? Vampires! No we don't believe in vampires. Of course we don't! Why do you ask?"

Inspector Bellamy was most vehement, spitting out the words. I immediately thought of the Bard's words in Hamlet: "The lady doth protest too much, methinks." Though in this case it was the police inspector not the lady, who was protesting.

"No especial reason, inspector," I said. "It's just that there has been so much publicity about vampires recently. It seems that never a day goes by without some reference to them in one of the newspapers."

My boss had been right and Inspector Bellamy had appeared backstage not a half-hour before curtain-up. I tried to explain that it was a bad time and that he couldn't roam the auditorium if that was what he had in mind, but he nonchalantly waved a hand at that idea.

"We are here to have a word with one of two of your actors, Mr. Rivers. This is a time when we know we will be able to catch them. Don't worry. We will not be in your way."

A police inspector wandering about backstage? How could he not be in our way?

"I understand that you view Mr. Guy Purdy with suspicion," I said.

He sniffed and looked down his nose at me. "We do have reason to believe that that gentleman may be involved to some greater or lesser degree."

"Why? Just because you've been told – misinformed, I might add – that he had a disagreement with Mr. Saxon?"

"A very heated disagreement, we believe."

"But in fact he *didn't*," I cried. "That was a story started by a past cast member who had an axe to grind. Guy Purdy and John Saxon were, in fact, good friends." I was beginning to get angry. This talk of the two old actors fighting over who should get which part had been fueled by backstage gossip started by a miscreant now languishing in jail. It was time to put a stop to it. But I could see that the inspector was not listening.

"We had it in mind to remove your Mr. Purdy to Scotland Yard, to undergo some rigorous questioning."

"You can't do that!" I cried. "Apart from anything else, he's needed in *Othello*. You can't start decimating the cast."

He pursed his lips and stood a moment in thought. "We have decided not to pursue that line *for the moment*." He emphasized the words. "But if he is to remain here at the theatre then we will need some assurance that he will not run away."

I could not imagine Guy Purdy fleeing the law, even if he were guilty of any offence. I tried to speak calmly. "Inspector Bellamy. I will be more than happy to take it upon myself to vouch for Mr. Purdy and to guarantee his continued presence here at the Lyceum, so that he is available to you whenever you need him."

Bellamy remained thoughtful for a few moments. Then, "Very well. Mr. Guy Purdy is, then, your responsibility, Mr. Rivers. We will, however, be placing a constable in the vicinity of the theatre – on the outside, you may rest assured – to make doubly sure that the suspect does not flee the scene. He will be responsible for Mr. Purdy's movements outside of theatre hours. Now we have questions to ask of your people."

He turned and disappeared in the direction of the greenroom. I breathed a sigh of relief, though wondered if I had made a wise decision. How was I to check on John Saxon's extra-curricula activities if I was anchored to Guy Purdy? But Bellamy had said that the police would take over that role during after-theatre hours. That's when I would have to do my probing.

Before the evening performance was over I'd had a chance to question Guy Purdy, Anthony Sampson, William Hammermind, Toby Merryfield, Arthur Swindon, and Bill Thomas. Of them all, only Bill Thomas was able to provide any helpful information. I should have thought to ask him in the first place. Bill Thomas, our theatre doorman, seemed to know at least something about everyone. I wondered what nuggets he treasured about myself.

"Oh, our Mr. Saxon was a tight one," he said. "Played it very close to the chest. Kept himself to himself, you might say. Any friends outside the Lyceum? Not so you'd know. Though there was one person he once spoke of. Young fella he knew in his early days, when he first got to treading the boards – or so he said. As I understand it, Mr. Saxon recently bumped into this man again. Let me see . . . name of Andrews, I'm thinking. Gilbert Andrews, I'm pretty sure it was."

I was unable to squeeze anything else out of Bill but that was a start. Gilbert Andrews. If this man had also been an actor, and it sounded as though he had, then I should be able to track him down through any number of theatrical agencies. I was excited. This was a good start, I thought. I looked forward to sharing the information with my boss.

Chapter Twelve

Thursday morning found me outside a frosted-glass-paneled door with the words *Theatre World* painted on it. It was two floors above the Admiral Duncan tavern on Old Compton Street. *Theatre World* was a professional journal for actors, actresses, back-stage staff, and any and all connected with the theatre. Although the magazine featured some few articles on various aspects of the profession, its main purpose, and source of revenue, was the advertisements that it carried. Along with company displays proclaiming the virtues of wigs, make-up, costumes, lighting, properties, and the like, it also bore announcements of casting calls, agents seeking clients, actors seeking agents, rooming houses catering to actors, and several pages of personal advertising by said actors and actresses. Here you could learn of an individual's talents, his or her experience, vocal range, abilities, and references. *Theatre World* had been a mainstay of the profession since 1837 and had become almost indispensible to anyone even remotely connected with the stage.

I had occasion to visit the publication a few months ago and nodded greeting to the office manager as I entered. He did not appear to recognize me however, peering at me questioningly over the tops of his steel-rimmed spectacles. He had a cigar clenched between his teeth – I'd swear it was the same one he had been chewing upon at my last visit – and hovered over a young lady who was pounding away at a typewriting machine.

"Yes?"

I introduced myself, though he did not respond in kind. However, I had learned that his name was Mr. Herschel.

"We are very busy, Mr. Rivers. What is it you want? Judy, hurry up with that!" This last he addressed to the young lady at the typewriting machine. She appeared to ignore him.

"I was wondering if you had any record of a Mr. Gilbert Andrews," I said. "He ..."

"Actor? Stagehand? Lighting? Be specific, sir. We are very busy here."

"Yes. Yes, of course. He is an actor. At least I presume he is still on the stage. I don't know if you keep a listing . . ."

"We do. We did. Judy would know. Right, Judy?" The typing continued unabated. "Listing not up to date though," continued Mr. Herschel. "Just can't keep up with it. Lead? Character?"

"I beg your pardon?" I said.

"Lead actor? Character actor? What roles did he play, Mr. Rivers? We are very ..."

This time I was able to interrupt him. "Yes, I know you are very busy, Mr. Herschel. But this is important. I really don't know much about the man but I would think he would play lesser roles, not necessarily leads."

"Pass me the book, Judy," he said. He worked in his waistcoat with his shirt sleeves rolled up. There was no sign of his jacket. I could see sweat stains under his arms, attesting to his claim to be extremely busy. The young lady continued banging down the keys of her machine, ignoring his request for a book. He reached across her and pulled a tattered volume, with many loose sheets projected from it, off a shelf and thrust it in my direction.

"Look in there. He may be in it, he may not. If he's not, we have plenty more volumes."

I thanked him and took the book to a nearby table, pushing aside the accumulation of papers and old magazines. I glanced briefly at the office staff. Mr. Herschel was extremely thin, clean-shaven, with gray hair plastered across the top of his balding head. The typewriter lady appeared young, but was wearing a lot of make-up that I supposed might be appropriate for someone working for a theatrical journal. She had a generally delicate touch on her machine but would occasionally pound down on the keys as though to emphasize what she was typing. The whole time I was there she completely ignored both myself and her employer, even when he addressed her directly. I presumed that it took much concentration to operate such a machine.

I worked my way through the book I had been given. It was an alphabetical classified listing of men and women, grouped under such headings as *Lead Actor/Actress, Minor Roles, Singer,*

Stagehand, Lighting, and so on. Many of the pages had come loose and were stuck back out of order. There were additions that had been written in and others crossed out and marked *Deceased.* I could find no mention of Gilbert Andrews in any of the classifications. I said as much to Mr. Herschel.

"Where'd you come across him?" he asked.

"I believe he might have been with a company up north," I started to say.

"Up north?" He actually removed the cigar from his mouth as he snorted. "Huh! Why didn't you say so? You are not the brightest light on the floats, if I may say so, Mr. Rivers. Lyceum or not!"

I was not used to being insulted and drew myself up to my insignificant height. "What do you mean, sir?" I demanded.

"Well, stands to reason. We only deal with the South of England area, with particular emphasis on London. If your man is up north – up above the Midlands – then you want to check with *Stage North*, or . . . what's the other one, Judy?"
There was no reply. He continued, "Oh yes, *Northern Footlights.*"

"Do they have offices in London?" I asked.

"Of course they do! Everyone has offices in London. Now, excuse me. You've wasted a lot of my time, Mr. Rivers. We are very busy."

"Very busy," I echoed. "Yes, I know. Thank you for your help, Mr. Herschel." I went out, banging the door unnecessarily loudly behind me. I don't think they noticed – they were too busy.

It was in my lunch hour that I came in direct contact with the "police escort" that had been attached to Guy Purdy. It consisted of a sergeant and a constable. I met them quite by chance in the Druid's Head, seated at the next table to mine. Sergeant Fairview was a short, gruff, overweight man with a cast to his right eye. He wheezed as he spoke – which was little; he was inclined to mutter short, staccato sentences – and had frequent spells of coughing. Constable Jimmy Hathaway, on the other hand, was a bright, breezy young man, new to the force. He seemed to take an interest in everything, constantly looking about him with his shining blue eyes.

"Our 'ost says as 'ow you was a big wheel at the Lyceum," said Jimmy, nodding toward where John Martin stood behind the counter, carving the roast beef. John was the tavern's landlord.

I smiled. "Not so much of a big wheel," I said. "I'm simply the Stage Manager. If there is any truly 'big' wheel, other than Mr. Henry Irving, it would be my boss, Mr. Bram Stoker, the Theatre Manager."

"Ah! I've 'eard of 'im," said Jimmy knowingly. "The inspector says to watch out for 'im."

"Watch your tongue, constable," snapped the sergeant.

"Yessir," said Jimmy, giving me a wink.

"'No fraternizing', said Inspector Bellamy." Sergeant Fairview cut into his roast beef and held his mouth in a firm, straight line until such time as he needed to open it to take in the meat.

"I understand you two gentlemen are keeping an eye on our Mr. Purdy during the hours he's not engaged in the theatre," I said.

"S'right," said the constable, unabashed by the sergeant's comment.

"And you watch him doing the play stuff," said Fairview. "Best you don't let him slip out any time."

I found it disconcerting to look at the sergeant, not being able to tell whether or not his right eye was looking at me or not.

"Have you been working with Inspector Bellamy for any length of time, Constable?" I tried to engage the younger man in conversation.

"He's new," said Fairview, and then broke into a fit of coughing.

"Brand new, you might say," added Jimmy, with a smile. "I didn't expect to start off at Scotland Yard but it seems that's what was meant to be, as the goose said when 'is 'ead was lopped off by the butcher."

I smiled. I imagined that Jimmy was a year or so younger than myself and I felt a certain sympathy for him. I remembered my early days at the Lyceum, little more than three years ago now. I had been unsure of myself at that time yet didn't have the Cockney self-assurance that Jimmy seemed to have.

"So how is it you are both sitting here having lunch?" I asked. "Curtain-up isn't until this evening, so I won't be watching Mr. Purdy till then."

Jimmy pointed his knife in the direction of the far corner of the tavern. I saw, through the tobacco smoke and dim lighting, that Guy Purdy himself was sitting with Arthur Swindon at a table in the corner.

"Ah!" I said. "I know some of the cast take most of their meals here but I hadn't realized that Mr. Purdy and Mr. Swindon were of that number."

"It seems 'e's decided to stay close to ''ome', as 'e puts it, while the inspector is investigating."

"Makes our lot a bit easier," grunted the sergeant.

"What you got planned for this afternoon then, Mr. Rivers, if I might make so bold?" asked Jimmy, putting his knife to work slicing through his roast beef and then speaking with his mouth full.

"As it happens, I have to go up to Euston and visit the offices of a magazine there," I said. I had ascertained that Euston was where *Northern Footlights* was located. It seemed that *Stage North* had gone out of business.

"Euston?" said Jimmy. "My old mum lives there. Anyfink I can 'elp you wif?"

"Constable Hathaway, you mind your business," said the sergeant, gazing down into his almost empty beer glass.

"What?" Jimmy sounded offended. "Can't I even make a comment, then?"

"Best keep your mind on your job," growled his superior. "Don't need no complications."

"What's to . . ." Jimmy trailed off, turned to me and again winked. I got the feeling that he didn't take his sergeant too seriously. To me he said "If there's anyfink I can 'elp you wif, Mr. Rivers, I know *my sergeant and me*," he emphasized the words; his boss ignored him. "We'll be only too 'appy to oblige. I'm sure that's what the inspector would want too." He sat back with a grin on his face. I found myself really liking Police Constable Jimmy Hathaway.

After lunch I took an omnibus along the Tottenham Court Road to Euston Road. The *Northern Footlights* office was to be found on Seymour Street, between Euston Station and St. Pancras Station. It was located in a back room on the ground floor of an ancient office building. A faded plaque on the wall beside the door proclaimed it to be the *London Offices of NORTHERN FOOTLIGHTS, mouthpiece of the theatre.*

I tapped on the door and turned the handle to enter. The door seemed to be stuck and did not open.

"Ye'll have t'give it a clout!" came a voice from within.

I applied my shoulder to the door and it suddenly sprang open, depositing me in the middle of a cramped little office that seemed to consist of shelves upon shelves of bound copies of the *Northern Footlights* periodical. Apparently this publication had been in print for many years and each and every one was preserved here in the Euston office.

Balancing precariously, standing on the seat of a stool and looking down at me, was a wiry gentleman of indeterminate age. His salt-and-pepper hair appeared wild, uncombed, and awry; his collar was askew. His pince-nez spectacles perched on the very tip of his nose (how could he look through them in that position?) and his waistcoat was unbuttoned and flapping about him. He wore his sideboards bushy and untrimmed, his eyebrows to match. I introduced myself.

"Harry Rivers, Stage Manager of the Lyceum Theatre."

"Would ye do a little managing here, Mr. Rivers?" he responded. "I fear I may have over-reached m'self."

His burr proclaimed him to be a Scotsman. I moved forward and took three weighty volumes from his arms and, with a sigh, he descended to the floor and indicated for me to put the books on the top of the sea of papers covering what I presumed to be a desk.

"Ye'll have come about the rent, I dare say," he said.

"Rent? No. I am trying to trace an actor."

He looked relieved and moved around to stand behind the desk. "Then ye have come to the right place, Mr. Rivers." He extended his hand, which I shook. "Malcolm Buchannan. Now then, who is this fine thespian for whom ye search?"

"A Mr. Andrews," I said. "Gilbert Andrews. I'm afraid I know no more than that. I understand that he played mostly in the north of England . . . and possibly in Scotland also."

"Andrews." He savored the name. "Andrews. Ah!" His eyes lit up. "Ye must be speaking about Tom and Ted Andrews. Double act that appeared for many years at the Glasgow Empire. Very funny. I saw them m'self many times."

"Er, no. I don't think so," I said. "I presume the Glasgow Empire was a variety house. Music Hall? No, this was not a double act. A single gentleman named Gilbert. Gilbert Andrews. A legitimate actor."

The theatrical world is divided into the legitimate theatre, which produces such works as those of Shakespeare, Johnson, Lytton, Molière, and Goldsmith, among others, and the non-legitimate theatre that indulges in pantomimes, musical comedies, music hall acts, and other entertainments. The one tends to be scornful of the other.

"Ah!" The Scotsman nodded his head understandingly. "Then ye'll have to look through one or two of our past editions. I'd suggest concentrating on Liverpool, Birmingham, Manchester, Leeds and Newcastle for a start." He waved his hand towards a set of books bound in dark red. "Those will give ye the theatres. The blue bound ones have plays and other productions, by title."

"Do you not have a simple listing of actors?" I asked.

"Well there is that," he acknowledged. "The green bound books over yon would be where ye'd need to look." He nodded toward another set of volumes. "They may not be right up to date, of course. Actors come and go, y'know."

It had seemed to me to be the obvious place to start, but what did I know? I moved across to the books bound in green cloth.

"There is no index, ye'll find, but the names are in alphabetical order . . . more or less."

"Thank you," I said.

The order turned out to be less rather than more. As I had found at the offices of *Theatre World*, names had been written in, others crossed out, whole sections were either missing or misplaced. However, I did eventually locate a number of people named Andrews. Running my finger down the page I finally found Gilbert Andrews written-in, incorrectly, between a Glen Andrews and a Graham Andrews. I gave a sigh of relief and copied down the details.

"How accurate is this information?" I asked.

Mr. Buchannan shrugged and gave me a wry grin. "Guid help is hard to find, sir. And devilish tricky to handle. We do the best we can."

"You are all by yourself?" I asked, thinking of *Theatre World* and its Judy the typewriting lady.

"Aye, that I am. But we manage."

It seemed I had made a start to finding the mysterious friend of John Saxon. If I could now track down Gilbert Andrews I might be able to uncover more of Mr. Saxon's past. I just hoped that the information I had obtained was accurate. It gave an address in Birmingham that had been crossed out, but it did also list an actors' agent in London. I hoped that he still had contact with his client.

Chapter Thirteen

Bram Stoker sat at his desk, his eyes focused on an empty envelope that he was tapping on the desk surface. There was a frown on his face.

"I think it would give us a more complete picture of John Saxon if we spoke with this lawyer," he said.

I sat in my usual seat in front of his desk, my notebook open on my lap. My boss and I were going over all that we had discovered about our late actor friend, hoping to find a clue that might point us in the direction of his murderer. Mr. Stoker had determined, in his own mind at least, that it was a case of murder and not suicide and I completely agreed with him. From all that we had heard – my new-found friend Constable Hathaway had helped here – Inspector Bellamy had also settled on murder as the cause of death.

The envelope that was our focus of attention was the one I had found in the drawer at Mr. Saxon's back room in Mrs. Stone's establishment. Although empty, it did bear the name and address of a solicitor on Serle Street, Lincoln's Inn Fields. The date stamped on the envelope was from many years in the past yet Mr. Stoker thought it was still worth pursuing.

"You have the details of Gilbert Andrews's agent, Harry. You might pay a visit to both gentlemen this morning, if you would. They are within confortable distance of each other, I believe. Oh, I think you'll be all right." He said this last, when he noticed me glancing out of the window in his office. The sky was overcast yet there seemed no hint of rain.

"That's fine, sir. If it should start to rain I don't think it will last long, and I can always shelter in a shop if necessary."

"Well done, Harry," he murmured. He passed the envelope across the desk to me and I tucked it into my notebook. "I have an appointment with a bank manager myself, this morning," he continued. "To see if he will divulge who it is receiving those checks that John wrote so frequently. He is manager of the local branch of the Manchester bank, so thankfully we won't have to go all the way there after all. But bank managers can be tenacious when it comes to preserving the anonymity of their clients so I don't hold out a great deal of hope, but I will glean what information I may."

I hesitated a moment before standing up ready to leave.

"What is it, Harry?" He could see that something was troubling me.

"It's just . . . what was Mr. Saxon doing up there in the gods? Obviously he was meeting with someone; the 'someone' whom we must assume was his murderer. But why up in the gods? And why at that time, when the auditorium was deserted?"

Mr. Stoker had also risen to depart but now he sat down again. I, too, resumed my seat.

"Good thinking, Harry. Yes, that has also been troubling me. We need to find out who he planned to meet and why. The one will lead to the other. For the meeting to be in the gods, it must have been pre-arranged. It was no casual happenstance. We need to hone in on this planned encounter, and thereby discover the murderer."

Lincoln's Inn Fields is the home of many lawyers attracted by the proximity to the Inns of Court, the professional associations to which all barristers must belong. At one time the Lincoln's Inn Fields Theatre stood there but it was demolished just over thirty years ago, although it had not been used for the production of plays for many years before that.

The solicitor I sought was one Thomas Redpole, Esq.. I quickly located his office, entered, and made myself known to the clerk in the outer room.

"And your business, Mr. Rivers?" asked this young man. He was little more than in his late teens. He had a pimply face and the wisps of hair that indicated a desire to grow a mustache. I could identify with that and so I gave him a smile.

"Merely to enquire regarding a past client of Mr. Redpole's."

"Mr. Redpole don't like to talk about no one as 'e does work for," he offered.

"No. I am familiar with a need for confidentiality," I said. "Please tell Mr. Redpole that I would like just a few moments of his time."

He disappeared but soon returned.

"This way, sir. Straight through the door." He held open the door from which he had just emerged.

The solicitor was a short, rotund gentleman with an abnormally red face. His bulbous nose bespoke of a love of port or brandy. His eyes were mere slits beneath bushy grey eyebrows. His face was unadorned with whiskers of any sort. On his head perched what, to my mind, was a badly fitting wig.

"Please take a seat, Mr. Dithers." He nodded towards the chair in front of his large, polished desk. His voice was hoarse, which I attributed to frequent representations in court . . . though it could have been due to equally frequent visits to the *Coach & Horses* tavern that I had noticed within walking distance of his chambers.

"Rivers," I corrected, though I don't think he was too concerned with the correctness.

"My time is valuable, sir, so I would appreciate it if you would state your business in as concise a manner as you are able."

I produced the envelope I had found in John Saxon's rooms and laid it on the polished desk, sliding it across to him.

"This, I believe, was sent from your office here," I said, "to the gentleman addressed, Mr. John Saxon."

He barely glanced at it.

"That much would seem to be obvious, sir. And your point?"

"As you may see from the date, it was sent some years ago. Mr. Saxon was employed at the Lyceum Theatre, where I am the stage manager. My employer, Mr. Abraham Stoker, was wondering if you could . . . if you *would*, be able to give us some idea of the content of the letter. You may well have a copy of it in your files, I would think."

"And why, pray, sir, would I divulge its contents to you or to your employer?"

"Mr. Saxon was recently murdered, Mr. Redpole. It is our belief that knowledge of the letter's contents may be useful in determining the person responsible."

There was a long pause. Mr. Redpole sat with his eyes fixed on the envelope in front of him. Finally he looked up at me.

"This is most irregular," he said. "Most irregular." He sat a moment longer looking at the envelope before lifting a small silver bell that stood on the corner of his desk. At its ring the door opened and the pimply youth appeared. "Bring me the file for Saxon, John," said Mr. Redpole. The youth disappeared and we sat there in silence for several minutes. Eventually the door again opened and the youth delivered a bulky file to the desk and retired.

Mr. Redpole opened the file and thumbed through it. He paused at one or two of the pages as he progressed. He finally closed it again and sat back. I sat with my eyes fixed on his face.

"There is nothing herein that would have the remotest bearing on anything to do with the death of the deceased," he said, his mouth set in a grim line.

"Surely you cannot know that," I said. "There may be nothing that is obviously connected but . . ." My voice trailed off. I really didn't know what to say, how to pressure the solicitor. Finally, seeing that he was not to be swayed, I said, "Inspector Bellamy of Scotland Yard may well pay you a visit, sir. I think he may be more persuasive than myself."

"Then I shall await his coming."

I made one final plea. "Can you not give me some slight clue as to the business that Mr. Saxon conducted with you, Mr. Redpole? As I said, Mr. Saxon was murdered. We really do need to know all that we can of his background. Any little thing may help in tracking down his murderer."

I like to think that it was my honest plea that tipped the scales. Or perhaps my innocent face? Whatever the reason, the solicitor did – grudgingly, I will admit – offer a clue.

"All I may tell you, Mr. Rivers, is that the letter was to do with Mr. Saxon's divorce. Now I must bid you good day."

It didn't take me long to locate Gilbert Andrews's agent a short walk away on Great Wild Street. His name was Phillip Whitstable, though I found that he pronounced it "Phillipe" as though it were French. However, the man spoke with the strong Yorkshire dialect that rather destroyed any such illusion.

"It's Gilbert you're after, lad? Aye, I'm his representative. I make the bookings for him. He's a good lad is Gilbert. What have you got in mind for him then? You're from the Lyceum, you said? That's a step up, if I may say so. The lad's been used to second-class parts in the provinces up till now, though he is in town at the moment, you know? Not that he's in need of looking for jobs, you understand? It's just that . . ."

I interrupted his flow of rhetoric. "No, I am not here to offer Mr. Andrews a part in a Lyceum production, sir. I merely wish to locate him. I have a number of questions I would like to ask . . ."

"You may ask me any questions you have, lad." It was his turn to interrupt me. "I represent him, as I like to think I made clear."

"No, sir. These are not professional questions; not to do with his career. They are of a more personal nature. Nothing to do with a part in a play."

I went on to explain about Mr. Saxon's death but I don't think Phillip Whitstable was interested in anything beyond possible bookings for his clients. However, I did eventually persuade him to let me have the address of where Gilbert Andrews was staying while in London. It was the Cardinal Wolsey Hotel, off Great Russell Street not far from the British Museum. I had heard of it. "Hotel" was rather a grand name for it, since it was little more than a rooming house popular with itinerant actors. I bade farewell to the agent and returned to the Lyceum.

"So what have we learned?" said Mr. Stoker, when we got together later that Friday morning. "For myself it was very little, I'm afraid. As I feared would be the case, the bank manager was very close-mouthed about his client. He did let slip that this Summerfield was a lady, rather than a gentleman, but other than that he would tell me nothing whatsoever."

"I had slightly better luck, sir," I said, feeling somewhat pleased with myself. "Like your bank manager, the solicitor was close-mouthed yet mentioned that his business with John Saxon had to do with Mr. Saxon's divorce . . . I hadn't even known that he'd been married. And then, going to see Gilbert Andrews's agent, I learned where Andrews is presently staying. I'm planning on paying him a visit after lunch and seeing if I can pick his brains about his old friend John."

"So Mr. Saxon had been married and was divorced?"

"Yes, sir. That surprised me. None of his friends here had mentioned such a possibility. I think they all believed him single. He certainly had been single for the years he had been at the Lyceum."

Mr. Stoker sat silently for a few moments, absorbing things. I tried to sit as quietly. Finally he looked up.

"Well done, Harry. Good thinking. Yes, if you can connect up with this Gilbert Andrews this afternoon we might learn more interesting facts about our late friend. Get off now and get some lunch so that you can make an early start."

I did as he suggested and had a good, if somewhat hurried, lunch at the Druid's Head before setting off for Great Russell Street.

It was easy enough to locate the Cardinal Wolsey Hotel, which was actually on George Street, just off the main road. It was adjacent to the Meux Brewery and was, as I had remembered, a somewhat seedy, rundown establishment in need of a coat of paint on its front door and around the windows. The brass door-knocker had not seen polish in many a long year and whitewash was unknown on the front steps.

I rang the bell that sat on the receptionist's counter. It went unanswered. I rang a second and then a third time. No one appeared. I was wondering what to do next when an elderly gentleman descended the staircase. He was obviously on his way out but glanced at me as he passed.

"Excuse me, sir," I said. "But do you happen to know of a Mr. Andrews, whom I've been given to understand resides here?"

He stopped and wrinkled his brow in thought. "Andrews," he mused. "Andrews? Would that be the north country gentleman on the third floor?"

"The floor I'm uncertain of," I said. "But yes, I do believe him to be from the north."

"Ah!" he nodded his head appreciatively. "Then in answer to your question, young man, yes, I do know of Mr. Andrews. But all I can tell you is what I have just stated . . . he is situated on the third floor. Good day to you, sir." And with that he proceeded on his way out of the hotel.

I don't know what information I had expected but at least the essentials were there. Mr. Gilbert Andrews was indeed staying at the Cardinal Wolsey Hotel and had a room on the third floor. I started the climb up the stairs.

I had no idea which was Andrews's room but there were only three doors on the floor. It was indeed more of a rooming house than a hotel. I took a chance and knocked on the first door I came to. There was no answer. I realized that it was early afternoon and so it was likely that anyone in the residence might well be out and about their business, but I persevered. I tried the second door, with the same result. With a sigh I knocked on the third door.

I heard someone inside make a movement, apparently knock over something, curse, and then approach the door.

"Yes? Who is it?" came a voice.

"Is this Mr. Gilbert Andrews?" I asked.

"It is." I heard the lock being turned and the door opened a short way. The face of a middle-aged gentleman looked out at me, his eyes appraising me. "And who might you be?"

Chapter Fourteen

Gilbert Andrews and I sat in the bar of the Crossed Arms, a glass of Meux porter apiece on the table between us. I had suggested we proceed to an ABC tearoom but he had insisted that he needed to wet his whistle at the bar, which was on the corner of George Street and the main road.

"John Saxon?" he said. "I can't believe he's dead. Why, I saw him not long ago. Him and me started treading the boards together many moons ago. We were both not much more than seventeen. Up north, you know? Manchester, Birmingham, Leeds, Sheffield, Newcastle. Aye! We played 'em all. Bit parts all the way up to . . . well, perhaps not leads, but good roles. Second line, you might say. Then John started getting ambitious. Said as how he could feel the draw of the footlights in London. Was sure he could make it there. And what if you can't, I said? We've got it good right here, I said. There's a thousand or more actors fighting each other to get on stage in the big city. Why go there to struggle? If you want to struggle then play the Theatre Royal, Glasgow, I said. That made him laugh."

I smiled. Mr. Andrews could certainly talk. He paused only long enough to take the occasional drink.

"But no, John had to give it a try. He had a long tussle, so I believe. I think he had hopes of joining the Charles Keene players at the Princess's Theatre, but I heard that didn't work out. I myself had to be away to a job up north. I lost touch with him, of course. Had to get on with my own life, you know?"

"But you said you saw him not long ago?"

Another drink. "Right. I had to come down to the Big Smoke to talk with my agent – you met him? Phillip Whitstable?"

I nodded.

"Thought I'd see if I could look up my old pal while I'm here. Didn't take long to find him. Phillip was a help there. Popped into your Lyceum a few days ago and had a bit of a chinwag with John. Good to see him. He seemed happy enough."

"You didn't spend any great time together?" I asked. "I would have thought, after so many years . . ."

"To tell you the truth we had a few words. Nothing serious, mind you. He'd lent me a few quid last time I saw him and do you know, he remembered that! I was sure he'd said it was a gift; told me to forget it – I'm still certain – but that's not the way John remembered it. Always was a bit tight with his money, was John. But he remembered that as though it were yesterday. Must be a bit short of change these days I'm thinking. Anyway, it kind of soured our reunion, you might say. Thought I'd give it a rest and get back to him before I head north again."

"Did he ever marry," I asked.

He took a long drink, set down the glass and waved to the barman for another round. "So I heard. Don't know no details. Didn't last long, of course. Actors shouldn't marry. Not when they're moving about all the time. Stands to reason."

"But John did," I persevered.

"Aye. I wasn't there when it happened but I heard, through the grapevine you know? An actress older than him. I think her name was Maggie or Marjory or something. Like I said, it didn't last long. You wouldn't expect it to."

"Where did John come from?" I asked. "Does he have any family?"

Another long drink, then "A mother as I know of. His father died when John was younger, which was why he took to the stage."

"His mother is still alive then?"

"Oh, aye. Last I heard. But she disowned John when he took to the theatre instead of following his father as a fisherman. She lives down on the east coast. Somewhere near Great Yarmouth, as I recall."

"Great Yarmouth?"

"Lowestoft!" he cried. "That was it. Just outside Yarmouth. His father had a fishing boat there, and also used to man the lifeboat, I think."

"You don't have an address, I suppose?"

"You're joking! If, as John said, his mother disowned him after he took to the boards, why would I have her address?"

"I just wondered," I said. Hoped, was more like it.

I spent another half hour or so drinking with Gilbert Andrews before bidding him farewell and returning to the Lyceum. It had been a worthwhile visit, I felt.

Early Saturday morning, at my boss's "suggestion", I caught the Great Eastern Railway's train from Liverpool Street Station to Lowestoft, on the Norfolk coast. It was a four and a half hour journey so by catching an early one I had hopes of being able to return the same day, though I realized that was far from certain.

Shortly after brief stops at Ipswich and Framlingham – with views of both a picturesque ruined castle and a fine church – it was a relatively short run to Aldeburgh where I caught my first glimpse of the sea. Dunwich then came and went, as did Halesworth.

We eventually steamed into Lowestoft, a fashionable sea-bathing resort of some 20,000 inhabitants. The old town, as it is called, is to the north of the harbor and the new town to the south. The new town is the favorite part for visitors, with a long Esplanade and a pier that is located in the center of the beaches. The beach south of Claremont Pier is referred to as Victoria Beach. All I really know of Lowestoft is that it supports a large number of fishing boats and that its lifeboat is famous for executing many a rescue when those same fishing boats get into trouble on the frequently rough North Sea.

I set out from the railway station and enjoyed a bracing walk following the stationmaster's directions to the local police station. My thinking was that they might have some sort of city directory where I could find the address for Mrs. Saxon. I was to be disappointed.

"No, sir, we don't keep any sort of a listing of residents here. With all the summer visitors and the like, there's no way we could keep up with such a thing, believe me." So said the tall, thin, police constable who manned the front desk.

I thanked him and turned to leave.

"You might find such a thing at the postal office," he added, as an afterthought.

But again I was disappointed. The post office in Lowestoft was closed on a Saturday afternoon. Mail delivery continued, I imagined, but the counter service was not available. I wandered out toward the harbor and thought about how to proceed.

My gaze fell on the lifeboat station, at the far end of the harbor. Since I was here, I thought, I might as well avail myself of a close look at such an establishment. I was unlikely to have such an opportunity again. It wouldn't take too much time out of the few precious hours I had available, and it would give me a chance to get my thoughts in order as to how to locate John Saxon's mother. I had, of course, been pondering this very question on the long train ride to Norfolk, but a workable solution had yet to present itself.

As I approached the harbor entrance, I could see the lifeboat itself up on the ramp that pointed out to the water. A cable was used to pull the boat out of the surf and crank it up to the top of the slipway. There it sat until called for. At such a call, the men of the crew would climb aboard, the brakes would be released, and the boat would slide down the rail, launching itself into the sea. There the men would man the oars and haul away to the craft in distress. At this time of year I imagined the station was generally quiet.

In fact I found a few men on duty. Three of them sat around a table, drinking tea and reminiscing about past exploits. A fourth, young man with sandy-colored hair and the start of a promising beard, greeted me.

"Welcome to the Lowestoft Lifeboat Station, sir. One of the oldest lifeboat stations in the British Isles. My name is Francis Stackpole; fairly new to the crew," he confided. "We were founded in 1824 as the National Institution for the Preservation of Life from Shipwreck."

"That's quite a name." I smiled at his obvious enthusiasm.

He grinned. "Well, thirty years later they made it the Royal National Lifeboat Institution, which is a lot better," he said. We both laughed. "What would you like to know, sir? We've done a lot of rescues at sea, most recently from a brigantine that foundered just north of Yarmouth. Very exciting that was. We joined with Great Yarmouth's boat on that one."

"To tell you the truth I'm here just out of curiosity, though perhaps you can help me?"

"If I can."

"Nothing to do with the lifeboat, but do you happen to know of a lady named Saxon? Mrs. Saxon? She lives in Lowestoft, I'm told."

"Along with a lot of others," said one of the men at the table behind us. His fellows laughed.

Francis Stackpole didn't laugh but gave the question some thought, his brow wrinkled.

"His father was a fisherman," I added. Then I suddenly remembered something that Gilbert Andrews had mentioned. "Wait a minute! I believe his father also used to man the lifeboat here, on occasion."

One of the men at the table got up. He was a burly fisherman with a weathered face and squinting eyes. Grey beard, mustache, and sideboards framed his face. His teeth were a deep, dark yellow; two of them missing. He had a knitted hat pulled down over his head and clenched an ancient pipe between his teeth. I noticed that the whole time he spoke with me he never removed the pipe from his mouth, speaking around it.

"This is the skipper," muttered Francis, out of the side of his mouth.

"Used to man the boat? When was this, d'you know?"

I did some quick calculating. "It must have been around 1850 or '55. I'm not sure exactly."

"Come with me," he said and, turning, made off along a corridor running back to offices at the rear of the building. Francis and I hurried after him.

At the back of the building the wall was covered with framed photographs of groups of men: the lifeboat crews from previous years. Our grizzled friend paused in the front of them and then started slowly moving forward again, peering intently at the names listed below each picture.

"Have a good look here, young fella. Should be in one or more of these. They takes 'em every year or so. Never seen the need a'fore."

It was Francis who found what we were looking for.

"Here! I think I've found him."

I looked at the faded photograph, trying to make out the faces. The list of names below it included one *Edwin Saxon, bos'n*. The date was 1855. With a full beard, he looked to be as grizzled a fisherman as the one standing beside me. All of the men in the photograph were dressed in oilskins and the cork lifejackets that had been introduced just the year before the picture was taken. I looked at the next photograph. He was not present in that one. I commented on it to our skipper.

"Let me go and look at the records," he said.

He disappeared into one of the small rooms and reemerged a few minutes later, carrying a well-worn cardboard folder. He had it open and prodded a handwritten sheet of paper with his forefinger.

"Next year – 1856 – him and two others was swept overboard in a big storm, when aiding the *Grace Worthington*. She went down with all hands, for all our efforts. Don't happen a lot but enough." His voice was tight and he kept his eyes down on the folder. "Something here for you too. Address of

Mister Saxon. Happen Mrs. Saxon might still be at the same address. Her as you was looking for. Name's Letitia, it says. Mrs. Letitia Saxon, next of kin."

Mrs. Letitia Saxon lived in a small but nicely kept cottage less than half a mile from the lifeboat station. She was a small woman, even shorter than myself, with her nearly-white hair drawn back severely in a bun chignon. She still wore widow's weeds with a single strand of jet beads the only jewelry beside the wedding ring she still wore. She looked far older than what I guessed her age to be. Her face was wrinkled and her blue eyes watery. She held a delicate handkerchief with which she constantly dabbed at her nose. I came to realize that it was a habitual movement.

"Mr. Rivers, you said? What can I do for you? You're not collecting money for anything are you?" Her voice was sharp; her brow wrinkled.

"No! No, I'm not," I was quick to reassure her. "I'm visiting from London and was just up at the lifeboat station. There I happened to see an old photograph of your late husband. The men on duty were kind enough to give me your address."

She still looked puzzled. I didn't want to get off on the wrong foot, talking about her son if she had truly disowned him, so I tried to work around to the subject.

"I understand that the late Mr. Saxon was a fisherman in addition to manning the lifeboat."

She nodded. "Best come in, Mr . . . what was it you said?"

"Rivers, ma'am."

"Best come in, Mr. Rivers. It's been a long time since anyone showed any interest in me or Mr. Saxon." I followed her into the neat, if small, living room. "Best you be seated. I'll put on the pot for a cup of tea."

When she said that I realized that I had had nothing to eat since fleeing Mrs. Bell's Chancery Lane establishment to catch the early train out of Liverpool Street. As if in response to my thought, my stomach rumbled. I hoped that Mrs. Saxon did not hear it.

"I have a bit of mutton left over from lunch, if you'd care for a sandwich? Perhaps with some of my homemade chutney and a nice cup of tea?" Mrs. Saxon, though seemingly not the friendliest of people, was the soul of discretion.

"Thank you, ma'am. I would like that."

While she fussed around in the kitchen, I settled into an overstuffed armchair close enough to the window to be able to peer out at any activity in the road outside. I imagined Mrs. Saxon must spend some considerable time doing just that. She soon rejoined me, bearing a tray containing a pot of tea, sugar, and milk, cups and saucers, and a plate of very solid looking sandwiches. I smiled at Mrs. Saxon.

She did not return my smile but, as she poured our tea and I settled to consuming the sandwiches, she started reminiscing about the late Mr. Edwin Saxon. She appeared to mellow a little as she talked and a faraway look came into her watery eyes. I would not go so far as to say she became friendly, but there was no longer the animosity I had first sensed.

"Now Mr. Rivers," she said, after we had enjoyed our repast. "You have told me your name and that you are from London, but other than that . . ? What is your particular interest in my husband? I don't quite understand. As I have said, Mr. Saxon died many long years ago, God rest his soul."

I was now hesitant. I presumed that she knew nothing of her son's demise. Who was I to break the news? How would she take it? I suddenly realized that I had jumped in with both feet, as it were, without considering her possible reaction. I took another drink of tea, put down the cup, and looked intently at the figure seated opposite me.

"I am afraid I have some bad news," I said.

She looked at me blankly.

"It's about your son."

"My son? Is he dead?" She asked with an unemotional voice. I was surprised.

"Er, yes. Yes, I'm afraid he is," I said.

There was a brief pause and then her head nodded. She said nothing, dabbed at her nose, and then refilled her teacup. "More tea, Mr. Rivers?" she asked.

"What? I – I mean, yes please, Mrs. Saxon."

As she poured she spoke. "You must wonder at my lack of display. I am sorry if I disappoint you. You see, to me my son died a very long time ago."

"I don't quite understand."

"It was the hope of Mr. Saxon and I that John would follow in his father's footsteps. We thought that he would work with my husband, gradually taking over the fishing boat, and the lifeboat station duties. But I regret he showed no inclination to do so. In fact, he claimed that he disliked the sea! Can you imagine? His heart, he claimed, was in the theatre."

It was the way she said the word "theatre" that said it all for me.

"Then, when Edwin – my husband – was lost from the lifeboat . . ." This time the nose dabbing was somewhat more prolonged, I felt. "When Mr. Saxon drowned, John proclaimed his need to 'tread the boards', I think was how he put it. The death of his father seemed to have removed any feelings of guilt and he declared that the greater the distance that he could remove himself from the sea, the better." This time she blew her nose.

"He left home? Left you here alone?" I asked, though it was obvious that was what had happened.

She sipped her tea, then replaced her cup and, now quite calm, nodded. "That was when I disowned him," she said matter-of-factly. "I haven't seen him since. Would you care for another sandwich?"

Chapter Fifteen

"It does indeed seem unnatural that a mother should so disown her own son," said Mr. Stoker the next morning, when I had returned from my trip to Norfolk and apprized him of what I had learned. "Yet I have heard of such situations before. I would not go so far as to say that such actions are common but they are certainly not unknown . . . especially with regards to sons and daughters wanting to tread the boards. I don't know why parents are so averse to the theatre as a profession, but that does seem to be the case."

"There was not a great deal more I learned from the good lady," I said. "As I told you his friend from the past, Mr. Andrews, knew of John's marriage and later divorce but had no details."

"And the mother?"

"She didn't even know of her son's marriage, least of all any knowledge of the bride. No, sir, I'm afraid there was not much in the way of rewards for the long journey to Norfolk."

"Nonetheless, Harry, we needed to ascertain what was known. There was always the possibility that you might stumble upon some important fact connecting to John's murder."

"Speaking of which," I said. "I think I did stumble on something, though not in Lowestoft."

"Oh?"

"Yes, sir. When I met with Gilbert Andrews he said that he had recently visited Mr. Saxon. It must have been at some time before the murder. He was most surprised to hear of John's demise. But it seems it was not a long visit and apparently it did not end well."

"Go on."

"Mr. Andrews admitted that the two of them had an argument – over some money owed – and parted on bad terms."

"Really? Most interesting. I wonder if their meeting took place up in the gods? And at what time? You must follow up on that, Harry. An argument over money might well have got out of hand."

"Yes, sir. I'd already thought about that. I'll make a point of connecting with Mr. Andrews again before he leaves London."

"Very good. You did well, Harry. Thank you."

Mr. Stoker's words pleased me. I was tired from having to take a late night train back to the city and then rising early to get in to the theatre to talk with my boss. I could never sleep on one of those wretched trains. The bed at my room in Chancery Lane was not the most comfortable, but it was my own and most welcome. My rush to return was due to my determination to be back in time for my Sunday assignation with Jenny.

It had become something of a Sunday tradition for Jenny and I to take a stroll around Hyde Park and to end up by the Serpentine, then partaking of a cup of tea and pastries at one of the teashops in the vicinity.

"Did you like Lowestoft, Harry?" Jenny's eyes were bright and shining, making my blood race as she gazed at me. I always had difficulty focusing on anything but the beauty of her face when my eyes met hers. "I hear that the sand there is almost white and so very fine."

"Yes. The beaches are magnificent," I agreed. "And very popular. Bathing machines are in abundance, despite the prevailing fears of men and women bathing together in public. There are a lot of hotels along the Esplanade."

"I've always wanted to visit that part of Norfolk," she said. "The beaches and, of course, the Norfolk Broads."

"Lowestoft is the ideal place to stay if you want to visit the Broads," I said. "I caught a glimpse of a section of it, with a very picturesque windmill, as the train drew into the station yesterday morning. Too dark to see anything coming back last night, of course."

We sat in the window of the teashop, looking out at the park across the road. Our hands had met on the tabletop and, refreshed with tea and petit fours, I felt extremely content. I had shared with Jenny what little I had to tell, of the lifeboat station and of Mrs. Saxon. Now we sat in silence for a while, absorbing each other's company.

"Who do you think murdered John Saxon, Harry?" Jenny finally broke the silence.

I shook my head, "I really have no idea, Jenny. I always liked the man. He claimed to come from a long line of Shakespearean actors, which we now know was not true. But I think I can excuse him that, knowing the seeming need of actors to boost their pedigree. From others in our Lyceum family, I hear that he was not good at remembering his lines yet would unhesitatingly fill in with his own words until he found himself again."

Jenny laughed.

"He had a bit of a reputation as being a ladies man, though how serious that was I don't know. He was about five feet and nine inches tall yet always referred to himself as 'just a little shy of six feet'. There! Now you know just about as much about Mr. Saxon as do I."

Jenny laughed again and squeezed my hand. It felt good to bring a smile to her face. But then she grew serious again.

"Someone must have disliked him a great deal to do such an evil thing," she said. "And what was he – what were *they* – doing up in the gods, that the person was able to push him over the balcony?"

"These are all questions that both Scotland Yard and Mr. Stoker and myself are trying to answer. Whether it was late at night or early in the morning – the police still haven't given us a time of death – it was most unusual for anybody to be in any part of the auditorium then. My guess is that John Saxon knew his killer and that he had met him there by pre-arrangement. Perhaps to discuss . . .

what? A debt? A new acting role? A dispute over a woman?" I gave a sigh. "It's all so . . . unknown. There's so much more we have to find out."

Jenny let go my hand and investigated the teapot, to see if there was any more tea available. There was not. I offered to order more but she shook her head.

"It's time I started back, Harry."

She looked at me and smiled one of her heart-melting smiles. Sunday afternoons seemed to fly by, yet I was grateful to spend any small amount of time with Miss Jenny Cartwright. I admitted to myself quite freely that I had lost my heart to the young lady.

Monday morning Inspector Bellamy tapped on the door and entered, unbidden, into Mr. Stoker's office as my boss and I were sitting reviewing the coming week's activities.

"Inspector Bellamy!" My boss's voice betrayed his irritation at seeing the policeman.

"Mr. Stoker," responded the inspector, as usual ignoring myself. "We are in need of solving this murder before you and your troupe disperse. Otherwise we will be forced to hold you all here until the matter is resolved."

"You can't detain Mr. Booth," I said. "He may have to return to America."

"In point of fact, Mr. Booth is making a brief tour of our British theatres before such a return," said Mr. Stoker. "But Harry's point is a valid one. I don't see that you would have any good reason to . . ."

"We have reason enough to hold everyone, if we so please," snapped Bellamy. "This, as you well know, is a murder case. We are Scotland Yard!"

"If you are Scotland Yard, as you put it," I interjected, "then why have you not yet solved this case?"

He turned his little beady eyes on me for a moment and then, with a very slight shake of his head, returned his attention to my boss.

"We have been advised that the time of Mr. Saxon's death was close to midnight, so it was at that time rather than early the following morning that interests us. Oh, and by the way, we are taking your Mr. Purdy into custody." He held up his hand as my boss opened his mouth to object. "For now, he is our prime suspect. It will be up to him to prove his innocence, we think."

Mr. Stoker got to his feet and looked down on the inspector. Mr. Stoker could be very intimidating when he chose.

"I think not, Inspector Bellamy! So far our arrangement of watching over Mr. Purdy ourselves, with your constable taking on that duty after theatre hours, has worked well. I see no reason not to continue it until after the final curtain on Saturday 25th of June. That is yet four weeks away. At that time you certainly may take Mr. Purdy into your charge . . . if by then you have not managed to find the actual killer."

Mr. Stoker sat back down again, as though everything was now resolved. He turned to the desk diary open in front of him and, in effect, dismissed the policeman. But Inspector Bellamy was not so easily done away with.

"We think that, as a precaution, it may be necessary to close off your top gallery . . . the gods, is it you call it? It is, after all, a crime scene."

I thought that he was possibly saying this as some sort of veiled threat, because of Mr. Stoker being, in the inspector's eyes, uncooperative. But my boss was not so easily brow-beaten.

"An excellent idea, inspector. We have been observing a decline in upper gallery sales of late anyway. That would not be a problem."

I thought I saw Bellamy's jaw drop momentarily, but he drew himself upright and, after a moment's pause, left the room.

"Are you really going to close the gods, sir?" I asked.

"Of course not, Harry. And if Inspector Bellamy gets upset, then it will be only a short while of back-and-forth play before we are at the end of the run, when it will make no difference to us whether the gods be open or closed." He sighed. "I have enough to worry about without the good inspector adding to things."

"Anything I can help with, sir?" I asked.

He looked at me briefly, smiled, and shook his head. "Thank you, Harry, but no. It seems that Miss Grey, who has been with us these many years, has handed in her resignation. Something about an offer of a leading lady position at a theatre in

Newcastle upon Tyne, I think it was. Or was it Leeds? She was a little vague about it. The Guv'nor has prevailed upon her to finish the run, of course, but I'm surprised at her decision to leave."

"I have overheard her complaining of no longer being offered younger roles," I said.

"She is no longer young."

"Well, that is certainly true. But I'm sure it's not easy for a woman to accept that fact."

We looked at some details for a cast party at the end of the run and then I returned to my own office and contemplated the whole John Saxon situation. We knew that he had been murdered and had not committed suicide nor fallen accidentally – the bent safety rails attested to that – and we had, to date, gathered a certain amount of material on Mr. Saxon's past life. Not that it had helped us a great deal, so far, though we did seem to have established that he had no obvious enemies. Certainly none who would have reason to do away with him.

We now knew that John Saxon had met with Gilbert Andrews at some point before John's death. I made a mental note to follow up on that, as Mr. Stoker had requested. It seemed doubtful that the meeting took place late at night but I needed to verify that. Scotland Yard had now given the probable time of death as shortly after midnight. Personally I couldn't see an argument between two old friends ending in murder, even if the disagreement was over money.

I was kept busy for most of the morning. There was no production scheduled immediately after *Othello*. The theatre would be dark for the always-slow summer season. The Guv'nor planned to re-open in September with a revival of the always-popular *Merchant of Venice*. Mr. Irving as Shylock was a guaranteed sell-out, which was a good way to start a new season. I decided to take an early lunch, stopping by Bill Thomas's booth on my way out. But it was empty; unusual for Bill, I thought. I made for the Druid's Head.

I found Guy Purdy lunching at the tavern once again in the company of Arthur Swindon, their heads close together over their meals. The two of them seemed to be spending a lot of time together these days, I thought. I wondered, briefly, if we had been too easily swayed by Mr. Purdy's always-friendly manner. Was there, perhaps, something to Inspector Bellamy's suspicions? *Could* he have killed John Saxon? But there was no way I could see the old actor in other than the light in which he always presented himself. Under no circumstances could I imagine him throwing his old friend over the balcony of the gods. Besides, he had neither the height nor the strength to do that. Although . . . another sudden thought! Could he and Arthur Swindon together have done such a thing? I stood there mentally shaking my head. I was letting my imagination run away with me.

Close by, at a separate table, sat Police Constable Jimmy Hathaway nursing a pint of stout, looking about him with his head continually turning. He broke into one of his broad grins the moment he saw me. I made my way in his direction.

"Afternoon, Mr. Rivers! Might o' known you'd be showing up 'ere afore long, as the poacher said when the gamekeeper grabbed 'im. Don't you worry none. I've got Mr. Purdy square in me sights."

I took a seat at his table. "I'm sure you have, Jimmy," I said. "And glad to see it. Inspector Bellamy must be grateful."

He snorted and took a drink of ale. Wiping his mouth with the back of his hand, his grin broadened. "I can't say as 'ow I've ever seen the inspector grateful to anyone for anyfink."

I ordered one of John's enormous sandwiches of sliced lamb liberally spread with mint sauce. The Druid's Head was busy, which was not unusual at lunchtime. The food there was good, not expensive, and served promptly for those, such as actors, who often had limited time available. Gwen Morgan the younger of the two serving girls – a pretty young Welsh woman who John had found somewhere – moved briskly through the crowded room, dispensing food and filling glasses and goblets. She made sure I had my porter right away. It was soon followed by the food.

"'As the inspector told you about that watch, 'Arry?"

"Watch? No I don't think he has. What's that all about, Jimmy?"

"Ah!" He chuckled to himself. "Seems to fink 'e's stumbled on some special clue . . . to somefink! I don't fink 'e knows where it fits in anywhere but 'e's sure it's important. That's the inspector for you!"

"Tell me about it, Jimmy. Whose watch is it?"

"Ah! That's the question, ain't it? 'Oos watch is it? Seems as 'ow Inspector Bellamy got it off a tooler,"

"A pickpocket?" I said.

He nodded. "Seems this 'ere pickpocket had on 'im a nice silver 'alf-'unter pocket watch. It's engraved to some foreign nob. Says 'e lifted it from a gent standing in line for one of your theatre's god seats."

This suddenly became interesting. We had all sorts wanting to be seated in the top balcony. The majority chose the gods because the seats were so inexpensive, but those who could actually afford better accommodation would many times want to sit there for personal reasons. Perhaps they didn't want it known that they were at the theatre that particular night, or perhaps they were in the company of someone they didn't want to be seen with. It was not for us to question them.

"So why does Inspector Bellamy find the watch so interesting?"

Jimmy finished his beer and gazed into the empty mug as though deciding whether or not to get a refill. "I fink it's the name on it," he said. "No one's reported it missing, what seems strange. Must be worf a penny or two."

"What is the name on it?"

"I dunno. Foreign. I fink 'e said it was Polish, but I'm not certain. Then, funny fing . . . the inspector started mumbling somefink about vampires, if you can believe that."

"Vampires?" I sat up and took notice. "What did he say about them?"

"You interested in 'em, 'Arry? I could never quite believe in 'em meself."

"What did he say, Jimmy?" I felt I had to know what Inspector Bellamy might have on his mind.

"'Ere! Don't go getting' mum and dad."

"Mum and dad?" I knew that Jimmy was Cockney so I expected him to use the occasional rhyming slang so loved by those born within the sound of Bow Bells, but mum and dad was a new one to me.

"Mum and dad. Mad."

I shook my head. I couldn't keep up with all the rhymes. I was sure many of them were made up on the spot so I didn't feel too badly about my ignorance. "Don't worry, Jimmy. I'm perfectly sane. Now, what did the inspector have to say on the subject?"

"I fink 'e was under the impression that this nob what owned the watch was a vampire."

"I wonder where he got that idea?"

Jimmy shrugged.

"You know, I think this might just be important enough that I actually need to go and speak to the inspector." I surprised myself saying it.

I ate my sandwich, trying to finish it quickly with large mouthfuls. Reluctantly abandoning part of it, I paid my bill and, leaving Constable Hathaway still watching over Guy Purdy, I went out and got a cab to Scotland Yard.

Chapter Sixteen

I had not gone far when I had the thought that Mr. Stoker might like to hear what the inspector had to say, if this watch was truly important. I had the cabbie make a brief detour to the Lyceum and then had him wait while I ran inside to speak to my boss, giving him the gist of the story about Inspector Bellamy's interest in the watch.

"It sounds very interesting, Harry," said Mr. Stoker. "Yes. Thank you for thinking of me. Let me get my hat, gloves, and cane and I'll join you in your cab."

Enquiring for Inspector Bellamy at Scotland Yard, we were told that he was out.

"Have you any idea where he might be?" asked Stoker.

The desk sergeant dug out a clipboard and ran his finger down the page.

"Says as 'ow 'e was going to Whitechapel," he read.

"Can you not be more specific?"

The officer looked uncomfortable. "I don't think the inspector would want me giving out that information, sir."

Mr. Stoker nodded. "I quite understand. He didn't, then, go to the Rose and Crown on Simpson Street?"

The sergeant again glanced at the clipboard, a frown on his face. "No, sir. It was the Dog and Duck on Hall Street, it says 'ere . . ." His voice trailed off as he realized what he had done.

My boss smiled, tipped his hat to the desk sergeant, and turned to leave.

"Come Harry. Let us not dally and miss the inspector."

"How did you know that we'd find him at the Dog and Duck?" I asked when we were safely outside.

"I didn't," he replied. "I just threw out the name of the Rose and Crown to see what it might produce. The desk sergeant was most obliging."

On the way to Whitechapel I shared with Mr. Stoker my recent thoughts on Guy Purdy. "He seems to have become very close with Arthur Swindon," I said. "Not that they weren't friends before – all of the cast have become quite close to one another – but it seems that their friendship has really developed of late."

"In what way, Harry?"

I shook my head. "It's not easy to put a finger on it. Previously I would occasionally see them together but recently it seems that every time I see Mr. Purdy he is in the company of Mr. Swindon."

"You don't think that it's simply the death of John Saxon that has brought them closer together?"

Again I shook my head. "I noticed this even before Mr. Saxon's death." I paused a moment. Then, "I was wondering if, perhaps, they were involved – together – in the death of Mr. Saxon," I said in a rush.

Mr. Stoker raised his eyebrows but said nothing.

"I know it sounds ridiculous," I hurried on. "Especially now that I say it out loud. No! Sorry, sir. Forget I said that." I felt embarrassed.

"Not at all, Harry," he said. "It is good to voice our thoughts; our suspicions. It is only by so doing that we can analyze them."

"Do you think there might be the smallest grain of truth in it, sir? Somehow I just can't see either Mr. Purdy or Mr. Swindon as murderers, especially of their long-time companion Mr. Saxon. Yet when I think of the two of them acting together . . ."

"What would be their motive, Harry?"

"Ah! There's the rub, as Mr. Shakespeare would say. I can't come up with a motive that seems the least bit plausible."

"Then let us set the idea aside for the moment, Harry, yet keep it in the backs of our minds. Now, tell me more about this watch in which Inspector Bellamy shows so much interest."

I again ran over what Police Constable Hathaway had shared, having already given Mr. Stoker the gist of it when I first picked him up at the theatre.

"He said that the inspector thought it belonged to someone Polish, though he didn't seem absolutely certain on that."

"And you say that Inspector Bellamy made a comment about vampires?"

I nodded. "That's what Jimmy – Constable Hathaway – said," I agreed. "He said that the inspector 'mumbled' something about vampires. Nothing specific."

"Nonetheless, we need to find out what Bellamy is thinking. Why does he connect this gentleman, through his watch, to vampires, especially when the good inspector claims not to believe in such creatures?"

"Suppose there really was a vampire in London, sir? How would you recognize him?"

Mr. Stoker smiled, a taut smile. "What sort of things to look for, Harry? It's not easy to recognize vampires. They can quite easily pass as ordinary people much of the time, which is the trouble."

"But there must be something, sir?"

"Well, for a start they certainly avoid the sunlight. It is said that you'll seldom encounter a vampire in daylight hours. Perhaps as a consequence of that they invariably have very pale skin; almost white in some cases. Their eyes are frequently red-rimmed."

"Do they really sleep in coffins? Sam Green said something about that."

Stoker chuckled. "No, Harry. That is a fallacy. They do not need to sleep either in a coffin or in a quantity of soil from their native land.

However, it is said that their teeth – the incisors – are pointed, to facilitate the bite, yet not obviously so. Unless you were especially looking for such denticulation you would not notice them."

"Anything else, sir?"

"I have heard it remarked that vampires have no reflection, but I find that difficult to credit, Harry. Perhaps we may confirm or reject that suggestion through our present investigation."

"If it's all the same to you, sir, I'd rather not get close enough to one to find out."

At that moment the hansom pulled into the curb outside the tavern in question and we alighted.

"Now to see if we are in time to intercept the inspector," said Stoker, paying the fare and then leading the way.

At that time in the afternoon there was not a lot of people in the place. We immediately saw Inspector Bellamy standing by the bar and speaking with the landlord. As we entered, he turned to see who had come in. His face changed when he saw Mr. Stoker and myself. It was a very slight change, he was never one to write his emotions on his face. A slight elevation of the eyebrows; a tightening of the mouth.

"Come, Harry." Mr. Stoker, his steps quiet on the sawdust-strewn floor, strode across the room to stand facing Bellamy.

"Mr. Stoker! Why are we not surprised to find you following us?"

"Not following, inspector. Merely making contact."

"And now that you've made it, what do you want?"

"I understand that you have acquired a timepiece. And that there is some sort of a story attached to it."

Seeing that we now had the inspector's attention, the landlord moved away and left us alone.

"Let's take a seat."

We all sat at the nearest table. I found myself looking about me in anticipation of a serving girl carrying beer but it seemed this was not to be a social meeting. The inspector reached into his coat pocket and pulled out something wrapped in a none-too-clean white cloth. He laid it on the table and uncovered it, disclosing an elegant silver pocket watch. Mr. Stoker leaned forward to look at it more closely.

"This is what we found on the person of a young pickpocket we apprehended a day or two ago."

"May I examine it?" my boss asked. The policeman nodded. Mr. Stoker picked up the watch and turned it over in his hands, holding it close to his face.

"Engraved on the inside of the back cover," said Bellamy.

Mr. Stoker popped open the case and studied the inscription. "To Menachem Klaczko, in appreciation," he read.

"Your eyes are good," conceded the inspector. "It took us several minutes to make out the name."

"Despite being on the inside, the engraving is somewhat worn, inspector. And it is, admittedly, a thin and fancy script that is not easy to read."

The inspector grunted.

"Why does it say in appreciation, I wonder?" I said.

"Probably presented at the gentleman's retirement, or some such auspicious occasion," said Stoker. "The fact that it shows signs of wear suggests something."

"Oh?" The inspector leaned closer.

"He was probably an elderly gentleman who, as I said, had the timepiece presented to him many years ago and who reminisced about his past. It's a shame there is no date. I would say that the watch and its engraving had great sentimental value to Mr. Klaczko. He possibly opened the back on many occasions, just to read that inscription and, perhaps, to run his fingers over the lettering thus bringing about the wear."

"Must have been an old codger," suggested the inspector.

"Exactly," agreed Stoker. "Did your pickpocket remember from whom he purloined the watch?"

"No. He'd been a busy little smug and had his pockets full of swag. All he could say was that he remembered lifting it from a gent standing in line at your theatre."

"Obviously a gentleman of taste," I murmured.

"I believe you have connected this, in some way, with vampires, inspector?" My boss looked hard at the policeman, whose face reddened as he sat back in his chair.

"Yes. Well, let us not go jumping to any conclusions, Mr. Stoker. We are still looking into this."

"Yet you have some suspicion on the matter?"

"We have not yet been able to track down this Mr. Klacky..."

"Klaczko."

"Whatever. The landlord here . . ." he nodded towards the man behind the tavern counter, ". . . says he thought he recalled hearing a name like that mentioned by a woman who sometimes stops in for a jug." He pulled out his well-worn notebook and thumbed through the pages. "Ah! Here we are. The woman's sister has a rooming house off Drury Lane, on Castle Street. She's a Mrs. Lublin. Mrs. Brajna Lublin – what is it with these names?"

"Polish, inspector. I'm sure they are not familiar with the name Bellamy."

He waved his hand dismissively. "Whatever. We are here in these British Isles. Now then, this woman said that her sister had a weird lodger named Klacky – if it's the same one – but that he was not such an old man."

"Had? You used the past tense, inspector. Is he no longer there?"

The inspector shook his head. "The point is, Mr. Stoker, the landlord said that this woman described her sister's lodger as a very pale-faced man with white hair and red eyes! Can you credit that? And she stated that despite his white hair, he seemed not to be an old man, though exactly what she meant by that we don't know."

"Go on."

"The woman said her sister claimed the man never went out in the daytime, only at night, or after the sun went down. Now, sir!" He looked hard at my boss. "Does that or does that not meet with what the public press has been saying is the marking of one of your vampires?"

Mr. Stoker pursed his lips and looked down at his hands. He thought for a few moments without saying anything.

"Harry and I were just discussing the hallmarks of a vampire. What you say certainly seems to fit with what we would expect. But every case should be treated individually. We cannot be absolutely certain until we have examined all of the evidence."

"Well, it's good enough for us," said Bellamy, pushing back his chair and getting to his feet. "The interesting thing is, if this watch really is so important to Mr. Klacky, why has he not reported it stolen, that's what we want to know? Must be worth a bob or two. Now we must get on. We can't be lallygagging about like you gents."

We watched the inspector stalk away, his brown bowler hat jammed down on his head. Mr. Stoker seemed in no hurry to follow.

"I think that, unlike Inspector Bellamy, we need to carefully plan our course of action, Harry."

"Yes, sir."

"My first inclination is to visit this Mrs. Lublin to get the full and correct story."

"You don't think the inspector has it right?"

He shrugged. "If we are to judge from past performances, I would say that I have my reservations. He is a little too eager to leap to conclusions . . ."

"Especially those that would bring about a quick conclusion to his case," I interjected.

My boss nodded. "Precisely. So let us consider what we have learned, Harry. The watch would seem to have belonged to an elderly gentleman yet Mrs. Lublin, according to the inspector, told her sister he was not so old. He was rooming with this lady but, just about the time the police start enquiring, he disappeared. His watch, that was apparently so dear to him, was stolen yet he has made no report of its loss to the police. Now then, Harry, what can we deduce from all of this?"

I scratched my head. Not that the action ever produced any results but I always felt it gave the questioner indication that I was seriously considering the matter.

"An old man yet not an old man and one dismissing the fact of a dear possession being stolen," I mused. I really had no idea.

"What if the old man – the true owner of the watch – had died and someone else had obtained it? Someone much younger than the original owner. And then that person, seeing the name engraved on it, had assumed that name," suggested Stoker.

"Someone else calling himself Klacky?" I said, adopting the inspector's bungling of the name.

"But why on earth would anyone want to pretend to be someone with a name like that?"

"The name is Klaczko, Harry. Get it right now, because we may well be working with that name for a while."

I obediently repeated it a few times.

"Good. Now there are many reasons for a person to adopt a false name . . . especially in this neighborhood."

I conceded the point. "Where would he have got the watch, sir?" I asked. "Supposing the old man had died, as you suggest, who would have got the watch?"

"There are again several possibilities, Harry, but let's follow the most obvious. Either, whoever acquired or inherited it is the person now impersonating Mr. Klaczko, or – and I think this the more likely scenario – the watch was pawned and the subsequent purchaser became the impersonator." He got to his feet. "Come, Harry. I think we need to speak with Mrs. Brajna Lublin. If we put our minds to it we may well be able to come up with some questions that the good inspector failed to consider."

Chapter Seventeen

Mrs. Lublin lived in a well-kept house on Castle Street. A hand-written sign in the window stated that there were rooms available for rent, to professional persons, at a reasonable rate. At our knock, a uniformed maid opened the door and showed us into a downstairs parlor.

Mrs. Brajna Lublin was a short, dark-haired, middle-aged lady with a no-nonsense manner about her. She wore a striped silk dress in shades of medium and deep blue, arm bands of jet jewelry, and little in the way of a bustle.

"Please be seated, gentlemen. Are you here seeking accommodations?"

Mr. Stoker and I remained standing, despite the invitation.

"No, madam," said my boss. "In fact we are here merely to ask one or two questions regarding a tenant of yours. Or, as I understand it, a past tenant. A Mr. Menachem Klaczko."

Her eyebrows rose briefly. "The police have already been here asking after Mr. Klaczko."

I noticed that she pronounced the name correctly and smoothly.

"So it is my understanding, madam," continued Mr. Stoker. "However, for reasons I need not go into, I would like to ask my own questions. Please bear with me if I repeat some that you have already answered. Firstly, how well did you come to know Mr. Klaczko?"

Mrs. Lublin herself sat and waved her hand to again suggest that we do the same. We did, seating ourselves on a most uncomfortable triple-arching-back settee, facing her.

"I do not make a habit of befriending my tenants, Mr. Stoker. It is neither my desire nor is it good business sense. However, in the case of Mr. Klaczko I think it would have been difficult if not impossible to grow close in any sense of the word. He kept very much to himself to the point of seemingly avoiding me at all costs."

"Did he not have to make contact when paying his rent?"

"He first took his room through the actions of an intermediary. A gentleman who paid the first three month's rent in advance for his friend. From then on Mr. Klaczko confined himself to his room at all times. I was aware of his going out late in the evenings but never actually encountered him at any of those time."

"Were you not curious?" asked Stoker.

"I do not have time for curiosity regarding my tenants, sir. I make a decision on their suitability for my premises when I first accept them as tenants, but from then on their lives and my own are completely separate."

"Of course," my boss murmured. "But you did actually see Mr. Klaczko on at least one occasion, I presume? The occasion of his first entering your establishment?"

Mrs. Lublin paused a moment before shaking her head.

"No. Now that you mention it, I don't think that I did. At least, not a good sight of the gentleman."

"Can you describe what you did observe?"

She thought before answering. "Of medium height, with white hair. I did notice that particularly, it was so completely white. It had no grey in it at all, which surprised me for he did not seem to be an elderly gentleman, if one is to judge from the way he moved. I had but the briefest of glimpses of his face, for he retained his hat pulled low. The face was extremely pale – I presumed he was perhaps unwell – and I did notice that his eyes were an extremely pale blue, with much red about the rims. This reinforced my sense that the gentleman was not in the best of health, despite his freedom of movement."

"Thank you, Mrs. Lublin. You are indeed most observant. May I ask if you were equally observant about the other gentleman; the one who brought him here and paid his rent?"

Mrs. Lublin shrugged. "I don't think that I was, Mr. Stoker. Perhaps because he was not so remarkable. Very ordinary, if I may use that term. Tall and thin, with a straggly mustache and beard. Not particularly well dressed. Indeed, I may not have accepted them into my home had I not been in need of another tenant. That room had been vacant for far too long a period."

"I understand. One last question, if I may? Inspector Bellamy – the policeman you spoke with earlier – had mentioned that Mr. Klaczko was no longer in residence. Is that correct?"

"Indeed it is, sir. The gentleman went out one evening, little more than a week ago, and did not return. He left with his room still paid for another six weeks or more."

"And you had no way of contacting the other gentleman, the one who originally delivered Mr. Klaczko to your house?"

"None whatsoever."

"May I ask?" I spoke up. "Did you not wonder whether or not Mr. Klac . . . your tenant had perhaps met with an accident, since he went out and didn't return?"

"That was my first thought," Mrs. Lublin replied. "I did enquire around, briefly. Not to make too much of it, of course . . ."

"You didn't go to the police?" I asked.

She looked horrified. "It was not my place, sir. Who am I to involve the authorities? People are a strange lot. They come and go as they please, in this city."

"Understandable, madam," agreed Mr. Stoker. "Is there anything else you can tell us about him? Anything at all?"

"Only . . . No! No, I do not believe so." Her lips formed a thin tight line across the lower part of her face.

My boss studied her silently for a moment before leaning forward slightly. "Please, Mrs. Lublin. There may well be much at stake here. Any information you can impart; any little detail, observation, comment . . ?"

She looked uncomfortable and studiously raised her eyes to the unlit gasolier above us, keeping them fixed on that object as she spoke. "In the old country, Mr. Stoker. We – my mother, my grandmother – we could 'sense' things. I am not making myself clear! We . . ."

"On the contrary, dear lady." Mr. Stoker smiled his lady-charming smile, and nodded his head understandingly. "I am Irish by birth, Mrs. Lublin. I believe that we have not dissimilar backgrounds. My own grandmother . . ."

I could not help letting a sigh escape me. If Mr. Stoker was going to get into his grandmother with her second sight and association with the fairies, then we were doomed to remain there for a very long time. But possibly my boss heard my sigh and recognized it for what it was. He stopped himself before enlarging on his maternal lineage.

"But, no matter. Suffice it to say that I am indeed well acquainted with any thoughts or feelings you have that may, to other ears, appear irrational. Please do continue, Mrs. Lublin."

The tight mouth loosened and her eyes descended to again engage those of my boss. "I do not believe that the person calling himself Menachem Klaczko was in fact that gentleman. I do not believe he was a Polish Jew. I'm very much afraid I don't know what I do believe." She looked to Mr. Stoker for help.

He nodded his head understandingly and pursed his lips, as he did when contemplating the best way to say something. "I have long ago learned to put trust in such feelings, madam. I am sure you have done the same." He came to his feet and I followed suit. "We do thank you for your time, Mrs. Lublin. You have been of inestimable help. May I return to speak with you again should I need to do so?"

She nodded her head almost enthusiastically, as she too arose. "Do not hesitate, Mr. Stoker. I will always be at home to you."

"Harry, how far are we from Gilbert Andrews's hotel? It is somewhere in this part of town, is it not?"

"Yes, sir. Probably within walking distance of here. Why do you ask?"

"Did we not decide that we needed to speak further with Mr. Andrews, regarding the hour of his meeting with John Saxon?"

I mentally shook myself. Of course! It had been on my list of things to do but had got temporarily lost in the shuffle. Thank the gods that my boss never loses sight of anything. I don't know how he does it, with so much always going on.

"He's just the other side of New Oxford Street, not far from here, sir. "

"Then let us pay the gentleman a visit. Lead on, Macduff!" As I started up Drury Lane he added:

"You know, of course, that is a misquotation, though oft repeated it seems."

"Sir?"

"Yes, Harry. The actual words, as written by the Bard, are 'Lay on, Macduff'; a totally different meaning. But we seem to be surrounded by ignoramuses."

I decided not to point out that by using the incorrect phrase himself he was pandering to the ignorant.

The Cardinal Wolsey Hotel was close by the Meux Brewery. The brewery announced itself by its pungency long before we came anywhere near to it. I don't know whether it was the hops or the yeast that delivered such an olfactory titillation but there was no mistaking it. Mr. Stoker took several deep breaths but refrained from comment. The Meux Brewery was dear to my heart since it was the last London brewery to solely produce porter, my favorite stout.

Sir Henry Meux, the original owner, died in 1813 and his son, Sir Henry Meux the Second, took over. The following year the securing iron hoops on a giant vat containing 3,555 barrels of porter snapped, allowing the vat to burst. It was said that a wall of beer nearly fifteen feet in height, took out the end wall and poured from the brewery. The resultant rush of liquid into the street caused the collapse of several houses and killed eight people. Many years later, in 1858, Sir Henry was declared insane. Yet despite all this, the brewery grew in size and fame, Henry Bruce Meux and Lord

Tweedmouth taking over management just two years ago.

This time there was a figure behind the Cardinal Wolsey reception desk when we entered. It was a slight shadow of a man, dressed in a shabby suit of faded grey. His well-worn appearance blended in with the nondescript background created by the ancient wallpaper. I wondered if, in fact, he had been there on my previous visit and that I had just not seen him, but dismissed the thought.

"Is Mr. Andrews in residence?" asked my boss, startling the older man whose attention had been fastened on a newspaper spread on the desk in front of him.

"Eh? What's that you say?" He cupped a hand to his ear.

"Mr. Andrews," I said loudly.

"Andrews?"

"Mr. Gilbert Andrews." Mr. Stoker's voice echoed off the ancient walls. "Is he in his room. We wish to speak with the gentleman."

"Ah! Well you'll have to speak up a lot louder than that to do so." A slight smile cracked the old man's face. "He's most likely halfway to Yorkshire by now."

"What do you mean?"

"He checked out late yesterday afternoon, sir. I've already let his room. You want to speak to Mr. Hanson?"

"Who's Mr. Hanson?"

"He's the gentleman as is now in that room."

"No I don't want to speak to Mr. Hanson!" snorted Stoker. "Come, Harry. This has been a wasted journey."

As we retraced our steps my boss muttered bitterly about the dearth of good help in public institutions.

"When I spoke to Mr. Andrews he had assured me that he would let me know if he was likely to be leaving town," I said.

"Well, let us be charitable and assume that he was suddenly offered the lead in some new play at the Doncaster Playhouse."

"He said he doesn't play leads, sir."

"Don't take me so literally, Harry."

We walked on in silence for a while. Our steps led us back to Drury Lane.

Chapter Eighteen

Mr. Stoker and I remained uncertain about Gilbert Andrews. Was he involved in the murder of his friend John Saxon? At what time of day, or night, had he argued with John? Why had he so suddenly left London and returned north? First thing Tuesday morning I made a point of paying another visit to Mr. Phillip Entwhistle, Gilbert Andrews's agent. He did not seem overjoyed to see me.

"Mr. Lyceum, isn't it?" he said, shuffling papers on his desk. I couldn't help noticing that some of them were unpaid bills.

"Harry Rivers of the Lyceum, Mr. Entwhistle. Yes."

"Well, what's to do now? Did you not meet up with my lad Gilbert?"

"Indeed I did," I replied. "And he promised to stay in touch and let me know if he was likely to be leaving London. Yet I find that he has suddenly returned to Yorkshire, or somewhere. It's important I speak with him. I wondered if you could enlighten me as to his present whereabouts?"

"Oh, aye!" I got the feeling that Mr. Entwhistle had been half expecting me. His answer seemed to come too readily. "Young Gilbert got a casting call from Doncaster Playhouse. Part of Charles Marlow in *She Stoops to Conquer*."

I was, of course, familiar with Mr. Oliver Goldsmith's play. "Surely Mr. Andrews would be miscast as Marlow?" I said.

Entwhistle looked up sharply. "What? Aye, well . . . One mustn't fly in the face of Providence, must one?"

"There are certain questions I must ask of Mr. Andrews. If I cannot ask them, then I believe that Scotland Yard will be looking to speak with him." I didn't know this for certain. Indeed, it was more likely that Inspector Bellamy would have no interest in Gilbert Andrews whatsoever. But Phillip Entwhistle wasn't to know that.

"Oh! Let me see. Now where's my calendar?" He rummaged around among the confusion of papers on his desk, finally retrieving a large desk diary and opening it. He turned pages back and forth. "Where . . ? Ah! Here we are." He held up the volume so that I could not see what, if anything, was written on the page and proceeded to apparently read from it. "Aye! I had forgotten. Our lad moved out of that hotel but has not actually left for Doncaster as yet. I believe he moved to another hotel – the Gloucester Hotel – close by Victoria Station so that he can hurry up to Doncaster the very minute they need him."

I thought of pointing out that trains for Doncaster would leave from King's Cross railway station not Victoria, but decided not to bother. The name of the hotel where Andrews was now staying was the important thing.

I again visited Gilbert Andrews, this time at the Gloucester Hotel. He was unapologetic about having moved without letting me know.

"You know the theatre business, Harry. Got to keep moving to keep up with yourself. I was offered a nice part in *The Good-Natur'd Man.*"

"Your agent said it was *She Stoops to Conquer,*" I said.

He waved a hand. "One of them Goldsmith plays. It was work – a good part – that was all I knew."

I shook my head resignedly. "Well there are some questions I would really like answers to, regarding when you last saw John Saxon."

"Of course."

"The main one is, at what time in the evening did you and John meet."

He turned away and busied himself rearranging some scripts on the side table. We were in his room at the hotel and it was sparsely furnished. He had half a dozen play scripts with him; I noted that none of them were Goldsmith plays.

"It was after that evening's performance, of course. He had invited me backstage after the final curtain. John had got out of costume and make-up. Must have been close to midnight."

"And you said that you argued. Over money. A loan he had made you many years ago?"

"John never forgot a thing . . . except his lines, once in a while. But as I told you, I had thought the money a gift. Certainly not worth fighting over." He stopped fiddling with the scripts and sat down in a chair opposite me.

"Where were you when this argument took place?" I asked.

"Where? I don't know! Somewhere in the theatre, I suppose. I wasn't looking where we were going. We just sort of wandered as we talked."

"It wouldn't have been up in the gods, would it?" I tried to make it an innocent question.

Andrews laughed. "Oh, I think I would have noticed a long climb up to the gods, Harry. No, it wasn't there."

"I'm surprised you don't remember."

"I can tell you it wasn't in his dressing room, but other than that . . . I'm not familiar with the layout of the Lyceum. All theatres are slightly different, as you know. Dressing rooms are upstairs or downstairs; wardrobe might be next to the greenroom; props is often tucked away in a corner. No two are the same."

I had to agree. I was very familiar with my own theatre but probably I could easily become disoriented in another.

"Anything else you can think of, about this argument?"

"It left me with a bad taste in my mouth, I can tell you that. After all those years! Between two old friends! I walked away, though I suppose I should have stayed and sorted it out."

"You had no trouble finding your way out of the theatre?"

He shrugged. "I suppose not. I'm here now,

aren't I?" He forced a grin, which I ignored. "Oh, one more thing. John did say that he didn't have a lot of time because he had to meet with someone else, even though it was so late."

"Someone else?" I was immediately alert. "Any idea who?"

He shrugged again and shook his head. "No idea. I just hoped John wasn't going to treat him as badly as he had treated me."

"Him?" I said. "It was a man, then?"

His brow wrinkled as he tried to think. "You know, I don't know. I assumed it was, though we both know he had an eye for the ladies. Hmm! Perhaps he did have a dollymop or a flame on the side. I never thought of that."

I got up to leave. "You will keep in touch this time, won't you?" I said, looking him in the eyes. "This is part of a murder investigation, you know. No running off up north without letting me know?"

"Well, if I get a sudden casting call – a part I can't turn down – then I may have to move fast."

"I thought you already had that, for Doncaster Playhouse?"

He didn't have the grace to look embarrassed, just grinned and said nothing. I left him there.

Inspector Bellamy seemed to have his mind fixed on Guy Purdy as the culprit but I thought that if I could somehow manage to expand the policeman's mind – something I very much doubted – then we might be able to move on and locate other more likely suspects. Little did I realize how quickly such a list could add up. But it seemed that I should strike Gilbert Andrews off the list. He had said that he never went up into the gods with John Saxon. I tended to believe him. If so, I couldn't see how he could have pushed John over the balcony.

On my way back into the theatre I came upon the Welshmen, Davey Llewellyn, speaking animatedly to Bill Thomas, at Bill's cubbyhole.

"I know it's not good to speak ill of the dead – or of anyone, if it comes to that – but I have to say what I feel, you know? Mr. Saxon was not a nice man, that much I can tell you. Oh, he might well have been a good actor – a real second Henry Irving, is it you're saying? – but what does that have to do with anything when you come down to it?"

"Here! You know how long I knew John Saxon?" demanded Bill.

"No, I don't know and I don't want to know. Is that going to help my friend? I don't think so!" With that, Davey Llewellyn turned and stalked off down the corridor leading back into the theatre.

I stopped at Bill's desk and watched the short figure bustle away, disappearing around the far corner.

"What was that all about, Bill?"

He pushed his half-glasses back up on his nose, where they had slipped down, and gave a sniff. "Welsh temper, I'd call it, Harry," he said. "Hasn't been here five minutes and he's defaming someone who can't talk back."

"He has a grudge against John Saxon?"

"You know what they say, Harry. A Welshman prays on his knees on a Sunday and preys on his friends the rest of the week."

"So what's this about Llewellyn's friend? Is that Lonnie Plimpton he's talking about?"

Bill nodded. "It is. Those two look out for each other, believe me. Thick as thieves. It seems that John used to pick on Plimpton. Not nice of him I know, but that was just John. Used to call the big man dumb and stupid and things like that."

I shook my head. "I didn't know that about Mr. Saxon."

"Got to admit that this Lonnie Plimpton isn't the brightest light in the footlights but there was never any call for John to harangue the poor man. The Welshman's got a point there. It seems that soon after this duo first got here Plimpton was standing in the wings, gawking at the action on stage, and got in the way of John Saxon making an exit."

"Plimpton definitely shouldn't have been there," I said. "But two wrongs don't make a right."

"Well, as you just saw, the little Welshman isn't going to forget it, even after John's murder."

Both Mr. Stoker and myself had acknowledged that the murderer was almost certainly one of the Lyceum family, as unpalatable as that might be. At my later meeting with Mr. Stoker I brought up this episode. I had been thinking about it ever since Bill Thomas had enlightened me and I had to admit that it had brought on a lot of speculation about Davey

Llewellyn and Lonnie Plimpton. Perhaps we were clutching at straws but if we were to recognize all possible suspects then this new revelation about Mr. Saxon's attitude towards Mr. Plimpton did put one, or both, of the duo onto our list. Davey Llewellyn had the temper to make him go too far in fighting back at John's taunts, and Lonnie Plimpton had the strength to put actions to those words.

"It is certainly worth considering," said my boss. "See if you can find out anything regarding the movements of the duo after the final curtain on the night of John Saxon's murder, Harry."

"I will, sir." I brought him up to date on Gilbert Andrews and then got on about my work.

It was while on an errand later in the morning that I had an inspiration. I was hurrying along Drury Lane, trying to get to our printer to drop off a job that Mr. Stoker wanted done, when I happened to glance up and my attention was caught by the sun shining on three gold-painted balls hanging outside a shop just around the corner from Drury Lane. A pawnbroker. There were few of them in this particular area; far more to the east where poorer families made frequent use of their services. In the East End it was not unknown for an indigent housewife to pawn her cooking pots and pans on a Monday and then retrieve them on Friday, when the husband got paid. Here, closer to the Lyceum, there was a better class of pawnbroker.

If I had stopped to think I probably wouldn't have entertained the thought, but on impulse I turned and went into the shop. A tall, thin, Jewish gentleman, with a thick black beard, stood behind the counter examining the stones of a necklace through a small magnifying glass he held tightly in his eye. Hearing the door open, he slipped the jewelry out of sight down behind the counter top and removed the glass from his eye.

"Pawning or redeeming?" he asked, his dark eyebrows drawn together in suspicion as he examined me from bowler hat to shoes.

"Neither one," I replied. "I just have a question for you."

His eyebrows knit even tighter together. "I don't answer questions."

"It's a simple one," I persisted. "Do you recall recently selling an old silver hunter inscribed with the name Klaczko?" I mentally thanked Mr. Stoker for making me repeat the name over and over until I had it right.

"I don't know no Menachem Klaczko."

This time it was my eyebrows that moved – upwards. "Did I say his name was Menachem?"

He waved his hands at me. "I am closing up for lunch. You must leave. This is not a good time. Shoo! Go away." He waved his hands at me, indicating I should get out.

I stood firmly at the counter, gripping it as though to do so would prevent him from ejecting me. He was certainly taller than me, but much older and definitely frailer.

"The watch, sir?" I said, firmly. "Just a question or two."

I think he sized me up in much the same

way that I had appraised him. He shrugged resignedly, pouted, and mumbled "What is it you want to know? You are not with the Peelers." It was a statement, not a question.

"No, I have nothing to do with the police. I am merely enquiring about this one particular item; the silver pocket watch."

His shoulders slumped resignedly. "I knew old Menachem. He was a good man. When he died his nephew inherited what few things he had. The nephew immediately pawned it all. He knew of me so he brought it all here. There was nothing worth anything except, perhaps, the watch. That too was not of very good quality but Menachem treasured it after his long years in the accounting office. I gave the nephew a few pounds for it . . . more than it was worth because I didn't want it going to some other broker."

"And yet you sold it," I said. "It wasn't precious enough for you to keep it?"

He waved his hands around to indicate the plethora of pawned items. "Even items from old friends can outstay their welcome. Yes, I had a customer liked the look of it and gave me more than I had paid the nephew." He shrugged. "Life goes on."

"What can you tell me about the man who bought it?" I asked.

Again he shrugged. "What's to tell? I think he was an actor. A lot of my customers come from the theatres around here. But anyway, it wasn't for him."

"Oh?"

"No. He said he wanted it for his brother. I don't know . . . perhaps a birthday gift or something? *Oy vey ist mir.* What do I know?"

"Just one more question," I said. "Was your friend Menachem a pale-faced gentleman with snow-white hair? A strange question I know, but I would appreciate knowing."

He slowly shook his head. "Menachem was as bald as these billiard balls here in this case. And his face was always red. Too much drinking I always told him. I think that's what finally killed him."

Pure chance, I thought to myself as I left the shop and walked away down Drury Lane. I had guessed that the pawnbroker used by Mr. Klaczko was in a slightly better area than Whitechapel but it was just coincidence that I happened upon the very one, though there were not a lot of pawnbrokers in this part of the city. Let us not look a gift horse in the mouth, as the good saint admonished us. I smiled to myself and started whistling as I walked.

Chapter Nineteen

Wednesday morning I was doing my usual check of props knowing that, with the matinee, there would be two houses that day. The curtains were open and while I was on-stage some of the front-of-house staff were on the other side of the footlights, talking amongst themselves. I couldn't help overhearing one of them calling to another.

"Did you see it too, Frank?"

"Couldn't hardly miss it, could I? Right up there looking down."

"Not the first time, neither."

"'S right!"

"You'd think they'd do sommat about it, wouldn't you? Complaining about the gods being 'alf empty and then puttin' up with this."

"Excuse me!" I had to interject. Mention of the lack of audience in the gods was definitely something I was interested in. "What's all this about then?" I asked. "What was up in the gods looking down?"

The tall, lanky man called Frank glanced about him and then, seeing that no one else was going to speak, stood up straight and hooked his thumbs into his waistcoat pockets as he fixed his eyes on me. "The vampire!"

"I beg your pardon?"

"The vampire. Leastwise that's what we figured it has to be, didn't we?" He looked around at his companions but they were all busying themselves picking up discarded programs from the previous night's performance and generally tidying up the auditorium. Frank shook his head at them and returned his attention to me. "That's what it has to have been. A pale face peeping out from the box up there. Gave me the creeps it did. And everyone else as saw it, whether they want to admit it or not." He looked scathingly at his fellow workers but they kept their heads down.

"This was during last night's performance?" I persevered.

"Right at the end, just before final curtain. As though it was having a last look around afore everyone cleared out."

"And it was the top box on this side?" I pointed up towards the box on the OP side of the stage.

Frank nodded. "Yes. Anytime we seen him it was always that side."

"Thank you," I said. "I assure you we will try to do something about it. Please be sure to let me, or Mr. Stoker, know immediately if it happens again."

"What about during the play?" asked the man who had originally called out to Frank. "That's when 'e's been lookin' down."

"Yes," I said. "Especially during the

performance. That way we can rush up there and see if we can catch him."

"Not wif me, you won't!" said the man.

"Nor me," added Frank.

"That's all right," I said. "You don't have to approach him. But do let Mr. Stoker or myself know about it. We will go up there."

I was more thrilled than frightened. I'm sure that when it came to it the idea of facing a living, breathing vampire – they did breath, I supposed? – it might be a slightly different story but right now I was simply excited at the prospect of finding the cause of our loss of revenue. I thought that Mr. Stoker would share that excitement.

As I had told the man Frank, it would be best to catch the creature in the act, as it were, but even so I made a point of climbing up to the gods again right away to have yet another look around. Perhaps I'd missed something vital the last time I had looked?

Reaching the top gallery, I took a moment to sit down on the end of the back row of seats and to catch my breath. I looked about me. All was still. It seemed that the cleaners who came up here swept through as quickly as possible and did not linger. I noticed one or two sweet wrappers and bits of paper still under the seats. They were not doing a very good job of cleaning and I needed to call them to task or at least to point it out to Mr. Bidwell.

I got up and moved along to the entrance to the box. It was mid-morning and I should have nothing to fear, I told myself, but still I held my breath as I turned the handle on the door and prepared to open it. My heart was thudding in my chest as I threw it open of a sudden. I was never happier to hear utter silence. There was no rapid retreat of footsteps or scampering of some creature across the carpet. There was nothing.

I moved into the center of the area. It was much like the last time I had been here, with the gilt upholstered chairs lined along the wall on one side of the box and the curtains pulled together across the front. Yet as I studied the row of chairs, something seemed different. What was it? They were not spaced quite the same, I thought. I seemed to recall that the last time I was here the chairs were all placed tightly side by side, yet this time in a couple of places there were small gaps between adjoining seats. It was not a big difference I had to admit, and probably had no significance, but if no one had been here since I had last looked at the chairs then who had moved them? And why? I shook my head. I was going crazy! Obviously the cleaners had been here . . . ? But the cleaners wouldn't even take the time to properly clean the upper gallery so why would they clean an unused box? As if to confirm this thought, I noticed an empty pork pie wrapper lying crumpled in the back corner. No. No one had been up here to clean. I left and returned to my duties on stage.

It was close to time for curtain-up for the matinee show when I again happened to bump into the man Frank. Normally front-of-house and backstage staff don't encounter one another but it seems that

Herbert Gardner needed someone to take a message through to Bill Thomas, about an expected delivery for the commissariat. Frank was nearby at the time and offered to go around for Mr. Gardner, since time was short. It was as I hurried along between Mr. Stoker's office and the greenroom that I bumped into him.

"Did you get a chance to look up in the gods yet, Mr. Rivers?" he asked.

"Oh yes, Frank. Right after I talked to you. Nothing there, of course."

"But we all saw it. The same figure. We even compared notes and we all agreed we'd seen the same thing."

"Oh, I don't doubt it," I said. "It's just that there was nothing visible up there when I went to look. That's why I'd like you to give me a call the next time you do see something, even if it's during a performance." I had a sudden thought. "By the way, how is Mr. Gardner doing with his supplies? He was missing stuff a week or so ago."

"I heard about that," said the lanky front-of-house man. "I think some of us were under suspicion for a while but it seems he's had no more trouble."

"Good," I said. "At least something is going right then. Now I must get on. It'll soon be overture and beginners. You'd better get back around front."

It was shortly after the start of Act Three Scene Four that the electricity failed again. Edwin Booth had just entered as Iago, with John Whitby as

Cassio, when all the stage lights went out. Mr. Booth had delivered his opening line and then, when we lost the lights, John Whitby "dried up". Happily, with a prompt from Miss Price he quickly regained his lines and the scene continued while house lights were brought up. Before the end of the scene the electricity had been restored but the Guv'nor was hopping mad. The blame was finally laid to a faulty main fuse but I couldn't help seeing it as an echo of the aggravations heaped upon the Lyceum when Ralph Bateman was causing so many problems. It may well have been a faulty fuse but I promised myself to ask Mario Pinasco, the electrician, if he would double-check everything possible. He did a quick repair job to get the play back on course, but I felt we needed to look more closely at the whole electrical set-up.

"Heard the latest stories, Harry?" It was Bill Thomas who addressed me as I was slipping past his post, out to the Druid's Head for a quick bite between houses.

"What's that, Bill?" I wasn't as taken with gossip as he was but it was difficult not to be fascinated by some of the stories Bill heard and passed on.

"It seems that the Lyceum has a ghost up in the gods that attacks people during the last scene of the play." He chuckled. "Why it waits till just before final curtain I don't know, but that's the latest chinwag."

"A ghost?" I asked. "Not a vampire then?"

He shrugged. "Who knows? One day it's a ghost, another day it's a vampire, another day it's something else. Not that I listen to them, mind you."

"Of course not, Bill." I smiled. "And these people who claim to have been attacked – have you seen any of them? Have they made official complaints?"

"I guess you'd have to speak to Mr. Bidwell about that, Harry. He's the one they would be complaining to. But I kind of doubt that there've been any actual cases. It's always someone who knew someone who was attacked, isn't it?"

So the stories wouldn't go away? At this rate we'd never get back to having full houses in the top gallery. "Have you been up in the gods yourself, Bill?" I asked.

It seemed to me that for some reason he avoided the question. Suddenly Bill turned away and busied himself with some papers he had on the shelf behind his desk. It wasn't like him to just break off a conversation. Bill loved to talk. Seldom would he let his work get in the way of a good gossip. I stood there a moment but he had apparently decided to become busy. I moved on and went out to the Druid's Head.

I found the tavern crowded, as was usual on a matinee day between houses. Some of the actors had dragged two tables together and were just getting seated. William Hammermind saw me and waved me over.

"Here, Harry! Come and join us."

I did. Toby Merryfield moved his chair a little so that I could squeeze in. Anthony Sampson,

John Whitby, Guy Purdy, and Arthur Swindon nodded in my direction. I waved to Jimmy Hathaway, our ever-vigilant policeman, and noticed Timothy Bidwell and Mario Pinasco sharing a table not far away. Lonnie Plimpton and Davey Llewellyn – permanently dubbed in my mind as "the duo" – sat close to the door and were constantly looking up as people came in.

I peered up to the chalkboard over the fireplace, to see what was on the menu, and decided on rabbit stew. The two serving girls, Penny and Gwen, together with the landlord's son Samuel, were kept busy in the dining room, rushing back and forth with orders. I quickly found my tankard of porter at my elbow and a bright-eyed Penny listened as everyone at the table tried to speak at once on their choice of repast.

There was a sudden sound of music as background to the babble of voices. I spotted a hurdy-gurdy man standing in a far corner. John Martin didn't usually allow entertainers in the dining room but the place was so busy he seemed to be tolerating it today. I thought I recognized the musician as one I had encountered in there on a previous occasion, though not playing his instrument at that time.

"Nice bit of music for our dining pleasure, Harry," said Anthony Sampson.

"Damn nuisance!" grunted Guy Purdy.

"Oh, leave him be," murmured Bill Hammermind.

The talk was the usual chit-chat and banter as we received our orders and started appeasing our appetites. It was not long, however, before talk got around to the rumors about apparitions up in the gods.

"Stuff and nonsense," said Toby Merryfield, reaching across the table for the salt cellar.

"People will see what they want to see," said Hammermind. "We've all heard the stories of the Man in Grey at the Theatre Royal Drury Lane."

"I don't know the details," said Toby. "I've heard talk of him, of course. Was he an actor?"

"Legend says that he's the ghost of a knife-stabbed man whose skeleton was found in a walled-up passage in the theatre nearly fifty years ago," said Anthony Sampson, with relish. "No one knows whether he was an actor or a patron."

"I've heard that he appears dressed as a nobleman of the end of the last century," added John Whitby. "Powdered hair under a tricorn hat, a dress jacket and cloak, wearing riding boots and carrying a sword."

"Joseph Grimaldi," said Guy Purdy.

"I beg your pardon?"

"Joseph Grimaldi. Another Drury Lane ghost but also seen at Covent Garden and Sadler's Wells," continued Mr. Purdy. "Started in the late 1700s as a child actor and eventually died in 1847. He's been seen a lot at all three theatres."

"And the ghost of actor Charles Macklin," added Sampson. "He' s supposed to haunt the Drury Lane theatre. He appears backstage, wandering the corridor. In 1735, he killed fellow actor Thomas Hallam there in an argument over a wig. 'Goddamn you for a blackguard, scrub, rascal!' he is supposed to have shouted, and thrust his cane into Hallam's face and into his left eye."

I shuddered. Anthony Sampson seemed to relish the image.

"So what about our own ghost then?" asked Toby Merryfield. "I've been up to the gods to look for him. Any of you?"

There were nods from a few of the actors. It surprised me. Generally actors seem to me to be a thick-skinned lot who believe in very little. They all have their superstitions, such as not whistling on stage, not wishing one another good luck, not wearing peacock feathers, and never mentioning the play *Macbeth* by name. I was surprised then, to find that all of the actors present took stories of our ghost to heart and believed in its existence.

"You've all been up to the gods to look for him?" I asked.

"Well, not specifically for him," replied Guy Purdy, slightly embarrassed. "Some of us older actors go up there when we can, when the theatre is empty, to practice our projection."

"That's right," agreed Hammermind. "The science of sound, they call it. But we just know that it helps us project."

"If one stands in the center of the upper balcony and projects one's lines, the sound of the voice will reflect off the various surfaces and one can develop one's voice to fully fill the theatre," added Mr. Sampson. "The Guv'nor himself gave me the tip. He used to declaim his monologues there for years, though he has not felt the need to in more recent times, it seems."

There was one other person I should check on I thought, as I sat finishing my meal with the chatter going on around me. I had first had this thought when I was returning from my time with Jenny on Sunday. How it managed to intrude on those joyful memories, I don't know. The thought was, where was Bill Thomas at the time of the murder? He almost certainly knew of Gilbert Andrews's visit to John. He would probably know where the meeting took place, and when. Bill was always the last to leave the theatre at night. He was the one who locked-up the stage door and left the theatre completely dark. So wouldn't he be the one who, if not involved in the episode in the gods, might be aware of it taking place? I had to speak with him as soon as I could make the time. It seemed I was adding murder suspects at a fast pace. When I later voiced my suspicions to my boss, Mr. Stoker did not make me feel foolish.

"A very good thought, Harry. Bill Thomas is one of those individuals who are so familiar they seem like part of the theatre furniture. Yet, as you so rightly point out, they are very tangible individuals running their own lives. Yes, he would – or should – have knowledge of anyone still in the theatre after hours. A clever deduction, Harry. That definitely needs following-up."

Chapter Twenty

I looked up in surprise, as did Mr. Stoker, when the door to my boss's office bounced open. The pair of Indian clubs standing behind the door was sent flying. On the threshold stood Mr. Henry Irving, Miss Ellen Terry leaning out from behind him to peer around his solid figure.

"Abraham!"

We both came to our feet. It was unusual for the Guv'nor to burst in without knocking and the two of us knew that something was very much amiss.

"Henry," said Mr. Stoker. "Do, please come in. Miss Terry. . . Harry get seats for our guests."

I scurried around, giving up my own chair and dragging a second one across from the wall behind me.

Mr. Irving held up his hand, as he did when taking command. "Stay, gentlemen. I am on my way out to a conference with Edwin but would leave Miss Terry in your capable hands."

"Of course, of course, Henry. Might I ask what is wrong?"

"Really, it's nothing," murmured Miss

Terry, maneuvering her skirts around the Guv'nor and seating herself on my recently vacated chair.

"I do not call it nothing," said Irving. "Sit down gentlemen and listen to what Ellen has to say. I will expect you to take appropriate action, Abraham. Please let me know the outcome when I return."

So saying, the tall figure swung around and hurried away, neglecting to close the door behind him. I moved across and did so.

"Miss Terry," said Mr. Stoker, re-seating himself and smiling at the leading lady. "What in the name of the heavens can be the cause of this distress?"

"Oh, Henry is taking it far too seriously I'm sure, Bram. It's just that . . . well, I mentioned to him that I was late leaving here last evening. I lingered to re-organize the costumes in my dressing room. Anyway, I happened to descend to the wardrobe room, to see if Miss Connelly had some dark blue thread left out that I might borrow. I was certain that I was alone in the theatre; everyone else had scurried off as soon as they could, of course, and I didn't plan on staying long myself."

"What happened?" asked Stoker.

She paused and her brow wrinkled.

"It was a sound. Not a voice, exactly. A strange sound that came up from below the stage."

"What sort of a sound?" I couldn't stop myself from interjecting.

Miss Terry glanced at me, the frown remaining on her brow. "Almost a moaning sound, as though someone was in pain."

"But you say there was no one else in the theatre?" asked Stoker.

She nodded. "Other than Mr. Thomas, who had not yet locked up, I had been sure of it. But it seemed I was wrong. This noise came from below stage and came and went. I could almost imagine someone sitting moaning, and rocking back and forth as they moaned. The sound rose and fell. It was eerie."

"Could you pinpoint from where, below stage, the sound issued?"

She shook her blonde tresses. "I've seldom been down there. It seems to me to be a veritable warren of passages and cubby holes."

I could sympathize. The original Lyceum theatre had been built in 1771. It was rebuilt in 1816 but was burned down fourteen years later. It was rebuilt and re-opened in 1834, being the first theatre in London to be lit by gas. Its foundations seemed to be a maze of tunnels and passages from previous incarnations and I had always tried to stay away from exploring them, being somewhat sensitive to enclosed spaces. I did have to visit the area immediately below stage a few months before, when Mr. Stoker discovered a secret room and evidence of strange rituals being performed there, but since that had been taken care of – or so I had been led to believe – I had avoided the area. I felt uneasy listening to Miss Terry's story and hoped it didn't presage my being sent below stage again to investigate. I should have known better.

"Harry," said Stoker. My heart skipped a beat. "Why don't you take a look down there and make sure we have no unwanted visitors?"

"Yes, sir." I moved to the door and smiled at Miss Terry. She returned the smile and I felt almost heroic. I stood up straighter as I opened the door and went out, but my shoulders quickly slumped and I wondered whether I should try to get Sam Green to accompany me. But Sam was at lunch, I knew, and there was no one else I could think of to pressgang into going with me. No, I would have to try to be the strong, unafraid young man that Miss Ellen Terry obviously thought me to be.

I descended the stairs down to the dressing rooms, greenroom, and wardrobe and then went on down to the below stage area. This was where the various stage trapdoors used in some of our productions were serviced. The space below stage was quite large, though low-ceilinged, and many disused properties and stage furnishings had been abandoned down there.

I quickly moved around but realized that I'd need a lantern to see properly. I went back up, got one, and set off once again. I reasoned that if Miss Terry had heard the noises from directly above, in the wardrobe room, then they had to have issued from close to that point. I did indeed find a passageway almost immediately below wardrobe, leading away into the darkness. Picking up a chair leg, and carrying it like a cudgel, I raised the lantern in my other hand and slowly advanced.

I was surprised at just how many alcoves and ledges there were, carved into the stone on which the theatre was built. Yet the passageway seemed empty, discounting an empty ginger beer bottle and an old pie wrapper that someone had discarded down there. I followed along the winding way but eventually came to a dead end. There were wooden boards closing up the way forward. I thought it might be that it was unsafe to proceed. Perhaps the roof was insecure? I knew that there was actually more than one level beneath the stage. A maze of passages and rooms, most of them unopened in many years, ran across the area immediately below where I was. There was also a half basement even below that, according to Bill Thomas. It tied-in to an artesian well that furnished the theatre with water. But such a subterranean city was not for me with my horror of enclosed spaces. I turned and retraced my steps.

I did discover a side passage that I had missed on my outward journey, but it was very narrow with a low ceiling so I didn't bother going deeply into it. No, I thought, if anyone – perhaps one of the stagehands who had been drinking? – had been down there, they had obviously gone now. I could report back to Mr. Stoker and Miss Terry with a clear conscience.

Miss Terry had left by the time I got back to Mr. Stoker's office.

"So, nothing and no sign of anyone, Harry?"

"Nothing at all, sir. Mind you, I think that if anyone wanted to hide down there, they'd have plenty of opportunity to do so. If one learned the layout one could probably move around and avoid contact with any searchers."

"Hmm. I'm sure you're right, Harry. I must get Sam Green to embark upon a systematic exploration one of these days. For now, I'll let the Guv'nor know that there is nothing for Miss Terry to fear."

"All the same, I wonder what it was that she heard?" I pondered. "Miss Terry is not the sort of person to be easily frightened."

"I'm sure the Guv'nor is taking it overly seriously. You know how protective he can be when it comes to Miss. Terry. But you are right. What can have disturbed her? What was the cause of the noise she heard?"

I paused. "You don't think . . . I mean . . ."

"Out with it, Harry."

"Vampires, sir! All this talk of vampires, and of the mysterious face up in the gods. You don't think there's any connection between what Miss Terry heard and that disturbance in the upper gallery?"

"Two totally opposite ends of the theatre? The highest point and the lowest? No, I don't think so, Harry. And besides, I still don't subscribe to the idea of there really being a vampire in our midst."

I remained silent. I was uncertain myself and didn't want to simply write off the notion.

It was late that afternoon when I encountered Bill Thomas and happened to mention to him my exploits in the below stage area.

"Ha! That old section of the Lyceum is full of secrets, Harry, you mark my words."

"What do you mean?"

"I've heard tell of a madman trapped down

197

there, back in the late 1700s, and then someone – an actor I think it was – who committed suicide there in the early days of this century."

"Really?" I said. "I didn't know that."

He nodded his head sagely. "Oh yes. You'd be surprised, Harry. All of these theatres have got their history."

"So I'm beginning to realize," I muttered.

"Strange sounds, weird cries, screams," he went on.

"Screams?"

"Well, maybe not screams exactly. But you know? Odd noises and things that you can't put a finger on."

I thought that Bill might be getting a little carried away but went along with him. "So has anyone heard this moaning sound that Miss Terry heard?" I asked.

He shook his head. "Can't say that they have. Of course, people *think* they hear all sorts of things when they're alone, don't they? Might really be nothing there at all."

It seemed to me he was now contradicting himself. I sighed. "Thanks very much, Bill."

"No! I'm not denying Miss Terry's hearing sobbing. And don't forget that room and the passage Sam Green had to seal up back at the start of the year. Went right out to the old tavern at the back of the theatre, didn't it? Well, who knows what other long lost rooms and tunnels there might be? Could be all sorts of things down there, I wouldn't wonder."

I had my doubts. From the possibility of a

few tucked-away areas in the foundations Bill was constructing in his mind a whole underground city of intrigue. "Thanks Bill. I must get on," I said. But his imagination had been caught. He wasn't going to let me get away so easily.

"Hold on, Mr. Rivers." He eased himself up out of his seat behind the counter. It would be extremely unusual to see Bill Thomas away from his desk and his *Sporting Times*. "I wouldn't mind taking a look down there myself. Been a while since I got below stage."

"Can you do that, Bill?" I asked. "I mean, it's not that long until this evening's performance. People must be starting to drift in already."

He paused, and then lowered himself back down onto his seat. "I guess you're right, Harry." He sighed. "Some other time I suppose."

"Right, Bill. Some other time. I'll be sure to let you know whenever I might go down there again." Which will be a long time from now, I thought as I hurried on my way.

I tried to put out of my mind the whole idea of some strange, unknown creature lurking down beneath the stage, but it persisted. I have a very active imagination and many a night I am unable to sleep from unsavory thoughts and disturbing ideas acting out in my head. Some years ago I had read *The Castle of Otranto* by Mr. Horace Walpole and been unable to sleep for a fortnight. The idea of vampires, madmen, and screaming ghosts inhabiting the Lyceum did not sit well with me. I needed to focus on my stage managing duties and put all other thoughts far from me.

Chapter Twenty-One

"How did you know, Mr. Rivers?" Mario Pinasco looked up at me with wide eyes.

It was Friday morning and I had prevailed upon the theatre electrician to humor me by inspecting the generator located outside the theatre, close by the alley leading out to Exeter Street. It was enclosed by a sturdy wooden fence and at first glance seemed to be well protected. I hated to think that I was succumbing to Mr. Stoker's repeated references to his old granny's second sight, but I really had no logical explanation for knowing that the generator had been tampered with.

"Just a hunch, Mario," I said. "How bad is it?"

"Well, someone has gone to the trouble of substituting inferior fuse wires. All different ones. Some of them are probably fine but one or two would pop when they got overheated."

"Can you change them?"

"All of them?"

"Wouldn't that be the safest?"

He nodded, rubbing his chin. "I can do it easy enough. Won't take too long. I'll have to turn off the theatre's electricity for most of the morning but we'll be all right for tonight's performance."

I walked around the small area. "Look at this, Mario. Someone pried open the wooden palings here so that they could get in."

"Lucky they didn't electrocute themselves." He shook his head in amazement. "Children these days!"

"Oh, I don't think it was children," I said. "No. I think that this was carefully planned and carried out by adults. Children might pry open a wooden fence but I doubt they would then play with dangerous electric wires. Even if they pulled out the fuse wires, they wouldn't replace them with different ones."

"No, I suppose not."

"Can you think of anyone who might do such a thing, Mario?"

He thought long and hard as he knelt and set to work replacing the wires. Finally he sat back on his heels.

"There's always Clement Eastbrook to consider, I suppose."

"Eastbrook? I'd forgotten about him," I said. A north country man, he had been in the employ of the Lyceum as an odd-job man and electrician before we hired Mario Pinasco. He had been dismissed for theft. "Yes," I conceded. "He did leave with bad grace. In fact – now that I think of it – I do believe that he threatened that we'd be sorry for sacking him."

"Where did he go after the Lyceum?"

I shook my head. "I'm not certain, but I have a suspicion it might have been Sadler's Wells.

If so then this mischief might well be at the instigation of Ralph Bateman. I'll have to do a little enquiring and see what we might turn up."

I had Sam Green inspect the fence around the generator and see if he could do anything to ensure its future safety. I also sent Mario off to the new Savoy Theatre, still under construction just around the corner on the Strand, to see what they were doing to make sure their generators would not be interfered with. I then found I still had a little time so I decided to follow through on my thoughts and pay a visit to Sadler's Wells.

A hansom took me to Rosebery Avenue in Clerkenwell. The neighborhood adjoining Islington is not the best by any means, though the theatre seems to do a good job of drawing patrons not only from there but also from many better areas. Sadler's Wells Theatre has seen better days, with such names as Edmund Kean and Joseph Grimaldi having graced its boards. But after many years of bad management, just three years ago it was condemned as a dangerous structure. At that time Mrs. Bateman left the Lyceum – when the Guv'nor embraced it – and took over Sadler's Wells. She brought it back to life. When she died her daughter, Mrs. Crowe, took over.

I went in by the stage door and quickly found who I was looking for – George Dale, the doorman. He was a contrast to our Bill Thomas. George was as likely to be found snoozing as not. He had straggly grey hair that looked as though it had never seen brush nor comb. His mustache and beard were unkempt. His eyes were rheumy and he wore dirty, finger-marked pince-nez spectacles permanently clamped to the end of his bulbous nose, always looking over them rather than through them.

"Hello, George," I greeted him.

He jumped, as though I had woken him.

"What? 'oo? . . . Oh, it's you, 'Arry Rivers What're you doing 'ere?"

"Yes, and it's a pleasure to see you again too, George," I said. "I was looking for some information."

"Ain't you always?"

"Mr. Clement Eastbrook. Do you know him? Is he employed here at Sadler's?"

"Maybe 'e is and maybe 'e ain't. What's it to you, Mr. Lyceum?"

"Now don't be like that, George," I said, smiling at him. ""We have been good friends in the past. Well, perhaps 'good friends' is over-stating it. But we have certainly been acquaintances on friendly terms, wouldn't you agree?"

He gave a belch, which he hardly tried to cover, and then scratched the top of his head. "I suppose you're right, young 'Arry. Still, I'm not supposed to talk to any Lyceum people. Strict instructions from Mr. Bateman."

"Is he about? Still trying to run things for his sister?"

"Nar! 'E's gorn more often than 'e's 'ere. Right now 'e's off over in Froggy country. Gorn to Paris."

"Has he been gone long?"

"About a fortnight, I'm thinkin'"

Then Ralph Bateman couldn't have been behind the electrical failures at the Lyceum, I realized. Nor could he have been spreading the rumors about vampires up in our gods. "What about this Mr. Eastbrook, George?" I asked. "Do you have such a gentleman employed here?"

He shook his head. "Nar! I think someone of that name was by a time ago, lookin' for work. But 'e got the push on. Might 'ave gorn to any one of the other London theatres. 'Oo knows?"

He was right. Without an indication of where he might have gone, all I would be able to do was go around to each and every theatre in turn and I wasn't about to spend my time doing that. No, if Mr. Clement Eastbrook was responsible for any of our problems then I would have to wait until there was a more obvious link. I thanked George and left, glad that I hadn't had to buy him a pint of Reid's stout at the Bag o' Nails tavern.

"Harry, I wonder if I might ask a favor of you?"

Mr. Stoker asking a favor was the polite way for him to give me an order to do something. I played along, as I always did.

"Of course, sir. What is it?"

"I've been thinking about your description of dear Mr. Saxon's rooms. A Mrs. Stone was it not, the landlady?"

I nodded. "Yes. A not very cooperative person."

"Mm. Yes, I remember you saying so. Well Harry, I'm afraid I'd like you to confront that formidable lady once again."

"More questions?"

"No, Harry. In your very full and excellent description of John Saxon's room at Mrs. Stone's you mentioned a picture on the wall."

I frowned. A picture on the wall? What was he getting at? I cast my mind back. "As I recall, sir, there were only two items breaking the bleakness. One was a picture of Kew Gardens and the other some old Christmas card that had been framed."

Christmas cards were a relatively new fad, started less than forty years ago. In fact they had really only taken hold in the popular mind as recently as a decade ago when Messrs. Prang and Meyer, a lithograph company, started producing such cards for the popular market for the Christmas of 1873. I suspected that the card on the wall of John Saxon's room was there more for its novelty value than for any other reason and said as much to my boss.

"You may well be right, Harry. Indeed, that had been my first thought, which is why I haven't made mention of it before now. But since we seem to be scraping the bottom of the barrel, as it were, in looking for clues to Mr. Saxon's murderer, it suddenly came to me that the card might well have been framed for a more substantial reason than simply its novelty value."

"Sir?" I was not really following his line of reasoning.

"The card may have been framed and hung on the wall because of some sentimental value that it possessed for Mr. Saxon."

"But we don't even know that it was John Saxon who framed it," I protested.

"Agreed. As I said, we are more or less clutching at straws. But just supposing, Harry, just supposing that it *was* John Saxon who framed the card and hung it on his wall. Why would he have done so? Not for any intrinsic beauty in the card, I'm sure. You said, did you not, that it was a winter scene of a thatched cottage?"

"That's right, sir." I could now see it again in my mind's eye. Some typical folksy cottage scene with just a touch of snow to give it the Christmas link.

"If, then, it was a personal connection, then would it not follow that there was an inscription on the inside of the card? Perhaps a clue to a person especially close to John Saxon? Someone we might be able to track down and speak with?"

I well knew who would be doing the tracking.

"So you want me to go back to Mrs. Stone and talk her into letting me look at the picture on the wall?"

"Precisely, Harry. We will need to take it out of its frame, of course. Perhaps you could offer to buy it from Mrs. Stone . . . I have a feeling that coins speak louder than words to that lady."

So it was that I once again approached the rooming house on Dickson Street. I saw that the sign had gone from the window, which would seem to indicate that Mr. Saxon's old room had been let. How was I to get into it now then, I wondered? I had no time to think when the door opened and I found myself confronted by Mrs. Stone. She seemed not to remember me.

"Yes?"

"Mrs. Stone. You may remember I was here when Mr. Saxon died, to look at his room?"

"You're too late. It's taken."

She made to close the door but I had expected that and stuck my foot in its way. I winced from the force with which she had been closing the door.

"Kindly remove your foot, young man, or I shall 'ave to call a policeman. I've told you the room is taken. Try next door. Old Mrs. Turpin ain't too perticler."

"No. You don't understand, Mrs. Stone. I don't want to rent a room. I want – indeed I need – to see inside Mr. Saxon's old room again."

She released the pressure on the door and re-opened it slightly. "What ain't you gettin'? There's another gentleman what's in that room now."

I took a deep breath. "Perhaps I should start again. I have no interest in renting Mr. Saxon's old room, or any room. However, there is something that was in Mr. Saxon's room that I would like access to." I remembered Mr. Stoker's words. "Something I would like to purchase from you, if I may?" I took out a handful of loose change and jingled it. My boss was right. Her eyes almost glazed over and fastened on my hand.

"What you talkin' about? Ain't nothing of 'is still in there."

"It's a picture that is on the wall."

"Picture? Ain't no picture there."

"Yes. Yes, it's a framed Christmas card. Right next to a picture of Kew Gardens, though it's just the Christmas card I'm interested in."

"What you want that for?"

"It's . . . oh, I don't know. . . . it was just something of John's. Of Mr. Saxon's. We were good friends." I felt my face reddening as I lied so blatantly.

"You said somethin' about buyin'." Her eyes fastened on mine.

"Yes. Oh, yes indeed." I extracted a half-crown from my handful of change and held it up.

"Something so dear to you, from an old friend must be worth a lot more than an Alderman. 'Alf a tusheroon? What d'you take me for?"

I added a second half-crown.

"A 'ole tusheroon, is it? Not much of a friend then, was 'e?"

I sighed, pocketed the change, and held up a half sovereign. "This is all my late friend was worth, Mrs. Stone. Take it or leave it."

"Half a bean? Half a quid?" she mumbled, but her hand sneaked out and closed on the coin. "Wait 'ere." She disappeared inside, closing the door as she left.

I waited a long time and wondered if she would ever reappear. Perhaps she had gone, with my half sovereign, and would refuse to open the door again. But just as I was about to raise my hand once again to the door-knocker, the door opened and she stood there, the framed picture in her hand.

"This it?"

I nodded. "Yes. Yes, thank you, Mrs.

Stone."

I reached out for it but she drew back and held it close to her bosom. "That's another two shillings for the frame," she said.

"I don't need the frame." I looked her steadily in the eyes.

She looked back at me just as steadily. "My new lodger 'as taken a fancy to this 'ere picture and don't want to part with it."

"I have already paid you for it," I said.

"Not for the frame."

I sighed, pulled out a florin and gave it to her. She handed over the picture.

"I was throwin' it out anyway. 'Ad to get it out o' the dustbin," she said as she closed the door.

Chapter Twenty-Two

It was Saturday morning before I had a chance to get together with my boss and examine the Christmas card for which I had paid so dearly. He had already removed it from the frame by the time I got there.

"My hunch was right, Harry. There's some interesting information here."

I moved around to peer over his shoulder at the card he held in his hands.

"It's quite a long note," I said.

Mr. Stoker read the inscription in his best stage voice. He had really been influenced by the Guv'nor, I thought.

"*Dearest John. Would you believe that I found this picture of 'our' cottage? Such wonderful memories of our Torquay days. When will we get there again, I wonder? I am trying out for pantomime in Skegness. Perhaps you can come north? I miss you. Margaret.* And then follows the printed greetings for the season, as you can see."

"As you thought then, sir. So where does this get us?"

"It gets us quite a way, Harry. You must read beyond the lines."

"Sir?" I could feel my brow wrinkling.

Mr. Stoker closed the card and turned it over to the back. "You will see that it is one of Messrs. Prang and Meyer's creations. And along with their name and device, they give the location of the picture on the front; the cottage. It is, as you can see . . ." he turned the card back to its front ". . . a photograph that has been hand colored. Quite nicely done, in actuality."

I murmured agreement, wondering where this was leading. He again turned to the back of the card.

"The cottage is apparently in Brixham, Devon, and known as Orchard Cottage. What a love the English have developed for naming their houses."

"Orchard Cottage, Brixham," I repeated. "So what does that tell us, sir? I'm afraid I still . . ."

"It gives us a place to go to start enquiries, Harry."

"Go?" My voice quavered a little, I know. Was I to be sent off to Devon, in the far reaches of the West Country, on another of my boss's whims? Tomorrow was Sunday, I thought. My day to see Jenny. Was I to miss that desired rendezvous again? I flopped down on my usual seat in front of Mr. Stoker's desk. "What do you think can be accomplished by going there, sir? Surely it's just . . . just a cottage."

"The inscription from Margaret, whoever that young lady might be, speaks of it as 'our' cottage. We must assume, therefore, that she and our John Saxon spent some time together there. If that be the case, then surely somebody locally will recall the couple. Discreet enquiries, of which in my humble opinion you have become expert, Harry, should reveal to us at the very least who this Margaret is. We then have the added information that she was in Skegness trying out for a part in a pantomime, so she was obviously an actress."

"We don't know that she got the part," I said.

"No, Harry, we don't. And we never will if we don't pursue it."

I sighed. I was trapped and knew it.

Othello had three more weeks to play. Twenty-one days in which to find John Saxon's killer. We had two or three possible suspects but really nothing concrete on which to proceed. Inspector Bellamy seemed to have settled on poor Mr. Purdy as the culprit for no good reason other than that he could find no one else to accuse. It did seem, therefore, that it was up to Mr. Stoker and myself to solve the case.

I sat in the corner of a South Western Railway carriage as it rattled over the rails bearing me westward towards Somerset, Devon, and Cornwall; the most beautiful part of England to my mind though I was in no mood to appreciate the fact. It was an almost five hour journey so I had plenty of time to think. I settled back and, in my mind, went over all I knew of Davey Llewellyn, Lonnie Plimpton, Gilbert Andrews, Clement Eastbrook, Guy Purdy, and Bill Thomas. It didn't take long. I realized that I didn't really know a great deal about any of them.

The scenery is most unattractive getting out of London, but once past Andover it improves immensely with a number of historical sites visible: Bury Hill, Quarley Hill, Old Sarum, to name a few. Beyond Salisbury the train passes through a 450-yard long tunnel, emerging at Wilton, its church tower visible above the trees.

I had studied the map to plan some sort of itinerary for when I arrived in Brixham and to learn something of the history of the place. I didn't know exactly where Orchard Cottage was located but hoped the locals would be able to tell me when I got there. I saw that Brixham was a small fishing town close to Torquay, mentioned by "Margaret" on her Christmas card. It was at the south end of the bay from Torquay.

Brixham is hilly and built around the harbor, which is usually filled with the red-sailed fishing trawlers that have been so improved in recent years. The red of the sails is from being coated with the local red ochre, for the sails' protection. I had read that over time hundreds of ships have been wrecked on the rocks around the town. Only fifteen years ago a sudden, terrible storm had blown up, the fierce wind keeping all the sailing boats from getting back into harbor. The beacon on the breakwater had been swept away so that, in the late evening and into the night, the men couldn't determine their positions. All the wives of the fishermen built a huge bonfire of furniture and bedding on the quayside to try to guide in the boats but more than a hundred lives were lost. It was said that the wreckage of fishing boats extended for more than three miles up the coast.

I had to change trains in Exeter with a half hour wait for the local Torbay & Brixham Railway. I spent the time pacing up and down the short platform to stretch my legs before getting on to the local train when it eventually arrived. This line carried me to my final destination, the stocky little engine puffing and panting as though it could only just finish its relatively short journey. The line then terminated a few miles past Brixham, at Kingswear. I decided to stay in Brixham at the Bolton Hotel, an ancient hostelry overlooking the harbor.

"You from Lon'on then?" asked the landlord as he showed me up to my room. It was small but clean, holding little more than a bed, chest of drawers, and nightstand. It did, however, look out over the water.

"Yes," I said. "And this is my first time out to this part of the West Country."

"Ah!" he said, the word a wealth of meaning. "You lucky to find a room 'ere. By this time next month there won't be no bed available for a 'undred miles or more."

"Is that right?" I tipped him a sixpence, since he seemed to be lingering in the doorway, and he went away happy.

It took me no time at all to unpack my few things and stow my valise under the bed. There was water, albeit cold, in the pitcher on the nightstand so I poured some into the basin and rinsed my face. It felt good to get the grime of travel off and I determined to have a late lunch before setting out to explore the town.

There were refreshments available at the hotel but I walked along the quayside to a small restaurant I found on a nearby corner. There I enjoyed a large Cornish pasty, the West Country delicacy. Its ingredients include chunky cuts of beef, turnip, potato, and onion, with a light seasoning of salt and pepper, in a golden flaky pastry pocket. They are good served hot or cold. There is nothing quite to compare and I vowed to enjoy many before I returned to London. This one was served hot, with peas and diced carrots and a liberal coating of beef gravy.

I spent what remained of the afternoon exploring the harbor and admiring the fishing trawlers. Most were out at sea, in the always-murky waters of the English Channel, but a number were docked at the quayside; enough to satisfy my curiosity. The town itself was exquisite, built up on the hill so that all of the houses had a view of the water. Most were painted a gleaming white though here and there were those of red brick. The Bolton Hotel was one such, making it stand out from all the other buildings along the front.

On King Street I found the Coffin House. It was a tall building, wide at the rear but coming to a narrow breadth at the front. Flights of stone steps rose up on either side of it. Legend has it that a merchant disapproved of the young man seeking his daughter's hand in marriage. The merchant said that he would see his daughter in a coffin before he would agree to the proposed marriage. Her suitor bought this house (others say he had it built), called it the Coffin House, and told the father that his wishes could be met. The father was so impressed that he gave his consent to the marriage. A nice tale if true, I thought. I was thankful I wouldn't have to build a strange house if I should ever wish to marry Jenny.

I decided on an early dinner followed by early to bed and I would start the investigation proper in the morning. It would be Sunday, so getting down to pursuing clues would, hopefully, take my mind off missing my regular meeting with Jenny.

I awoke to an overcast Sunday morning. I was wakened by the screeching of the seagulls seemingly right outside my window. I had slept with it open and now crawled out of bed and stood up just sufficiently to close the window with a bang. I staggered back to bed, hoping for a further few minutes of sleep, if not a half hour. It was not to be.

Despite the window being closed, I was able to hear the gulls crying as they wheeled back and forth across the harbor. And then I was actually taunted by the smell of cooking bacon, which was somehow seeping up through the ancient timbers of the inn to assail my nostrils. I was on the first floor, apparently above the kitchen. Smells of breakfast created in my mind pictures of eggs, bacon, kidneys, mushrooms, and all the other delights of a full country breakfast. I could not win. Knowing it to be a losing battle, I again crawled out of bed and prepared to face the day.

"Slept well, I'm bettin'" said the bright, cheery serving maid, when I settled into a table in the hotel dining room. "Folks allus does, 'ere," she concluded with a warm smile. She set a board of still warm bread on the table, along with a mountainous serving of freshly churned butter.

"It's a bit gloomy outside," I said, not really wishing to break her happy mood.

She waved a dismissive hand. "Oh, 'tis nothin'. 'Twill be clear as a bell with the sun shinin' down by ten of the clock, you mark my words."

And so it was. I was actually out on the quayside by nine but I could see that the early morning fog was already clearing. Boats were going out with the tide and, as I looked about me, I could see the whole harbor was alive with people.

"Gives folks time to do their observance," the hotel landlord had said. "But once they're back from church then we're all alive and kicking through the afternoon. It's the season, you know? Got to go with the visitors while we can."

I had studied my Baedeker's to see what

attractions there might be but could see no mention of an Orchard Cottage. Not that I really expected it to be listed in such a major travel guide. I realized that such a cottage must be but one of many similar local beauties. I enquired at the hotel but no one there had heard of it.

"Best ask around," the serving girl had said, not too helpfully.

I did just that. I received directions to Honeysuckle Cottage, Primrose Cottage, Apple Cottage (close, that one), Crabapple Cottage, Foxglove Nook, and recommendations to stay at Brixham Bungalow, Queen Anne's Hideaway, and Yew Tree House. I politely passed on them all.

I had a pleasant lunch at a little café overlooking Tor Bay, north of town. From where I sat I could make out the pier at Paignton, the neighboring town, and determined to visit there that very afternoon.

Chapter Twenty-Three

I expected another long and frustrating search for Orchard Cottage but was pleasantly surprised to locate it almost immediately upon arrival in Paignton. I had taken a char-a-banc from Brixton and alighted at Paignton pier. There I found a newspaper kiosk and enquired of the vendor if he had heard of a cottage of such name. He scratched his head for a very long moment before, with a bright smile lighting his face, he nodded and confided: "Why yes, sir. I do believe I know such a place. On the Brixham side of town. You just take the old footpath that starts alongside the post office and within about three miles you'll come to a crossroads. Turn onto the left hand path and you'll come to the cottage directly. You can't miss it."

I thanked him and followed his pointing finger to the post office. Sure enough, there was a footpath that swung off around behind the building and then ambled away from the line of cottages, in a southerly direction.

The day was rapidly warming, with the sun shining, and I strode along feeling happy and content. I was missing seeing my Jenny, of course, but if I had to be off on one of Mr. Stoker's wild errands, then this was a beautiful part of the country to which he had sent me. At the crossroads I turned onto the left hand road and continued. I caught a glimpse of a red fox disappearing into a hedgerow, listened for a while entranced to the beautiful singing of a song thrush, and breathed in the good country air. I won't say that I missed the fog that floated so persistently off the river Thames – "missed" would be the wrong word – but I was very much aware and appreciative of the clarity of the atmosphere in Devon. It would not be easy to return to the city and all its smoke.

About a mile from the crossroads I espied a building set off to the right of the road. As I approached, I saw that it was a thatched cottage. Not just any thatched cottage but the very one that Mr. Stoker and I had admired on the front of the Christmas card in John Saxon's old room. I hastened my step and was soon looking over the low picket fence and privet hedge. There was no sign of an orchard, belying the cottage name, but the setting was idyllic. Honeysuckle framed the doorway and a variety of flowers lined the pathway leading there from the front gate. I hesitated briefly then raised the latch and swung open the gate. I had hardly entered the front garden when the door to the cottage opened and I faced a giant bearded figure, who had to stoop as he stepped out from the interior of the cottage.

"Beautiful morning," he said to me, as though it was natural for him to exit his home and find a stranger on his front garden path.

"Indeed it is, sir," I replied. "Might I assume

that this is Orchard Cottage?"

"You might." He nodded. "And you would be right, for Orchard Cottage it is. Not that I am the owner, much as I enjoy the place. I have rented it for part of the summer season. My wife and I, that is to say."

I explained my arrival. "I am wanting to verify the names of the people who were here at the cottage a few years back," I said. "One of them was a Mr. John Saxon. He was accompanied by a young lady – I presume his wife at that time – whose first name was Margaret."

"How many years back are we talking?" asked the giant. "I have been familiar with this part of the country for a long time; long before my wife and I started renting Orchard Cottage." He extended his hand. "The name's Raber. Michael Raber."

I shook it; a firm, hard-working hand. I introduced myself.

"From London, are you? Now there's a place I have yet to visit."

"Trust me," I said. "You are far better off here in Devon." I looked about me. "The beauty that abounds here can never be matched in the city."

We strolled together around the cottage garden, admiring the myriad of flowers and herbs. Michael Raber had what seemed a limitless knowledge of the vegetation, reciting not only names but qualities, aromatic and healing properties.

"You must be a botanist, Michael," I said.

He laughed. "If so, then it is as a poor amateur. No, Harry, I have a great interest in, and appreciation for, all of nature. Living here it seems a natural inclination. By trade, I'm a blacksmith. I have a small forge over in South Brent, on the edge of Dartmoor. The moor has its own beauty, I won't deny it, but I have to have a breath of sea air every summer so we escape here."

I nodded. I could understand that. Now that I had been initiated into the heart of the West Country, I felt that an annual visit for myself would not go amiss.

"So who actually owns the cottage, Michael?" I asked. "Do you think he would have records of who has rented here in the past?"

"Oh, I am sure of it!" He smiled. "Miss Witherspoon is the owner. An elderly spinster. She is the village postmistress and keeps meticulous records of just about everything that goes on in Paignton." He chuckled. "She works behind the post office counter but somehow she finds time to peer out of the window in all directions, at all hours of the day and night."

I also smiled. I knew many people like that in the theatre world. And not all of them were elderly spinsters.

"Would that be the post office alongside which the footpath leading here branches off?"

"Aye. That's the one. You'll have seen it then. That's the Paignton station and Miss Witherspoon is the station mistress."

After a few more minutes with Michael Raber I thanked him and bade him farewell, returning my steps from whence I came. I passed the crossroads, continued to the village, and emerged alongside the post office. I peered in at the front window and jumped back when I found a face on the other side with an eye looking into mine. A sudden introduction to Miss Witherspoon, I thought. With reddened face, I proceeded to the front door and entered.

"You'll be the young man as went past here not an hour ago."

The lady, now behind the counter, made the statement without looking up, busying herself with weighing a brown paper-wrapped parcel tied up with string. She was shorter than I was, had her silver-gray hair pulled back in a severe bun, and wore wire-rimmed pince-nez spectacles clamped to her nose, a black silk ribbon attached to them falling to her deep blue dress and pinned to her bosom.

"Er, yes. Yes, ma'am. The name is Harry Rivers." I briefly raised my straw boater – the favored headgear for young men visiting the seaside.

"You're not staying in Paignton." Again it was a statement not a question.

"No, ma'am. No, I'm over in Brixham." How did she know I was a visitor, I wondered, though I imagined it was a pretty safe bet at this time of the year?

She nodded and entered the weight of the package in a ledger beside her.

"I understand that you are the owner of Orchard Cottage," I continued, in as friendly a voice as I could muster. I smiled at her.

She didn't look up but moved on to the weighing of a second package that lay on the counter. She again nodded. "We're all booked up for the summer, young man."

"Rivers. Harry Rivers." I repeated the information. "No. I'm not looking to rent the cottage." I smiled till it hurt. "I am looking for some information regarding someone who did rent it, but a few years ago."

She did pause at this, looking up at me and, for the first time, looking me full in the face. "And why should I share such information with you, Mr. Rivers? Are you some sort of private enquirer, I wonder? What is it they call them? Investigator, is it?"

"No, no." I tried to keep smiling. "Not at all. It is . . . well, a good friend of mine stayed at your beautiful cottage some years ago. He was with a young lady. I am not entirely certain whether or not she was his wife at that time, but I would like to ascertain her name. All I have is her first name. Margaret."

The first hint of a smile touched her lips but did not linger. "My own name," she murmured.

"The gentleman was Mr. John Saxon."

She frowned as she cast back her mind. "No. No, I don't recall a Saxon."

"Do you keep records, Miss Witherspoon?" I asked.

"Why of course I do, young man. What sort of a person would I be if I did not keep records?"

I took it to be a rhetorical question.

She moved along to an ancient wooden filing cabinet on the back wall of the office. She slid out one of the drawers and carried it over to the counter.

"What was the date you said, Mr. Rivers?"

"I didn't," I responded. "I am not completely certain of the date but I believe it was somewhere near 1858 or 1859."

She carefully turned back cards covered with tiny, neat writing. I strained to see what was written on them but was unable to. She turned through more and more of them.

"Do you enter them by name or by date, I wonder?" I said, mindful of similar records I had made to Mr. Stoker's prescription over the past few years.

She looked up at me briefly, said nothing, and returned to her search. Suddenly she paused, a gnarled finger holding the place.

"Mr. John Saxon, did you say?"

"Yes, ma'am." My heart beat in my breast.

"Early June of 1858 and then a return visit the following year, at the same time. I remember them now. A charming couple."

"They were married?" I asked.

"Of course they were married," she snapped. "I do not let my cottage for wild liaisons, I will have you know!"

I lowered my gaze. "They were, then, Mr. and Mrs. John Saxon? No record, I suppose, of the lady's maiden name?"

"Why on earth would they share that?" asked Miss Witherspoon.

"I – I was just . . . hoping," I said. "It's the young lady I am trying to trace. She is no longer married to Mr. Saxon and I'm hoping that if she reverted to her maiden name then it might make tracing her easier." It all poured out as I tried to relieve some of the frustration that had been building with us since John's death. "She was an actress, you see. They both were. Actors, that is. If I can discover her maiden name then that is probably the name which she uses on the stage."

Miss Witherspoon withdrew her finger and returned the file drawer to its home. When she came back to the counter I felt that her face had softened a little.

"Yes. I recall now that they spoke of the stage. I had not met with thespians before and was pleasantly surprised, after tales my father had told me. They seemed a very nice couple, as I have said. But I'm sorry, they did not speak of stage names or the like."

"It was straw-grasping, I know," I said. I had an idea. "Did they by any chance spend any time with anyone else while they were here? Strike up a friendship with another couple, of anything like that, do you know?"

She thought for a moment. "I believe they had a nodding acquaintance with one or two couples, most of them holidaying like themselves. I doubt you could find any of them after all these years." She thought a moment longer. "I suppose you might ask at the Old Anchor Tearoom. They stopped there most afternoons."

I didn't ask how she knew where they stopped. "Thank you, Miss Witherspoon. Thank you. Where is the Old Anchor Tearoom?"

"Oh, it's closed up now, now that I think

about it. After George Fordson died – he had a heart attack, you know – his widow didn't have the heart to carry on. But you can probably find Doris, his widow, at the pier teashop. She went from being a proprietor to being a regular customer, you know?"

I wasn't sorry to leave Miss Witherspoon and her post office. She had certainly been informative, but it had taken some chipping away to get down to the kernel of worthwhile information. I directed my steps back to the pier, where my acquaintance with Paignton had first begun. A visit to a teashop sounded like the perfect thing for this time of day.

Chapter Twenty-Four

The Paignton pier is 780 feet in length and boasts a fine grand pavilion at the seaward end. It had been officially opened in June of 1879, just two years ago, and is already a major attraction for visitors to Devon. In July of last year Mr. D'Oyley Carte's full company presented a production of Mr. Gilbert's and Mr. Sullivan's *HMS Pinafore* in the pavilion, to great success.

There is a teashop as part of the pavilion and it was to this that I made my way. I took a seat at a table looking out on the south side, affording a fine view along the coastline to Brixham. A young waitress took my order and when she returned with it I asked her: "Do you, by any chance, know a Mrs. Doris Fordson? I'm given to understand that she is a regular customer here."

"Mrs. F?" Her rosy cheeks allowed a broad smile, revealing bright white teeth. "Why yes, sir. Everyone knows Mrs. F. Mrs. Fordson, that is, sir. But we all call her Mrs. F." She giggled. "She's a one, I can tell you. Ever so nice. Bit scatterbrained, I think you'd call it. But then, at her age . . ."

"Yes. Thank you," I said, breaking into the flow. "Is she here now, by any chance?" I looked all around at the many customers then, hopefully, back to my waitress.

"Oh, she won't be in till three o'clock, sir. She likes to take a little stroll along the front after her nap. She takes an early lunch and then a short nap . . ."

"Yes. Thank you," I again broke in. "Perhaps you would be so kind as to point her out to me when she gets here?" I pulled out my old silver half-hunter and studied it. There was still almost an hour to go before three of the clock. "I might take a stroll myself before then, but I will be here at three."

I had my brief repast and then did take a turn along the pier, taking in the amusements and arcades set up to entertain the tourists. I even left the pier for a short while and stood at the edge of the waves gently lapping the sand, thinking of my Jenny. I vowed I would never again allow two weeks in a row to pass without seeing her, no matter the urgency of any business presented by Mr. Stoker.

It was still five minutes of three when I returned to the same table at the pier teashop. The waitress lost no time in coming to me.

"Mrs. F. is here, sir. Just came in, she did. That's her, sitting over by the potted palms in front of the piano player. She's wearing a big, white hat."

I saw the lady she indicated. A somewhat frail-looking lady with bright sparkling eyes. She had just been served a pot of tea and was in the process of pouring herself a cup before peering about her. I left my table and crossed to stand in front of her. She looked up, smiling. The bright eyes were a watery grey but constantly moving.

"Do I know you, young man?" she asked.

"No, ma'am, though I do know you. Or rather, I know of you. Mrs. Doris Fordson, I believe?"

She nodded enthusiastically. "And may I have the pleasure of knowing who is addressing me?"

"Mr. Harry Rivers, ma'am. I am stage manager at the Lyceum Theatre, in London. The theatre's business manager, Mr. Bram Stoker, asked me to seek you out."

"Did he indeed? Oh, please sit down, Mr. Rivers. You'll give me a crick in my neck if I have to keep looking up at you!"

I apologized and took a seat opposite her. "To be more accurate," I continued. "Mr. Stoker send me here to Devon on a quest, but I recently heard of you and am hoping that you might be able to bring that quest to fruition."

"Would you care for a cup of tea, Mr. Rivers? I can ask Janet, the waitress, to bring us some cakes if you would like. I love their Swiss roll, here." She leaned forward and confided: "They have a chocolate flavored one."

I smiled back at her. "No. Nothing, thank you. Mrs. Fordson . . ."

"Call me Mrs. F. Everybody does."

"Mrs. F. I wonder if you recall back a few years . . .1858 and 1859. There was a young couple . . ."

"Ah! My George was alive then. We had the

Old Anchor Tearoom, you know?"

"Yes, so I've heard," I said. "I spoke with Miss Witherspoon . . ."

"Margaret? Oh, it's been too long since I talked with her. Thank you for reminding me, young man. What did you say your name was?"

"Rivers, ma'am. Harry Rivers."

"Oh, yes. At some theatre in London, you said. The Stoker? Or was it The Lyceum?"

I decided not to worry too much about getting all the details right for the lady. I needed to find out about John Saxon and his wife.

"I believe that at that time you became friendly with a young couple who were renting Miss Witherspoon's cottage."

"Orchard Cottage." She smiled and nodded her head as she recalled it. "So pretty, George always said that we would have done better to have owned a cottage rather than a tearoom."

"Do you recall a young couple . . . Mr. and Mrs. John Saxon?" I asked. "They were here in 1858 and again in 1859. It's a long time ago I know, but Miss Witherspoon seemed to think that you came to know them quite well when they were here."

"Saxon?" Her brow furrowed as she thought back over the years. "Saxon. They weren't the couple from Wigan, were they? Couldn't stand them. So full of themselves."

I shook my head. "No. John and Margaret Saxon from London. Miss Witherspoon said that they spent a lot of time at your Old Anchor Tearoom . . ."

"Ah yes. You are right. John and his wife Margaret. She was quite a bit older than him, you know. But a lovely couple. In the theatre, I think they were. You should know them. You are in the theatre, didn't you say?"

"You do remember them, then?"

"Why of course I do! I may be an old lady now but my memory is as sharp as it ever was! What did you say your name was?"

"Rivers, Mrs. F. Now, in talking with the Saxons, I don't suppose that at any time the wife, Margaret, made mention of her maiden name, did she?"

Under the table I crossed my fingers as I held my breath and waited for her reply.

"Why on earth would she do that?"

I let out my breath but kept my fingers crossed. "It's not uncommon for a young lady of the theatre, on marrying, to retain her maiden name as her stage name. The name she uses as an actress," I explained.

"Ah! Well of course. That makes sense, does it not?"

"So did she mention it?" I pressured.

"Yes, she did mention her stage name, now that you mention it, young man. Or rather, as I recall, it was the husband who said it. He said something about them hoping to appear together in a play by Mr. Shakespeare. Now what was that?" Her brow wrinkled again as she poured herself another cup of tea. She selected a small sandwich from the plate the waitress had deposited, and then sat back and gazed about her. I decided not to press her but let her take her own time. I just hoped that she had not forgotten what I had asked. Eventually she nodded her head and looked me in the eye.

"Ah, yes!"

I uncrossed my fingers and leaned forward.

"*Romeo and Juliet*. That was the play!" she cried triumphantly.

It had been a long day and I was glad to finally return to my room at the Bolton Hotel. After much verbal sparring back and forth, I had finally pinned down Mrs. F. and learned that the name I was seeking was Margaret Green . . . or possibly Brown. "It was a color, I remember," she had said.

I think Mr. Stoker had been right to pursue this avenue. Knowing the name, and that she had been hoping to appear in pantomime in Skegness, I should be able to trace her to a particular theatre – I think there are but one or two in that seaside resort – and then follow a trail that might ultimately lead to her present-day whereabouts. Who knows what worthwhile information that might then bring? We had few enough leads so this was definitely worth following. I would be very grateful to return to London, even though it meant leaving the balmy, sunny West Country.

On my return I found the Lyceum in a state of near turmoil. I had arrived at Waterloo railway station close to noon and had taken a quick lunch in the station restaurant before getting a hansom to the theatre. As I came through the stage door I was greeted by an excited Bill Thomas.

"A fine time of day to be coming in, Harry, if I may make so bold."

"I'm just back from a trip for Mr. Stoker, Bill," I said, feeling that I really owed no explanation to the stage doorkeeper for my comings and goings. "What's the matter? Can the Lyceum not function for five minutes without my presence?"

"You'd better see Mr. Bidwell. He's been asking for you a dozen times in the past hour."

"Is Mr. Stoker not here?" I asked.

"Him and the Guv'nor stepped out early this morning. Don't expect 'em back till mid-afternoon."

"Any idea what concerns Mr. Bidwell?"

He shrugged. "Something about vampires, Harry. I don't know. It's beyond me."

I hurried off to the front of house. I had almost forgotten about the supposed "vampire problem" in my sojourn to Devon. Now I was back to the harsh reality of London, it seemed.

"It's my staff, Mr. Rivers," said Timothy Bidwell, when I located him at the back of the stalls. "Two of my young ladies claim to have been frightened by a vampire that almost attacked them early this morning. They had gone up to the gods and say they nearly bumped into him outside the OP box. They say they nearly tumbled down the stairs getting away from him."

There were one or two questions that immediately popped into my mind.

"Where are these ladies?" I asked. "I would like to hear from them directly."

"Of course, Mr. Rivers. Come with me. They are both resting in my office. I thought you'd want to see them."

The two young ladies concerned seemed to be recovering well in Mr. Bidwell's office. They had been given cups of hot tea and were resting comfortably on a small couch there. They rose as I entered the room.

"Please sit, ladies," I said, remaining standing myself. "Now then, what is all this about a vampire?"

They both started to speak at the same time. I held up my hand.

"One at a time, please. One at a time. You first, if you'd be so good. And let me know your name." I pointed to the darker-haired one of the two.

"Yes, Mr. Rivers. I'm Rosemary Best. This 'ere's Dora Spinks. We both been with the Lyceum front-of-house for two years now." She glanced at her companion, as though for reassurance. The other girl nodded and Miss Moss continued. "Me and Dora, 'ere, was up in the gods . . ."

"And why were you up there?" I asked.

"Oh, Mr. Bidwell asked us to make sure it was all clean up there, for the Monday night performance. 'E's very fussy . . . I should say, 'e's very particular about there being no sweet wrappers or orange peel or anything lying under the seats. 'Specially at the start of the week."

I nodded. "Yes. I see. Go on."

"Well, we was just getting started – we go down the center aisle and then, from there, along the rows. Me on the left side and Dora on the right."

"Though sometimes we do it the other way 'round," put in the blonde-haired Dora.

"Yes. But anyway, that's 'ow we started," continued Rosemary. "We'd only done about three rows . . ."

"Less than that," cried Dora. "I think it was only two."

"Never mind. Go on," I said. "You had barely got started?"

"Right." Rosemary nodded. "When suddenly there was this noise of someone coming and me and Dora looked up thinking as it was Mr. Bidwell come to check on us."

"He does that sometimes," Dora contributed.

"But it weren't Mr. Bidwell!" cried Rosemary. "It was this vampire!" Her hand went to her heart and her eyes were wide. Dora – equally wide-eyed – nodded vigorously.

"Now just a moment," I said. "You say 'a vampire.' What do you mean by that? How do you know it was a vampire?"

"Oh, we knew." They both again nodded. ""Is 'air were all white and so was 'is face, and . . ."

"And 'e 'ad these red eyes," said Dora.

"My 'eart missed a beat, I can tell you, Mr. Rivers."

"We thought we was gonners!" added Dora.

"So what did you do? What did this – vampire-like figure do?"

"'E 'ad come from over by the box and when 'e saw us 'e stopped dead in 'is tracks."

"Eyeing us, 'e was!"

"Right! So me and Dora – being so close still to the top row of the seats – we ran up there and then away from 'im, out the end door and down the stairs."

"I nearly fell down 'em," said Dora. "We couldn't get down fast enough."

"We went straight to Mr. Bidwell."

"What time was this?" I asked.

"Oh, about nine of the clock," said Rosemary. "We start at half after eight but then, once we've been given our duties, there's the long climb up to the gods."

"We was out of breath when we got there."

"Yes. Takes a minute to get your breath back."

"And you say that the figure came from the far end, over by the OP box?" I asked.

Rosemary nodded. "S'right."

"Have you been back to look since then?" I asked.

They both vigorously shook their heads. "Cor, no!"

"Not likely."

"Has Mr. Bidwell been up there?"

They looked at each other and then shrugged. "You'll 'ave to ask 'im, Mr. Rivers."

"My guess is no," said Dora.

"Hmm. Very well. Thank you, ladies. I think you may now return to your duties . . . away from the gods, of course."

I thought it likely that the ladies were right and that Mr. Timothy Bidwell had not himself gone up to check on things. With a sigh, I started up the stone steps myself. It was a long climb but obviously the two ladies had dawdled along the way if it had taken them nearly half an hour to make it to the top.

I came out at the end of the walkway across the back of the gods, connecting the entrances to the two boxes. I made straight across to the far, OP, box. I hesitated outside its door. I reminded myself that I did not believe in vampires . . . or I didn't think I did. On the other hand, there had been no previous occasion to test such belief. I'm sure Mr. Stoker would have seen this as a wonderful opportunity, but I was not quite of my boss's metal. Still, I did have a job to do. I reached out and grasped the door handle.

The inside of the box looked almost exactly as it had done the last time I had been there. With one exception. One of the chairs that had previously been standing alongside the others, lined across the side of the box, now lay in the middle of the floor space on its back. Had the two ladies knocked it over in their rush to get out? But no! They had not been in the box, according to what they said. They had restricted their work to the space between the two boxes; the seating of the upper gallery itself. How, then, could the chair have got knocked over? Perhaps others of the cleaning crew? But they would never have left it like that, surely? I decided it was time to find Mr. Stoker.

Chapter Twenty-Five

"The information you obtained in Devon is excellent, Harry," said Mr. Stoker. "Margaret Green, or possibly Brown. That is a good start. We will have to pursue that. I think you may be able to trace her using the various publications and theatrical agencies. There's obviously no point in having you travel up to Skegness to enquire there after all these years."

I breathed a sigh of relief. I did not want to miss another weekend with Jenny. And my boss was right. If I did travel up north it might well be to discover that our Miss Green had long since come back to the London area.

"I know it's a slim chance, sir," I said. "But if we can find her then we might well learn much about John Saxon's private life, and learn of others who might just possibly be involved in his death."

Stoker's big head nodded up and down. "Quite right, Harry. But in the line of criminal detection slim chances are often the only chances one has. I seem to remember Inspector Bellamy saying something to that effect at some time."

"Did he?" I was surprised to hear of something making so much sense having come from the police inspector.

"Now then. What is all this I hear about a vampire up in our gods?"

I told him what I had learned from the two young ladies. "I did make a point of going up to the gods myself, sir, to have a look around." I told him of the displaced chair in the box.

"You're right, Harry. The cleaning crew would never have left a chair upended like that. No."

He pursed his lips and narrowed his eyes, as he often did when considering a problem. I waited.

"Harry, it would seem that the only logical explanation is that this – character – is somehow located in the box area. Yet as we have both seen, there is nothing there . . . nothing but an empty room. Harry, I think that 'empty room' calls for closer scrutiny." He got to his feet. "Come! Let us put it to the test."

I once again made the long climb up to the roof of the Lyceum, following in my boss's footsteps. He led the way around to the OP box and threw open the door. It was as I had last seen it, except that the upturned chair was now right way up, in line with the others across the wall of the box. Mr. Stoker looked at me, saying nothing but with his eyebrows raised questioningly.

I also said nothing but merely shook my head slowly as I surveyed the scene. My boss advanced on the line of chairs and then, to my surprise, dropped to his knees.

"What . . . ?" I started to say.

"Ssh, Harry!" He leaned forward and peered

between the legs of the chairs, looking down at where the wall met the carpet. He pointed to that join.

"What do you see, Harry?"

I saw nothing out of the ordinary, but that was not what I needed to say. Happily Mr. Stoker continued without waiting for my reply.

"Would you not expect the carpet to be curtailed where it meets with the wall?" he asked.

I realized he was right. Normally carpet is laid up to the wall and then is cut off and fastened down. Peering now at the join I could see that in fact this floor covering seemed to continue on under the bottom of the wall! How could that be, I wondered?

"Get Sam Green up here, Harry."

"Yes, sir." I got to my feet. "Do you think . . . ?"

"Yes. I think that someone has constructed a false wall here. We can easily verify that by measuring the distance between the walls in both this box and the box on the far side of the proscenium. They should both be the same. I think we'll find that in fact the distance across in this box is considerably less than in its sister box. Something not easily noticed on casual observation. Get Sam up here, Harry, and tell him to bring some tools with him." As I started for the door, Mr. Stoker began pacing across the box. "While you are gone I will measure the width between the walls here and compare it to the other one," he said.

I hurried away.

Sam Green arrived and set to work taking

down the wall. It was, as Mr. Stoker had surmised, a thin false wall that had been set up to create a narrow hidden room. There was, in fact, so little space between its walls that I did not envy whoever had been living there. "Existing" might have been a more accurate term. There was a thin, narrow mattress in the space. Discarded wrappers from pork pies together with orange peel, a withered apple core, and an empty lemonade bottle drew my mind back to Mr. Herbert Gardner's complaints of thefts from the theatre commissariat. The breaking-in to his larder was now explained. Whoever had been living here had drawn from Mr. Gardner's stock for sustenance. The question was, where were they now obtaining their food, since we had secured the lock on the pantry door?

"So this would appear to be our vampire," I said. "Not any supernatural creature but one of flesh and blood who needs food and rest."

"Yet who is this creature and from whence came he?" posed Stoker. "I would warrant he has not been a part of the Lyceum for many moons. Certainly not the years that have graced Drury Lane with its Man in Grey. So how and why did he appear and – perhaps more importantly – who constructed this false wall?"

"The choice would seem to have been a good one, sir," I said. "This box, of all of them, is certainly the least used and therefore the least likely to be discovered."

"To answer my own question," continued my boss. "The wall must have been planned and constructed by one of our own. Someone who is a part of the Lyceum family yet someone who has reason to be secretive."

"Probably put up late at night, when we all thought – and I'm sure Bill Thomas thought – that the theatre was empty."

"This all extremely disquieting," said my boss.

"'Ere's the way in and out, sir, beggin' your pardon," said Sam, who was still working on dismantling the false wall. "'Ere, up at the end. Very nicely done, if I may say so. A loose flap what can be swung back just enough for someone to slide in or out of the space."

"If the intruder was here when the two front-of-house ladies were up here," I mused, "he probably went back into his hiding place when they saw him. How is it, then, that he's not here now? With the theatre now busy with workers, surely others would have seen him moving about?"

"I think he may well have been here when we first arrived, Harry," said Stoker. "And it is partly my fault that he got away. I was so intent on comparing the widths of the two boxes that he almost certainly was able to slip away while I was on the far side, pacing across in the opposite box."

"But he would still be spotted when he moved out, wouldn't he?" I persisted.

"If he ducked down the stairs quickly enough, he could then have turned off at the next level down, the Upper Circle, and avoided meeting you on your and Sam's return."

"And what then? Is he still just below us?"

"This, I think," said my boss, "is where the

collaborator comes into it. The man who constructed the false wall. Our lodger, if I may call him that, must have somehow made fast contact with that person and been spirited away to another hiding place."

"There's plenty of 'em," put in Sam. "The 'ole theatre's a rabbit warren down below stage. Several levels. I ain't even been in 'em all meself."

"Unfortunately you are correct, Sam," said my boss. "It may have taken a little while to slip down there, past the odd crew member, but yes, if he did make it to below stage then he could well now be safely ensconced somewhere there."

"Not as dry and cozy as his top-floor-flat up here, I think," I said.

"One thing which troubles me," said Stoker, "is the vampire aspect. This person is almost certainly our suspected vampire but, if so, why or how the pale face and red eyes? This troubles me. I do not know that I actually believe in vampires themselves, I have to say. Yet what other explanation can there be? Theatrical make-up, perhaps? But why?"

"What about the food and drink, sir?" I asked.

He waved a dismissive hand. "I could see that a true vampire – if such should really exist – might need rather more nourishment than simple occasional sucking of blood. That act, I think, belongs strictly to folklore. The blood might be essential yet not be the total sustenance needed. Hmm! But I wonder if I should not do a spiritual cleansing of the whole theatre, just to be on the safe side?"

"A spiritual cleansing, sir?" I had encountered Mr. Stoker's metaphysical bent on previous occasions. Somehow I knew that whatever he had in mind would involve myself in one capacity or another. I really didn't have time for such excursions. "If you don't really believe in them, sir," I said, hopefully, "then why bother with anything like that?"

"Did not Alexander Pope, the poet, say 'How prone to doubt, how cautious are the wise!'? I think we might err on the side of caution, Harry."

"Beggin' your pardon, Mr. Stoker sir," said Sam, "but 'ave you done with me? I've got a load of work waiting down the apples and pears, and I'm done with takin' down this bit o' wall."

"Yes. Yes, thank you, Sam. We'll close off this box for a while so you can come back later and remove what you've taken down. And I'd like you to get rid of this bedding also."

Sam gathered up his tools and left Mr. Stoker and myself contemplating the now open hiding hole.

"Quite ingenious, actually."

"Yes, sir."

"Well, alert everyone – cast and backstage crew – to be on their toes and to keep an eye open and an ear aware of any unusual sights or sounds. If nothing else we may have removed the 'scourge of the gods' and get our audience back. Now come. We have work to do."

It was an unsettling start to the week.

My boss's idea of spiritually cleansing the theatre consisted of burning incense and hanging pieces of garlic in strategic places. It was necessary to send out someone to purchase the garlic and incense before we could get started. Finding purveyors of either was not easy and the stagehand delegated to shop for them returned empty-handed.

"Surely it should not be so difficult," said Stoker. "A good greengrocer must carry garlic and any of the churches scattered about us must surely have some stock of incense."

"There has been much debate recently about the use of incense, sir," I suggested.

"What some have termed, the 'bells and smells' of the Catholics encroaching on the ritualism of the Church of England. Yes, I know, Harry. The recent Public Worship Regulation Act and all that. Yes, but there are many churches that still hold to ritualism. Find someone who knows what they are doing or, if necessary, go out yourself, Harry. I do believe this is something we need to get done . . . just in case, if you like. It will certainly do no harm to the theatre, and should there in fact be such a creature lurking in our depths then we must exorcize him. And I think we do need to concentrate our efforts below stage."

It took until within an hour of that evening's curtain call to do all that Mr. Stoker requested. He and I descended to the catacombs below stage level and there we burned our incense and hung our garlic. I was glad that my boss contented himself with "sealing", as he termed it, the nearest ends of the several mysterious passages without insisting on actually traversing them and probing their far ends. It was with a sigh of relief that I was finally dismissed to seek a quick dinner before the evening performance. I heard later that the Guv'nor had come upon the sprig of garlic hanging in his dressing room and cast it into the dustbin.

Chapter Twenty-Six

Tuesday morning I spent checking the agencies and the publications for mention of a Margaret Green. I drew a blank. I knew it would be a long shot, and exactly where connection with her would have led I wasn't sure, but with that trail petering out I could now concentrate on other business. When I got back to the theatre, I was greeted by Mario Pinasco.

"I've found Clement Eastbrook, Harry. Or rather, I've found out where he's currently employed. I haven't actually been there or seen him."

"Well done, Mario. Where is he?"

"Collins's Music Hall, Islington Green."

"Collins's?" I wasn't sure I had ever heard of it.

"It's a music hall, Harry. A tanner up to three bob. Twice nightly at 6:30 and 9:00 pm. I hear it's not too bad; not as bad as some of them."

I knew what Mario meant. Music halls varied greatly. Unlike the so-called legitimate theatre, which presents plays, the music halls offer a wide variety of entertainment such as pantomimes, musical presentations, individual acts, even circuses. I like to think that the Lyceum productions are not only entertaining but also educational, where the music halls offer pure diversion - one might almost say distraction – from everyday life.

We needed to face Mr. Eastbrook about the malicious damaging of our electrical generator. If he had not been responsible, then we should continue that investigation to find out who was. I resigned myself to traveling out to Islington Green. It was not, as so many similarly named areas around the capital, the remnants of an old village green but a surviving patch of common land carved out of old manorial wasteland, where local farmers and tenants had free grazing rights. Today, within a mile and a half of it, over a thousand public houses and beer shops have grown up. The Collins's Music Hall was originally a public house itself, named the Lansdowne Arms. The theatre probably did very well in that location.

I had an early lunch and took a hansom to the theatre. When I arrived I found there was nobody at the stage door to check on cast, crew and visitors, so I walked in unannounced and made my way to the backstage area. There I was finally apprehended by a short, plump, large-bosomed lady of indeterminate years, who demanded that I state my name and business.

"I am Mr. Harry Rivers and I wish to speak with Mr. Clement Eastbrook. I understand that he is employed here."

The lady had straw-colored hair piled high on her head in an elegant yet artificial style that made me suspect that it was a wig. She probably wore it to give herself greater height and a sense of importance. She now studied me through narrowed eyes, a frown on her face.

"Mr. Eastbrook is contracted to Collins's Music 'all so if you was lookin' to steal 'im away you can just forget it." Her mouth set in a firm line.

"Madam, I have no intention of trying to take him anywhere," I said. "I merely have one or two questions that I am hoping he can answer. Questions relating to the time he spent in the employ of the Lyceum Theatre."

She sniffed. "Lyceum? That's legit, ain't it?"

I didn't want to be drawn into conversation with her so I simply said, "Is Mr. Eastbrook available?"

She continued with her hard stare for several moments before pointing a long-nailed finger off to her right. "You'll find 'im at the 'lectric box in the back corner. Don't go keepin' 'im from 'is work. Time is money, you know."

I found my way across the unlit stage and into the wings on the far side. Off to the side I saw a lantern hanging, giving light to a man working on a metal box attached to the wall.

"Clement Eastbrook?" I asked.

The man looked up. "Who wants to know?"

"I don't know if you remember me," I said. "We didn't have much contact with one another when you were there, but I am the stage manager at the Lyceum."

"Lyceum!" He snorted in disgust and spat into the dark corner on his far side. "Don't go mentioning that name to me."

"I believe you left there in bad grace," I said.

"Bad grace, is it? Ha! You threw me out for no good reason."

"To my understanding you were found guilty of appropriating various tools and other items that did not belong to you," I said. I had no wish to get into an argument concerning Mr. Stoker's reasons for dismissing him, but I did want to find out if it was he who had damaged our generator. "I have heard it said that you vowed to 'make the Lyceum pay' for your loss of the job."

"And what if I did? What's that to you?"

"Have you in fact acted out on that threat, Mr. Eastbrook?"

He grinned, for the first time a smile on his face. "Maybe I did and maybe I didn't. That's for me to know and for you to find out."

"Have you been interfering with the Lyceum generator?"

The smile left his face as quickly as it had come. He glowered at me. "When I was there I was the theatre electrician. Changing fuse wires was my job."

"Did I say that fuse wires had been changed?" I challenged.

He sniffed and returned his attention to the electrical box he was working on. I waited. He said nothing more, but I felt that I had got my answer.

"I must warn you, Mr. Eastbrook, that should it be found that you have been trespassing on the theatre property we will have no hesitation in contacting the Metropolitan police and directing them to you here at this music hall."

He maintained his silence and after a brief wait I turned and left him there. I felt that I had more or less confirmed that he had been responsible for our electrical problems and had given him sufficient warning that we knew it was him and would act appropriately should he try that sort of thing again.

I returned to the Lyceum and brought Mr. Stoker up to date on Clement Eastbrook and the interference with the theatre's electricity supply. As I sat there, Bill Thomas came in with one of his atrociously strong cups of tea for my boss. How Mr. Stoker managed to drink them I don't know but he seemed completely unfazed by their intensity.

"Oh, by the way, Bill," he said after sipping the drink. "I've been meaning to ask you . . . about your whereabouts at the time of John Saxon's unfortunate demise?"

"My – my whereabouts, sir?"

I had thought Stoker had forgotten to question Bill. I know we had talked about it some time ago – the fact that Bill would, or should, know who was the last to leave the theatre of an evening – but Mr. Stoker hadn't mentioned it again so I thought he had dismissed the idea. I was glad to see that he hadn't.

"Yes, Bill. You are the one who locks up the theatre at night, are you not?" Bill nodded. "And I understand that you always make certain that the place is completely empty before doing so?"

"It's something of a pride with me, Mr. Stoker. Yes, I have a quick walk through before locking up."

"Backstage and front of house?"

"I do sometimes rely on Mr. Bidwell to give me the nod on his way out, that the f.o.h. is all tight and secure. But yes, sir, I personally walk through backstage and make sure there's no one asleep in the dressing rooms, or anything like that."

Stoker nodded, and sipped more of the tea. "And you did that, of course, on the night that Mr. Saxon fell from the top balcony." It was more of a statement than a question.

There was a barely perceptible pause before Bill agreed. Yet both Mr. Stoker and myself did notice that hesitation.

"It's usually after midnight when you do your round, is it not, Bill?"

"Yes, sir. By the time the performance is over and everyone has cleaned up and gone home, it's usually well after the 'witching hour. Of course, if it's one of the Guv'nor's Beefsteak Dinner nights then they can go on all night and I catch a bit of a kip back in my cubbyhole and don't even go home."

"Very commendable," muttered Stoker. "I'm sure the Guv'nor is appreciative. But tell me about that last check-up on Mr. Saxon's night, if you would, Bill."

"Tell you about it?"

"Yes. Step by step. For instance, did you – or do you normally – go up to the top gallery to make sure it was empty?"

"Like I said, Mr. Stoker, if I get the nod

from Mr. Bidwell then I don't need to go there."

"And did you 'get the nod' that particular night?"

"Yes, sir, though . . ."

"Though what?"

"Well, Mr. Bidwell had said that all was clear but when I was crossing the stage – the curtain was down, of course – I did hear voices up in the gods."

"Voices?"

"Yes, sir. Angry voices, I'd be so bold as to say. Anyway, I did go 'round the back and up the stairs to see who was there. As I got close I recognized Mr. Saxon's voice, and a woman. I thought at the time that her voice sounded somewhat familiar but I couldn't place it."

"And you still can't?" I interjected.

He shook his head.

"So what did you do then?" asked Stoker.

"Well, seeing as how it was Mr. Saxon, I figured it was none of my business. Some of them go up there to practice, you know. To 'project', I think they call it, their voices. So I figured that was what was happening."

"Even after midnight?" I said.

"Who knows?" He shrugged his shoulders.

"Go on," urged Stoker. "Did you see who it was, with Mr. Saxon?"

"No, sir, I never did. I went on about my checking – the dressing rooms, wardrobe, the greenroom – and by the time I got back all was quiet in the auditorium and I figured they'd all gone home. So I locked up and went home myself."

"And by that time John Saxon lay dead and the unknown woman had fled." Abraham Stoker pushed his empty teacup away from him and sat back in his chair.

"It might have helped if you'd come forward with this information earlier," I said to Bill.

He shrugged. "Don't see how."

After Bill Thomas had left, Mr. Stoker and I went over all we had learned.

"I have to say that, other than letting us know that John had a woman up there with him before he got murdered, it doesn't tell us a lot," I said.

"No," Stoker agreed cautiously. "It might or might not have sent Inspector Bellamy off on another wild chase, so it may be as well to keep this information to ourselves for the time being."

"But you don't think it was this unknown woman who killed John, do you, sir? Surely a woman couldn't have been responsible?"

"And what would be your explanation, Harry?"

"Well . . . well, I don't really know. Perhaps someone else slipped in as the woman was going out? That's a possibility, isn't it? I mean, I can't see a woman murdering John Saxon."

"Oh, you'd be surprised what women are capable of, Harry."

Chapter Twenty-Seven

The next day, Wednesday, Inspector Bellamy was at the theatre bright and early to start his own wild goose chase. It seemed he had got it into his head that the murderer might have been one of the front of house staff. Exactly what led him to this conclusion I don't know, especially since he had seemed so certain that poor Guy Purdy was the culprit.

"Top gallery – your 'gods' as you call them – that's all part of the auditorium, which is your front of house. Are we not correct?"

"You are indeed, inspector," I said. Mr. Stoker had not yet come in so Bellamy had to deal with me. "All parts of the auditorium are classed as front of house."

"So where's your man Sitwell? We'd like a word with him."

"Bidwell," I said. "Mr. Bidwell is front of house manager. I would doubt he is in yet, though it is a Wednesday."

"What's Wednesday got to do with it?"

"A matinee day," I explained. "Any other day, with only an evening performance, I wouldn't expect Mr. Bidwell to be on the premises until late afternoon at the earliest but on a matinee day he's here by mid-morning at the latest."

"Hmm." The inspector looked about him as though he might perhaps discover the manager lurking in the vicinity. We were standing on stage. The curtain was raised and I had been double-checking the positioning of various props set out for the opening scene later on.

"Where do we find your Mr. Bidwell's office?"

I directed him and watched as he went across to the pass door at the end of the orchestra pit and carefully negotiated the stairs down into the auditorium.

"If you go straight back and through the double doors you'll find yourself out in the foyer," I called. He waved a hand in acknowledgement and continued on his way.

It was nearly an hour later that Herbert Gardner came to me in my office.

"Mr. Rivers," he said, a worried look on his face. "I think you should come up front. There's something going on in Mr. Bidwell's office. An argument of come sort. I can hear Mr. Bidwell and another gentleman shouting at one another. Shouting!" He was wide-eyed. "I could hear them in the commissariat. I was checking supplies ready for this afternoon and I heard this – this – hullabaloo coming from downstairs. It's not at all like Mr. Bidwell to raise his voice."

"You're right," I said, getting to my feet. I knew immediately to whom the other voice belonged. "Don't worry, Mr. Gardner. I'll take care of it. You can get back to your commissariat." As he hurried away, concern still written all over his face, I debated whether or not to disturb Mr. Stoker, who must have been in his office by now. I decided to investigate myself first. Mr. Stoker probably had plenty to occupy his time.

When I arrived at Mr. Bidwell's office, the door was wide open and Inspector Bellamy stood framed in it. His ancient notebook was in his hands, with a stub of pencil being waved above the pages. "We can take you down to the Yard for questioning, you know. In fact why don't we do that? Get some sense out of you!" he barked.

"You are a fine one to be talking about sense!"

I had never, in my years at the Lyceum, heard Mr. Bidwell raise his voice the way he now did. Over the inspector's shoulder I could see the front of house manager's bright red face as he stood behind his desk, facing the policeman. An inch or two shorter than the inspector, he was obviously taking no accusations lightly. Mr. Bidwell was known for his diplomacy and his ability to smooth the ruffled feelings of patrons who felt they had been offended in any way. Mixed-up seating, overlong waits, misunderstood ticket prices, perceived slights by staff, were all dealt with smoothly by Mr. Bidwell with the patron always leaving feeling he was the recipient of special treatment which, in a way, he was. But never, ever, did Mr. Bidwell lose his temper nor raise his voice. Until today.

"We are talking murder here!" snapped the

policeman.

"Murder, in *my* theatre!" came back Mr. Bidwell. "Do you not think that we take this matter seriously? It was one of the Lyceum actors who fell to his death. Right here in *my* auditorium! And you have the audacity to question me on my movements and those of my staff? You insinuate that I may have had something to do with the unfortunate man's death? How dare you, sir! How dare you!"

"Gentlemen, gentlemen!"

I turned as Mr. Stoker came up behind me, his rich deep voice taking immediate command of the situation. I should have known to call on him in the first place. Once I knew that Inspector Bellamy was intent on implicating Mr. Bidwell in the murder I should have gone to him. Ah, well . . . he was here now.

"Mr. Stoker, sir!" Mr. Bidwell turned pleading eyes on my boss. "This . . . this *person* has suddenly taken it upon himself to accuse the front of house staff, and myself specifically, of throwing one of your actors over the front of the gods, down onto the stall seats below. Have you ever heard such nonsense?"

"Nonsense, is it?" retorted Bellamy. "Nonsense?"

"Gentlemen, gentlemen," Mr. Stoker said again. He held up his hands as he moved forward. Inspector Bellamy lowered his notebook and moved to one side to allow my boss to enter the office. Mr. Bidwell, his face already slightly less inflamed, came around from behind his desk.

"Inspector Bellamy," said Stoker. "I am

surprised to see you here at this hour. What is it that has brought you here to disturb the tranquility of the Lyceum Theatre? Is not all well at Scotland Yard?"

"No, all is not well at Scotland Yard! Nor will it be while a murderer runs loose among your people. We have reason to question your front of house manager here, and he is refusing to cooperate. Such refusal can only be treated by us taking him down to the Yard where we might the better deal with him."

"Intimidate him, you mean?" My boss turned his back on the inspector. "Relax, Mr. Bidwell. No one is taking you anywhere. Any necessary questioning will be done right here; in front of me." He half-turned to again include the inspector in what he said. "It was my understanding that statements were already made; made at the time that Mr. Saxon's body was first discovered. Is that not so, inspector?"

Bellamy flicked through the pages of his notebook but without really looking at them. "We have moved on from there, Mr. Stoker. Further questions need to be asked. At the time of the initial investigation our focus was on the body, of course. Now our focus is shifting to those who might be directly involved."

"You mean you haven't got anywhere so now you're going to browbeat poor Mr. Bidwell!" I couldn't contain myself. I had to join in the conversation.

"All right, Harry," said Stoker. "Let it go. Let the inspector do what he apparently feels he needs to do and then we can perhaps correct the direction of his thinking." I thought I detected the slightest sign of a wink but couldn't be certain. I said no more.

"Now then, inspector," my boss continued. "What possible link do you have to connect Mr. Bidwell directly with the fall of Mr. Saxon from the gods?"

Bellamy's brow furrowed and one eye closed. He pursed his lips for a moment before speaking. "Your Mr. Bidwell, here, has admitted to losing his temper."

"Never!" cried the front of house manager. "I said no such thing."

Stoker again raised his hand for a moment. "Gently! Now what is this, inspector? When do you claim he lost his temper, not that I can imagine such a thing."

The policeman referred to his notebook. "Did you or did you not say that you had a dispute with one of your patrons as a result of his fingers having been closed in a door?"

Mr. Bidwell threw up his hands in despair and sank down onto his chair behind the desk. "That was two years ago," he said in a quiet voice. "As I told you, the gentleman's hand got accidentally shut in the door as I was closing it. He thought it a deliberate act on my part and, being of an excitable temperament, he almost came to blows with me. I was, however, able to mollify the person and all ended amicably. It was a long time ago and a minor incident, as I have already told you."

"That's what you claim," said the inspector.

Stoker looked amazed. "What on earth has

this to do with the murder of John Saxon years later?"

"There is no connection," I cried.

"That's all very well," said Bellamy, snapping his notebook closed. "But we can see that as an indication of a short temper . . . the very thing that could trigger a major argument leading to you, Mr. Bidwell, pushing your actor over the balcony! We have seen stranger things at Scotland Yard, I can assure you." He looked very smug and pleased with himself.

"How did this hand incident even come up?" asked Mr. Stoker, looking at Bidwell.

Mr. Bidwell, shrugged his shoulders and gave a great sigh. "The inspector badgered me for anything in my past that showed a dispute, an argument of any kind. I had to search back in my memory to even recall this little event. It was nothing!"

"Of course it was nothing," agreed my boss. He turned to face the inspector, standing up to his full height that he might look down on the policeman. "Really, inspector! Is this the way Scotland Yard operates? Are you this desperate to solve the murder that you have to try to sully the reputation of someone – anyone – to claim to have found a suspect? I would have thought that even you were above that sort of tactic."

To his credit, the inspector looked somewhat abashed. He made a vague hand gesture, waved his notebook, and cleared his throat. "It is our job to explore all possibilities. You of the general public, who are not privy to the machinations of the

Metropolitan Police department, and the fine tuning of Scotland Yard in particular, cannot fathom the many subtle avenues we must explore in order to eventually lead ourselves to the truth."

"Subtle?" echoed Mr. Bidwell.

Just then there came a commotion from within the theatre. Sergeant Fairview, whom I had met when first encountering Police Constable Jimmy Hathaway, came out through the auditorium doors and stood looking about him. He breathed heavily from hurrying, attesting to his overweight stature. He broke out in a fit of coughing then, spotting the inspector, hurried forward to Mr. Bidwell's office and joined the rest of us there.

"Inspector! Inspector Bellamy!"

"What is it, sergeant? Please don't raise your voice. There's no need. We can hear you quite well."

I almost laughed. This from the inspector, so soon after he had been shouting and screaming at Mr. Bidwell loud enough to cause Mr. Gardner to seek me out.

"Sorry, inspector. It's just that you are needed. I have a police wagon waiting at the stage door in case you need it. There is a big disturbance at a tavern. People hurt."

"People drinking too much! Don't they know we have better things to do? Can you not handle that, Fairview?"

"They say it's really serious," added the hapless sergeant.

"Oh, very well." Bellamy looked briefly at Mr. Stoker. "This is not done with, sir. Not by a long chalk. We will be following through with our questions." He turned and strode away, the sergeant scurrying after him.

"What a waste of a morning," said Mr. Stoker as we returned to his office. He pulled out his gold pocket watch, a treasured gift from the Guv'nor. "What do you say, Harry? Shall we partake of an early lunch so that we may then cruise on into the matinee performance with no further interruptions?"

I thought it an excellent idea and we left the theatre, heading for the Druid's Head. It was when we rounded the corner at the end of the alley cutting through to the hostelry, that we saw the commotion. It seemed that the Druid's Head was the tavern indicated by Sergeant Fairview. A large number of policemen stood about outside, where a large black police wagon sat at the curb, its horses snorting and pawing the ground.

"What have we here?" said Stoker.

"This must be what Inspector Bellamy was called away to," I said. "I didn't realize it was the Druid's Head."

"Indeed. Let us proceed with caution, Harry, and see what's afoot."

As luck would have it, Constable Jimmy Hathaway appeared at the door just as we got there.

"'Ere! Just the gents we need. Seems two of your boys lost it inside."

"What do you mean, Jimmy?" I asked.

"'Two of our boys'?" added Mr. Stoker. "What exactly do you mean by that?"

"Yes, sir. You got a Taffy with a quick temper and a giant what looks out for 'im?"

"Davey Llewellyn and Lonnie Plimpton!" I said. I turned to my boss. "Two new stagehands, sir. I'm sure you know of them. Sam Green seems pleased with them."

"Ah, yes." He simply nodded his head.

"What have they done, Jimmy?" I asked.

"Well, right now they've scarpered," he responded. "The inspector's not pleased. Not pleased at all." Jimmy himself looked delighted.

"Scarpered?" I said. "You mean, they've run away?"

"Too right. Best come on inside and speak to 'is nibs." The constable turned and led the way into the tavern. We followed.

Inside, the normally well-ordered dining room was a shambles. Benches around the fireplace area were thrown about; some on top of others. Two tables had been overturned. Three or four men sat on one of the upright benches, a couple of them nursing their heads. On the floor directly in front of the fireplace lay a body. Inspector Bellamy stood over it, his stubby pencil scribbling into his notebook. He looked up when Jimmy led us over to where he stood.

"How come your Lyceum Theatre is nothing but trouble for Scotland Yard?" he asked.

"What, exactly, has happened here?" asked Stoker.

"What, indeed?" He sniffed, licked the tip of his pencil, and continued scribbling. When he had completed what he was doing he put away the book

265

and waved an arm to indicate the area. "Two of your actors went berserk, it seems. Aren't you paying them enough, Mr. Stoker? First one throws himself off your balcony and then others try to destroy the neighboring tavern."

"I can almost guarantee, inspector, that there is no connection whatsoever between what has happened here and the death of Mr. John Saxon. Not only that, but while Mr. Saxon was one of our actors, it would seem that this disruption was orchestrated by two of our stagehands. Not actors."

John Martin walked over to join us. He shook his head sadly as he surveyed the devastation. "They made a right mess, I'm thinking." He stood an overturned bench back up on its feet. "Not that I can really blame 'em for starting it."

"What do you mean, John?" asked Stoker.

"Well, it was some of the usual layabouts who come in 'ere. They started poking fun at your Welsh boy. What's 'is name? Davey, was it?"

I nodded. "Davey Llewellyn," I said.

John grunted. "Nice enough boy. 'E's been in 'ere often enough, along with that big fella."

"Lonnie Plimpton," I supplied.

"'E never says much. Leaves the talking to the Welshman. And 'e's never been no trouble before. But 'e sure looks after his little friend. When they started poking fun at Davey – and I think someone emptied his beer over the boy's head – well, that's when the big man lost it. Picked up a bench and started swinging it. Hit quite a few of 'em."

"Well, he's certainly in trouble now," said

the inspector. "Big trouble. He's killed a man."

"What?" Mr. Stoker and I both spoke together.

Bellamy indicated the body on the ground at his feet. "Looks like this poor beggar got his neck broken."

Chapter Twenty-Eight

Neither Mr. Stoker nor myself got any lunch that day. We waited for Dr. Cochran to arrive and confirm that the victim had a broken neck. With Inspector Bellamy, we interviewed the survivors and ascertained that what John Martin had said was correct. A group of men, who had enjoyed a liquid lunch, started picking on Davey Llewellyn, probably thinking that because of his diminutive size he would be an easy target. They reckoned without big Lonnie Plimpton. Those two looked out for one another. Lonnie had picked up one of the heavy oak benches and swung it around as though it were just a stick. Other benches and tables went flying and very quickly the whole group who had done the taunting lay scattered about the inn. The one who had poured his beer over Davey's head had suffered the most; probably from the first vicious swing of the bench. It had smashed his head and snapped his neck.

By the time Inspector Bellamy arrived, with his band of policemen, Davey and Lonnie had gone. I doubt that they realized how seriously they had hurt anyone but, as John Martin said, they had paid back in full for what they had received and had not stayed around to pick up the pieces.

"What a temper!" Bellamy said. "Now we know who was responsible for your Mr. Saxon's murder. That big one would have had no trouble picking him up and tossing him over the balcony."

Mr. Stoker looked hard at the policeman. "Are you, then, changing your mind again, inspector? Is Mr. Bidwell now to be let off the hook, as it were? First it was Mr. Purdy, then Mr. Bidwell. Now Mr. Plimpton. I can see how a dead body must speak louder to you than does a couple of fingers trapped in a closing door, but . . ."

"Police business, Mr. Stoker. Police business. We cannot expect you to understand the workings of the police mind . . ."

"Oh, that is certain, inspector!"

"Always supposing that the police have a mind," I muttered.

"You see," continued the inspector, obviously highly pleased with himself. "It all fits together. We knew that it would, of course, if we gave it long enough. Your big man there, what was his name?"

"Lonnie Plimpton," I said.

"Right. Him. He was a walking time-bomb. Much like those used by the Irish dissidents. It didn't take much to set him off, and see what it's done? We can be sure this is what happened with Mr. Saxon."

"Come, Harry," said my boss. "Let us return to the theatre and to sanity. We have much to discuss."

"Don't you worry," called out the inspector, as we made our way to the door. "We'll catch your stage actors. They won't get far."

"I don't think we have any choice in the matter, Harry."

I didn't know exactly what Mr. Stoker was about to say but I had a sinking feeling that it was going to involve me, in some action or actions.

"Meaning what, exactly, sir?"

"We have to find Messrs. Llewellyn and Plimpton ourselves. Before Inspector Bellamy does."

"It does seem that Lonnie Plimpton killed a man," I said, uneasily.

He nodded. "Indeed it does, Harry. And that is unfortunate. But we need to make certain that he is apprehended and brought back to be judged in a court of law. Was he defending himself and his friend? Was the death accidental? What were the exact circumstances? And did this really have any connection with the murder of Mr. Saxon? I don't think it did. No, I don't think we can simply leave it to Inspector Bellamy and his minions to find them and especially to treat one of the Lyceum family with due restraint. The inspector could become over-zealous in exactly the same way that Mr. Plimpton was over-zealous. Two wrongs will not make a right, Harry. We need to find our man before Scotland Yard does."

"Yes, sir." I knew he was right. "So what would you like me to do?"

"It is curtain up within the hour, Harry. Have Sam Green keep an eye on properties for the performance and you get on this right away. See if you can determine where the two of them might have gone to hide. Track them down and then talk them into returning here, giving themselves up, and then going to face the music with myself accompanying them. Do, please, let them know that the Lyceum is behind them. We will see to it that they get a fair trial."

"Yes, sir."

Once again I was to set off on a hunt. At least this time I did know who it was I was hunting. But where to start looking? So far as I knew Davey and Lonnie were both fairly new to London and the theatre world. I didn't even know if they had any friends in the area. Where was I to start?

I had to speak with Sam Green, to see that he kept an eye on things on-stage while I was gone. I imagined that he had spent some time getting to know the two men since they had started working for him. That was obviously the starting point. I set off back-stage to find him.

"No, 'Arry, I've no idea where they might have gone," said Sam. "Cor! What a turn-up, eh?" He chuckled. "I'd 'ave loved to 'ave seen Lonnie in action there. Swinging one of them benches about and laying 'em out!"

"He killed a man," I said.

"Yes, so I 'ear." His face became serious again. "Yes. That ain't no laughing matter, that's for sure. Mr. Stoker's right. We need to find 'em." He tipped his cap and scratched his head. "Now let's 'ave a think. I believe young Davey did mention something at one time. What was it 'e said?" More head scratching. Then he settled his hat back on, a satisfied smile on his face. "Lambeth. That's what 'e said. They got a room on Princes Street, if I'm not mistaken. Yes, that's it. Princes Street. 'Cos I remember thinking that the less like princes they were ..."

"Across Waterloo Bridge, in Lambeth?" I said. "Thanks, Sam. I knew I could count on you. Now if only they have gone back there."

"Where else would they go?"

"Well, that's what I'm going to have to find out."

I didn't know the south side of the Thames very well but I did know that Lambeth was the first district you came to once you had crossed the river. It must have been a bit of a walk for the two of them, to and from the Lyceum every day, but not too far. I grabbed a hansom and asked the driver to drop me at the end of Princes Street.

It turned out to be off Commercial Road. Princes was a long street, crossing Upper Stamford Street halfway down. I walked the length of it. There was no sign of our two men, but then I hardly expected them to be standing outside their lodging waiting for me – or the police – to come along to them. I stood at the south end and pondered what to do next. I was standing outside a small church, where the road ended. It was St. David's, a Methodist church. On a hunch, I went inside. I had half hoped to find the minister there but the only occupant was an old lady arranging flowers at the altar.

"Good morning," I said, coming up behind her. She took no notice and went on fixing the blooms. I repeated myself, a little louder.

"Oh! Goodness me!" She stepped back, turning to face me, her hand on her heart. "You startled me."

I raised my bowler hat. "My apologies, ma'am."

She was about my height, dressed all in black, a cameo brooch at her throat. A black bonnet was pulled low on her silver-haired head. Her eyes were watery and her face well wrinkled. I suspected that her hearing was not all that it might be so I kept my voice raised.

"I am looking for two men," I said. "I just wondered if, by any chance, they were regular congregation members here. It's a long shot, I know, but you might know them. One is a Welshman, Davey Llewellyn, and the other is a very big man named Lonnie Plimpton."

"Eh?" she said. She cupped her hand to her ear.

I sighed. I had been right about her hearing. I repeated myself, my voice even louder. She nodded slightly as she listened to me. I think, however, that she was nodding to indicate that she could hear, rather than to affirm that she knew the men I was talking about.

"Are you familiar with these men?" I asked.

She continued nodding and I was about to thank her and turn away.

"Mr. Llewellyn is a new member," she said. "I don't know the other gentleman you mention but Mr. Llewellyn I do. He has a fine voice. Used to sing in the choir back in Llandudno, he was telling me."

My heart jumped. If this was the same Llewellyn then I had struck lucky.

"Really? Thank you, ma'am. Thank you. Tell me, do you know where Mr. Llewellyn lives? It is somewhere on Princes Street, I believe. I need to speak with him but I don't have his exact address."

"Well, I . . ." she hesitated.

"Oh! I am Mr. Rivers," I said. "I work at the Lyceum Theatre, where Mr. Llewellyn works."

Her face brightened. "Oh, I love the theatre! Mr. Llewellyn has promised to take me there, one day."

"Wonderful. Yes, I know you will enjoy it. But, please, do you have Mr. Llewellyn's address? It is important that I speak to him."

"Can you not speak to him at the theatre?" This lady was not above exercising caution when it came to being approached by a stranger. I put it down to living in Lambeth. A district known for crime.

"He is not due to be at the theatre today," I lied. "But I do need to speak with him. That's why I've come all this way to find him."

"And yet you don't know exactly where he lives?" Her watery eyes never left my face.

I smiled my warmest smile and shrugged my shoulders. "I must admit that I rushed out without noting the street number." I shook my head. "Foolish of me, wasn't it?" Another warm smile.

It seemed to work. The lady turned back to her flower-arranging saying, "It's just down at the corner, on the right. The corner of Thomas Street. Number 21, Mrs. Jones. She keeps a tidy house. Comes here regularly, of course."

Mrs. Jones might have kept a tidy house but, not unlike the church lady, she did not seem inclined to welcome strangers. After repeated knocking with the well-polished brass door-knocker, she eventually came and spoke to me through the door, without opening it.

"Who is it?" Her voice was strong.

"Mrs. Jones? My name is Rivers," I said, bending so that my mouth was at the letterbox. "I would like to speak with Mr. Llewellyn, if he is home."

"And your business?"

"That is between myself and Mr. Llewellyn," I replied. "Is he at home?"

There was a long silence.

"Hello!" I called, holding open the flap of the letterbox.

"I will have to see if he is receiving," said the voice and I heard unhurried footsteps moving away.

If he is receiving? That was the sort of thing you expected to hear from a footman at an upper class residence in the west end, not at a rooming house in Lambeth. I straightened up and eased my back, looking about me up and down Princes Street. The houses looked as though their owners had at one time been prosperous but that – as with many areas on this side of the river – they had long since fallen on hard times. I was interrupted in my reverie by the sound of bolts being drawn on the inner side of the door. I was surprised that bolts were necessary, even in this part of the town. The door inched open and a steely eye looked out and down at me seemingly from a height. It was a thin-faced woman in a dark green dress devoid of any sort of decoration. Her lips were thin and pressed together in obvious disapproval.

"We do not encourage visitors at all hours of the day. I have advised Mr. Llewellyn of this and he should be well aware of it."

"May I enter?" I asked.

She paused a brief moment before opening the door just enough to allow me to slip inside.

"Thank you," I said.

She closed the door behind me, sliding the bolts back into place. Then she pointed to a narrow staircase, its carpet runner well worn. A collection of framed silhouettes decorated the walls up the stairs. "Second floor. Wipe your feet."

I dutifully wiped them on the mat inside the door and then proceeded up the stairs. I almost expected Mrs. Jones to accompany me but she disappeared into the back rooms on the ground floor.

"Mr. Rivers." A voice with the Welsh lilt to it addressed me as I reached the upper landing.

Once again a face peered at me from behind a door held only slightly ajar.

"Davey?" I said.

He opened the door, looked carefully up and down the stairs, and then waved me inside. The room was small and dark, the curtains drawn across the one window. It was sparsely furnished. Prominent in front of the empty fireplace was a large armchair occupied by the bulky figure of Lonny Plimpton. He nodded at me, his face impassive.

"How did you know where to find us?" asked Davey, drawing up a straight-backed chair for me alongside Lonny's. I sat down.

"It wasn't too difficult, Davey," I said. "And I imagine it won't take the police long to get here either."

"The police?" He seemed genuinely surprised.

"Yes. Lonnie's hay-making at the Druid's Head had its consequences," I said. "Are you aware that he killed a man?"

"What? What are you talking about?"

"One of the men he hit with that heavy bench he was swinging nearly took the head off him. Apparently he died. The police were there, swarming all over the place."

Davey's face had gone chalk white. Lonny still seemed impassive, his brow slightly furrowed as though he was trying to process what I had said. "I – I knew Lonny had done some damage to them," said the Welshman. "I thought, 'Good! That'll teach 'em to pick on the little man.' But I didn't know he'd hurt them that much."

I nodded. "As I understand it, it was self-defense . . . or rather, Lonny defending you. But that was the consequence."

Davey paced around the small room, running his hands through his hair. "What should we do, Harry? Lonny was just protecting me! I don't want the police taking him away."

I stood up. "Time is important, Davey. Mr. Stoker said that the Lyceum will back you, though I must admit I don't know just what he can do. But look, Davey . . . better you go to the police than they come after you. You and Lonny come with me back to the theatre. Mr. Stoker will know exactly what steps to take." I hoped he would, anyway. "Get your things and we'll find a growler. We can be back at the Lyceum while the police are coming here."

Chapter Twenty-Nine

It was Thursday evening, just at the end of the first act, when Mr. Stoker came to find me. I was backstage, of course, and he slipped quietly across to where I stood close to Miss Price, the prompt, looking over her shoulder and following her script. I knew that all props were in position for the start of the next scene.

"Harry, I need you." He hissed the words so as not to be heard on stage. The scene was all set for Act Two; Scene One, the seaport. As the curtain went up, I had a last quick glance around and then followed him away from the wings and out to the passageway beyond.

"What is it, sir?"

"We have to leave, Harry. Inspector Bellamy left word with Bill Thomas. The inspector was passing by and took a moment to look in."

"I don't quite understand, sir," I said. "Inspector Bellamy called in? Is this about taking Davey and Lonnie into custody?"

"No, Harry. That's all been taken care of. But apparently the inspector was on his way to a disturbance, near the Old Nichol Street Rookery. He said it was a vampire sighting, or some such."

"And he took the time to advise us?" I was surprised.

My boss nodded. "I know. It's almost unbelievable isn't it, that the good inspector should give us passing consideration." He thought for a moment. "I suspect that there is more to his action than meets the eye."

"Well, he is aware that you know more about vampires than he ever will," I suggested.

He nodded. "There is that, I agree." He straightened up. "Well, let us not look a gift horse in the mouth, as Saint Jerome said. Come, Harry. Let us be off to Old Nichol."

It was almost an hour's drive to that part of the East End. Even I knew the reputation of it. The lowest lodging houses in London were situated there; streets of attached houses between High Street, Shoredith, and Hackney Road. Spitalfields, another slum area, was immediately to the south. The main streets within Old Nichol were Boundary Street, Old Nichol Street, Half Nichol Street, and The Mount and Church Street. Inspector Bellamy had left the address to which he had gone, which was on Old Nichol Street itself. The area was home to nearly six thousand people, squeezed into about thirty streets and courts. Along with the houses there were workshops and stables.

"You probably know a little of Old Nichol," said Mr. Stoker, as the cab lumbered along the cobblestone streets.

I nodded. "A little, by reputation," I said. "I've never actually been there."

"Count yourself blessed," he said. "There was a big 'revelation' a few years ago when it was disclosed that in constructing the houses at the cheapest possible costs, the builders used a cement known as 'Billysweet' instead of the traditional lime and mortar."

"Billysweet?"

"Yes. Apparently it was much cheaper and for good reason. It seems it never stops drying out and thus has led to sagging and unstable walls. The houses are not only unsanitary but also extremely unsafe. Some have already fallen down; others lean precariously. There's a lack of foundation on many of them. Floorboards are laid on bare earth. Cheap timber was used throughout. It's not uncommon for a roof to fall in."

"Goodness," I murmured. "And people actually live there?"

He chuckled humorlessly. "Indeed, Harry. For most of them have nowhere else to go. Backyards have been built over, to provide more living space, and therefore more revenue to the owners. There is not even room now for privies. One house with five or six rooms must hold twenty-four persons. There is no running water. A tap at the back of one of the houses runs for ten minutes or so every day, except Sunday. Even the basements, dark and damp as they are, are rented for two shillings a week."

I couldn't help thinking that Mr. Stoker exaggerated in order to make an impression of some sort, but then the hansom turned onto Old Nichol. The moment we alighted the cabbie spun the vehicle around and goaded his horse into a gallop in order to leave as quickly as possible.

The inspector had left the address and we went straight to it. Even in the rapidly-fading evening light I could see that the houses were indeed in dilapidated condition. Windows were broken, front doors were missing, roofs had gaping holes in their tiles. A small group of Metropolitan policemen were gathered outside the house, surrounded by a strangely silent crowd of what turned out to be local residents, many of them from the house in question. Inspector Bellamy strode up and down in front of them in a state of agitation. We joined the group and he nodded greeting to Mr. Stoker.

"What's happening, inspector?"

"We've emptied the house; got all the people out. Not that there were many still in there. Never seen so many empty rooms in this area. It seems that 'it' is up in the attic, whatever 'it' is. One of our officers went up there but he came scurrying back. Said something about a vampire sucking blood, if you can believe it."

There were mutterings and the occasional exclamation from the gathered crowd. The police constables huddled together, eyes cast down so as not to catch the inspector's attention. One or two mumbled something but I was unable to catch what it was. They all looked very ill at ease.

"Have you not gone up there yourself?" asked Mr. Stoker.

It was the inspector's turn to look uneasy. "It's our place to remain where we can oversee the entire operation," he said.

"It doesn't seem like much of an operation if you can't get anyone to go up and investigate," I couldn't help observing.

"Do *you* want to go up there?" Bellamy turned to me and snapped.

"Come, inspector," said my boss. "Mr. Rivers is not one of your constables."

"No, sir!" I cried. "I'd be happy to go and have a look. I've never seen a vampire before."

"There!" cried the inspector triumphantly. "You see? Mr. Rivers volunteers."

I think it was the first time he had addressed me by name. But then I realized what I had volunteered for. To go and face a vampire? I reminded myself that Mr. Stoker had said he did not believe in them . . . or I think that was what he had said. I looked toward him to see what he might indicate, but he was looking around at the crowd that had gathered and was now growing.

"Yes!" I spoke up. "Yes, I'll go and see just what's going on . . . and I'll come back and let you know," I concluded quickly.

I sprang forward to act before my courage gave out. I entered the house through the doorless opening and made for the staircase. It was a rickety affair with half the banister missing, and I made my way cautiously up to the first landing. I thought I heard movement above me and I looked around to see if there was anything I might use to defend myself should I need to. Why hadn't I asked one of the policemen for his truncheon, I thought? I spotted a broken section of handrail lying at the top of the staircase I had just climbed and I managed to pry loose a spindle from it. It wasn't much but it was something. Inspector Bellamy had said that he'd cleared everyone out of the house . . . everything except 'it'! My mind conjured up a wild variety of creatures that could be dismissed as 'it'. None of them gave me comfort.

I advanced up another rickety flight and stood on the second floor landing. Yes, there was definitely movement from the attic above. I stood there undecided for a long moment. Then a figure appeared in the opening at the top of the attic steps. An *aluka*? At first I couldn't make out what it was, then I realized that it was an old woman. She was rail-thin, her cheeks sunken in and her eyes deep in their sockets. Her arms, poking through torn slits in a once-white shift, were like those of a skeleton. Her hair, what little there was of it, stuck out from her almost bald head. It looked as though clumps of hair had been torn out leaving behind blackened and still blood-red sores. But what drew my eyes and almost made me faint was what she held in her hands; held up to her broken and yellowed teeth. It was a human arm, as thin and scrawny as her own, but missing some of the fingers from the hand. She stood looking at me, chewing at the withered flesh, her eyes wide and wild.

"My god! It's a vampire!" I murmured. I had never seen one before, of course, but somehow I knew that this was what I faced.

Suddenly, as quickly as she had appeared, she turned and went back into the attic room. I noticed that her feet were bare and blackened.

"Harry! Harry! Are you up there?"

It was Mr. Stoker's voice coming up the stairwell behind me. I was never so glad to hear it.

"Yes! Yes, sir," I cried. "Up on the top floor."

He came round the corner and started up the final flight of stairs, but when he was halfway up, there came a creaking and cracking and the stairs began to break up and fall away. Mr. Stoker lunged forward and managed to get his arms up onto the landing where I stood. I immediately bent down and grabbed his jacket. There was no way I could haul up my boss's weight, of course, but with much wriggling and kicking on his part, we eventually managed to get him up onto the top floor.

"Thank you, Harry. Phew! That was a close one."

"What are you doing here, sir?" I asked. "Not than I'm not pleased to see you, believe me. You don't know how pleased!"

"Harry, we've got to get you out of here. Inspector Bellamy is losing control of the crowd down there and they are talking about setting fire to the house."

"Setting fire to it? But that would . . ."

"Yes. That would fire all the houses on the street. The flames would leap from house to house in no time, the timbers are so old and dried."

"Sir!" I felt that whatever might be with the crowd, I should relate what I had encountered. "Sir, there is an old woman up here. Up in the attic. But now that I think about it, I don't think she is a vampire."

"You don't?"

"No, sir. Though seeing her standing with a bloody arm to her mouth I can understand why the residents might have thought her to be one. She looks to me to be a crazed old woman who has perhaps lost her mind. And I don't think she's alone up there."

"What do you mean?"

I told him of the gruesome appendage she was gnawing on. "She looked half-starved," I said. "I'm guessing that some other or others have also been up there with her and that they may have passed away."

"And she is so hungry she's feasting on their bodies," Stoker concluded.

"Exactly."

"All right," he said, dusting himself down. "We'll get her out, and anyone else up there who is alive, and make sure no one tries to set a fire."

"How will we get down this collapsed staircase?" I asked.

"We'll manage somehow. Perhaps we can find some old bedding or curtains or something to make a rope. One thing at a time, Harry. Let's go and look at your vampire."

We had guessed fairly accurately. In the confined space above we found the old woman crouched over the body of an old man. Possibly he had been her husband. One of the corpse's legs bore teeth marks, as did the upper part of the arm that she still held jealously to her mouth.

"Too late for him," said my boss. "Come on, Harry. Let's see of we can rescue her."

"Sir!"

"Yes? What?"

"Sir, I smell smoke!"

"Damnation!"

We both moved to the end of the attic space and looked down the attic stairs. Smoke, rapidly thickening, was starting to issue from the stairwell.

Chapter Thirty

There was no time to lose. Fire would spread rapidly through the ancient timbers of the house.

"How do we get out, sir?" I cried.

Mr. Stoker looked around and then ran to the far end of the attic, past the old woman who still crouched cradling the remains of her companion. My boss pounded on the wall at the far end.

"Here, Harry! Come and help me."

I joined him, beating on the wall with my fists. I quickly saw what he had in mind. The partition between the attics of the houses was of laths and plaster; a thin partition rather than a solid wall. It was the cheapest of materials and fell apart easily as we struck it, the plaster crumbling away and allowing us to tear away the thin wooden laths. It was not like the more solid walls between the houses on the lower floors. We soon had made a hole large enough to squeeze through.

"Help me with the old woman, Harry. We must force her through, if necessary."

It was necessary. She clung to the partially rotting corpse and we had to wrench it from her so that we might push her through the opening. The smoke was now thick and, looking back to the attic opening, I could see the bright red and orange of the flames roaring up through the stairwell. It was no time to dawdle.

Mr. Stoker pushed me through the opening after the old woman, and he followed. But as we stumbled out into the bare attic of the next house, the old woman suddenly slipped past us and thrust herself back again through the hole. I moved to follow and get her.

"Harry! No!"

Flame had already engulfed the space we had just left. I was aghast. The old woman was almost immediately enveloped in the fire. She made no sound; no cry escaped her. I stood there unbelieving. Then my boss grabbed me and pulled be back and away from the hole.

"She didn't utter a sound, sir!"

"I know. No time, Harry. We have to keep moving if we're to stay ahead of the fire. Come on!"

I tried to shake the image of the old woman from my mind and ran after him to the far end of the attic we were now in. Once again we started pounding on the dividing wall. The partitions might have been thin but they were starting to take a toll on my fists. How many of these barriers would we have to beat our way through if we were to outrun the fire?

In the next attic we discovered a broken chair. Mr. Stoker forced it apart and gave me the seat and back, taking the legs himself. Armed with these we attacked the next wall with renewed vigor and made slightly faster progress.

But the fire pursued us relentlessly. It seemed to me that it was gaining in strength. Over the sound of the burning and falling timbers I could make out the bells and the loud alarm rattles of the fire brigade in the street outside. So, they had got here . . . but I held out little hope that they would be able to help us. They were best known for wetting down the remnants of a house. Seldom did they seem able to halt a blaze, especially one of this magnitude. Still, perhaps they would at least be able to restrict the fire to Old Nichol Street, and keep it from spreading on from there. I did not want to become a part of the next Great Fire of London. There are only 378 firemen for the whole of London and the city experiences over fifteen hundred fires every year. The newer steam-powered engines are quite successful at reaching even the tallest buildings when in flames, but the East End is sparsely covered by the insurance companies, who manage the brigades. The old hand-primed pumps have to suffice here.

I tried to think back to when we had first arrived at Old Nichol Street. How long a street was it? How many houses? We had entered the building about halfway along, so how much farther to the end? How many more walls did we have to break through? Then a thought struck me . . . what happens when we reach the end house? Surely the final wall would be if bricks and mortar not laths and plaster; impossible to beat our way through. What then? I should have known that my boss's mind was not idle.

"We have to get far enough ahead of the flames that we can move down, Harry. Down to the floor below the attic. Below that too, if possible. Ideally to the ground floor, of course."

"Yes, sir. I'd been thinking the same thing."

Spurred on by that, and the image of a solid wall ahead of us, we attacked the next partition with renewed vigor. We broke through fairly quickly and Mr. Stoker risked a quick look behind us.

"I think we've made a little headway, Harry. Come on!"

He led the way down the stairs of the attic we were then in; down to the second floor. But we might have placed ourselves in greater peril. The flames were moving from house to house much faster than we had guessed. They were already starting up the staircase of this house.

"Quickly, Harry!"

Mr. Stoker ducked into the room beside us. The fact that none of the rooms still had doors was to our advantage, since we didn't have to worry about them being locked. Stoker led the way across to the far wall and used the chair legs he still carried to beat out the window frame. He stuck out his head, had a quick look around, and then withdrew it. He was about to speak but his eyes widened at what he saw behind me. He grabbed me, spun me around, and said, "Come on, Harry! It's moving too fast. We must get back up to the attic where we can at least break our way along."

It was close but we did make it up the attic stairs again and along to renew our pounding on the partition walls. From then on it seemed a blur. I remember beating on walls and breaking through, one after another. Never any end. The back of the piece of chair I was using came apart and I was quickly left with only the seat to use as my assault tool and weapon.

But somehow we did manage to gain a little time. It was just as well because my hands jarred as I beat on the next barrier. The wall did not give. It was a brick wall!

"We've reached the end of the row of houses, Harry! It's now or never."

"For what, sir?" I asked in despair. I was exhausted.

"Last effort, Harry! Follow me."

He rushed down the stairs and I followed, stumbling as I went. On the floor below we peered over the banister rail and saw that, below us, the fire was already eating into this the last house. It would not be possible to descend any farther so we moved into one of the top floor rooms and, again, over to the window. Once more Stoker beat out the ancient window frame and had a quick look outside.

"It's a fair drop, Harry, make no mistake. But I think there's a way you can make it," he said when he turned back to me.

"Me, sir? But what about you?"

He ignored my question. "I'll hold you by the wrists and lower you, Harry. No! No time for questions; just listen to me. I'll lower you as far as I can. If I can then swing you, like a pendulum, enough to give you some momentum I can probably drop you so that you hit on the outhouse roof off to the right."

Probably, I thought?

"You can slide down the tiles," he continued, "and then it's not too much of a fall to the ground."

"But. . ." I started to say.

"No time!" he cried. "The fire is upon us!"

He was right. The flames roared up outside the room we were in. Mr. Stoker grabbed me by the arms, spun me around, and half lifted me onto the window sill.

"Remember, slide down the tiles," he said. His voice was hoarse and I detected a slight tremor in it. He grabbed my wrists and lowered me over the edge of the window. I was aware of him leaning out and swinging me back and forth. As I looked down, in the light of the burning houses I could make out the outhouse roof he was aiming for. It looked to be a long way off.

"Now, Harry!"

He let go of me and I went falling through the air. I tried to reach out as I fell and, by pure good fortune I'm sure, managed to hit the outer edge of the outhouse. I twisted, wrenching my back, and desperately grabbed for the slippery roof. I fell onto the tiles and, with no effort on my part, half slid and half rolled down the roof. I hit the lower gutter and bounced off it, finally dropping down to land on the solid ground. A sharp pain shot through my leg. I knew I had either broken my ankle or at the very least severely sprained it. I collapsed on the bare ground.

I tried to catch my breath and then I rolled over onto my back, reaching down to feel my foot. I looked up at the window from which my boss had lowered me. It was filled with flame. Mr. Stoker was no longer there.

Chapter Thirty-One

There was no way anyone could have survived the flames that must have rushed into that room right after my boss had dropped me from the window. I tried to come to terms with the situation. Abraham Stoker – my employer, my mentor, my . . . how could I define him? – he was no more. He must surely have perished in the fire. I looked back at the line of attached houses, flames still issuing from many windows as the interiors were destroyed. I was aware of roofs falling in and great spirals of smoke, flames, and sparks rising into the murky sky above. It was three days short of the full moon yet the only light in the sky came from the burning houses.

I lay on the ground at the rear of the last house. I could hear the shouts and noises of the fire-engine out on the street, its hand-primed water hoses fighting a losing battle with the conflagration. I thought I could make out the hoarse voice of Inspector Bellamy shouting orders though I couldn't be certain. I closed my eyes and wept.

Mr. Stoker had become a father-figure to me. I realized that now, though I would never have thought in those terms before. He was my guide; my rock in the ever-changing world of modern London. The theatre, the Guv'nor, the cast and crew of the Lyceum had become my world. We were an island in the midst of traffic, mystery, murder, intrigue. I thought back to when I had been lost with Mr. Stoker and a young boy in a London sewer, with rising waters and no hope of an outlet. Yet he had somehow led us out and to freedom. I thought of how he had led the battle to rescue my beloved Jenny from certain death by crazed fanatics in an underground cave. And then I thought of my boss and I going through the London newspapers to see how the opening night of a new play had been received by the critics. I sat up, leaning forward with my head between my knees and I cried. I had not cried so much since I was a little child but I could not stem the flow. The tears flowed and I wailed.

I became aware of a figure sitting down behind me, taking my shoulders and gently pulling me back to lean against him. I presumed it to be Inspector Bellamy, having made his way around to the rear of the houses. But in the back of my mind I could not really see the gruff, unfriendly policeman being so personal. I thought to turn around and see who it was but could not summon the energy to do so.

"There, there, Harry," said a voice. "Let it all out. There's no shame in it. Let it go. You'll feel better."

The figure hugged me and I felt comforted. But the voice . . . ? It sounded oh, so familiar. It's funny how the mind plays tricks in times of crisis. Mr. Stoker would have had an explanation, I know.

Mr. Stoker?

I spun around, as much as I could in that position. I gasped. The figure holding me tenderly to him was . . . Abraham Stoker!

His face was bleeding and black with smoke. His coat sleeve had been torn off, along with the shirt sleeve beneath it. His cravat was gone and his collar askew. But it was Bram Stoker! It was my boss!

"I – I . . . Sir! What . . . ?" I was at a loss for words.

"Gently, Harry," he said, relaxing his hold on me a little yet not letting go completely.

"Sir! How . . . how . . . I mean, I thought you were dead!"

"Ah! So did I, Harry. It was a bad time there for a while."

"But – what happened?"

He let go of me and rubbed his arm, which was obviously paining him.

"After I dropped you out of the window, you mean?" I nodded, mutely. "Well I must admit that I thought my time had come, Harry. Things did not look promising. The flames seemed to leap into the room behind me."

"How did you . . ." I started to ask.

He held up his hand for a moment, and eased his arms and shoulders. Then he continued. "It seems that the fire had taken its toll on the lower floors. I was contemplating leaping from the window after you, and trusting to providence to spare me on hitting the ground far below, when suddenly the whole floor collapsed."

"What?"

"Yes, the floor fell out from under me and I went hurtling down to the floor below. That, apparently, could not then take the extra weight and that floor too gave way. Along with burning floorboards and the good lord knows what else in the way of burning embers, I continued my descent to what turned out to be the ground floor." He again rubbed his arm and wriggled his shoulders. I let him take his own time. "As I tried to collect myself amid the flaming wreckage, I saw the open window beside me and managed to hurl myself through it. I landed heavily but it was on the ground floor. I then managed to crawl away from the house far enough to collect myself."

I didn't know what to say. Here I had been sitting blubbing and feeling sorry for myself and all the time Mr. Stoker had been fighting for his life. I wiped away my tears and attempted to stand up. A searing pain shot up my leg and I collapsed onto the ground again.

"Harry! You're hurt."

"Just a sprain, I think, sir. Nothing to worry about."

Late on Friday morning Mr. Stoker and myself – each cleaned up, freshly dressed, and somewhat rested – took a cab to Scotland Yard. I had borrowed a sturdy walking stick from the theatre properties department and was able to hobble about without too much pain. Dr. Cochran had proclaimed that my ankle was not broken but merely sprained; "merely" was his word. Inspector Bellamy admitted us promptly and I thankfully sank down on to a chair in his office.

"Not much left of Old Nichol Street, I'm guessing," said Mr. Stoker.

"Complete destruction," agreed the inspector. "And all because of some hothead – appropriate term, we're thinking – getting hysterical and setting fire to just one house in the street."

"At least it has allayed your reports of vampires," said Stoker.

The inspector snorted. "Vampires! We knew there was no such thing right from the start."

"And yet you were not prepared to enter the house and prove it," I said.

He glared at me. "As we stated at the time, it was important that we stay in front and direct the whole proceedings."

"And see where that got us," murmured my boss.

"We will admit that things got a little out of hand once the fire took hold."

"A little out of hand? The whole row of houses was destroyed, and the old woman who was mistakenly believed to be a vampire was lost in the flames." Mr. Stoker glared at the inspector.

He was silent for a moment. Then, "It was indeed fortuitous that you and your . . . Mr. Rivers managed to escape."

"No thanks to the Metropolitan police force," I said.

"Had you stayed in one place we would have known where to find you and might then have affected a rescue."

"If we had stayed in one place we would have been burned to a crisp," I retorted.

"Harry. Let it go," said Mr. Stoker.

Inspector Bellamy shuffled some papers on his desk. "Be all that as it may," he said, "we would like to return to the business we had in hand before this vampire nonsense took over your actions."

"*Our* actions?" I cried.

"Harry!"

"Yes, sir." I sat and seethed.

"The business of your two miscreants," continued the inspector.

"Mr. Llewellyn and Mr. Plimpton," provided Stoker. "We delivered them into your hands after they had surrendered themselves to me at the Lyceum. It is my understanding that you have them here in custody?"

"Oh yes, sir. Yes, we have them here."

"Good. Then indeed let us examine their case."

"What's to examine, Mr. Stoker? Your larger gentleman killed a man with an oak bench, on the premises of the Druid's Head tavern, after causing a disturbance. It would seem to us that in itself is ample evidence of the man's temper, not to mention his strength and wildness, such that he was almost certainly the murderer we have been seeking. To wit: the killer of your own Mr. John Saxon."

"Now hold on, inspector," said Stoker. "The one action does not necessarily connect to the other. And if we are to closely examine the one action, the death of the man in the Druid's Head was accidental. In fact it could be ascribed to an act of self-defense."

"Self defense?"

We had been over all of this before, when we had got Davey and Lonnie to surrender themselves to Scotland Yard. Mr. Stoker believed that it was only by going through the due process and following the rules – such rules as Inspector Bellamy claimed existed – that we would sort out the whole mess.

"Yes, self defense, inspector. Although technically Mr. Plimpton was defending Mr. Llewellyn rather than, or in addition to, himself. The disturbance, as you term it, was started by the man now dead and by his fellows, when they chose to pick upon Mr. Llewellyn. They had done so simply because of Mr. Llewellyn's Welsh origins and his small stature, thinking him an easy target."

"Your Taffy has only himself to blame for that."

"He is to blame for where he originated?"

"We were not present at the outset of the disturbance, nor are we able to produce those who were, so exactly who started the fracas we are unable to say."

"Fracas? That's a big word for you, inspector," I couldn't help saying. My boss waved a hand to silence me and Bellamy totally ignored me, as I knew he would.

"Have you in fact officially arrested my two men? Are they being charged with murder? If so, inspector, how can you charge both of them?"

"Taffy aided and abetted the big man. He must, then, pay the price. And as for Mr. Plimpton himself, yes, we do believe him to be the murderer we sought and he will also be so charged. We might add that your Mr. Purdy is no longer of interest to us. We never really seriously considered him. We shall remove the two officers from keeping a watch on him."

"This is all preposterous. We will not let it rest there." Mr. Stoker got to his feet. I struggled to mine. "The Lyceum does retain a solicitor, inspector. A very competent one. I shall consult with both him and with Mr. Irving and we will proceed from there. I think you will discover that you do not have the necessary evidence to succeed in what you are trying to do. Come, Harry!"

He turned and strode from the office. I hobbled after him as quickly as the pain in my foot would allow me.

Chapter Thirty-Two

Theatre life continues no matter what other dramas may be playing out. On Saturday morning I sat with Mr. Stoker, the Guv'nor, and Miss Ellen Terry, in the fifth row of the stalls, ready to watch the ladies who wanted to audition for Meg Grey's roles . . . the roles that Miss Grey would have played had she decided to remain at the Lyceum. Apparently her determination to leave and pursue this offer in the north of England had not abated. There were only two more weeks of *Othello* and it seemed strange to think of her no longer being with us. Miss Grey had been a part of the company for as long as I had been there.

"Who is first on the list, Abraham?" asked the Guv'nor.

Mr. Stoker looked at his sheet of paper. "A Miss Henrietta Butterforth. She's from the West Country. Played the Royal Court Theatre, Torquay, for the past year. Before that she was in Bude."

"Bude? I didn't know that Bude had a theatre," said Miss Terry.

"Nor I." Mr. Irving agreed.

"I strongly suspect it was an amateur production," said my boss. "She was a little vague about the details when I interviewed her."

"Hmm. And then just a year at the Royal Court," mused the Gov'nor. "What did she play there?"

"She claims to have played Calpurnia in *Julius Caesar* and Portia in *The Merchant*."

"We'll need a strong Portia, when we come back," murmured Miss Terry.

The Guv'nor nodded. "Indeed we will, but I think maybe one with somewhat more experience than it would seem Miss Butterforth possesses. No, let her go, Abraham. Who is next on the list?"

Two more hopefuls were dismissed without actually being heard and then a third given a very brief time on stage. I had learned that Mr. Irving was well able to assess an actor's potential based solely on his or her previous experience. He did, however, give as many people a chance to perform as time allowed. Halfway through the morning, and after a brief review of her theatre background, a Miss Mary Worthington took the stage.

"What have you chosen with which to amaze us?" called the Guv'nor.

"Katharina's speech to Petruchio at the end of *The Shrew*, sir."

"Good choice," murmured Miss Terry. "A little ambitious, perhaps. Let's see how she does."

"Go ahead," called Mr. Irving, and we all sat back to listen.

Miss Worthington did very well. Even I, as a humble stage manager, could appreciate her performance.

"Good projection," was Miss Terry's only comment. I took that to be approval. Apparently so did the Guv'nor.

"Do you have anything else, Miss Worthington?" he called out. "Perhaps something from *The Merchant*?"

The Lyceum was going to open its new season with *The Merchant of Venice* so I guessed that Mr. Irving was impressed enough to look forward to Miss Worthington possibly playing in that. She went on to deliver two more soliloquies, both of which Mr. Irving and Miss Terry discussed between themselves, their heads close together.

"Thank you, Miss Worthington," the Guv'nor finally called out to the woman on the stage. "Please don't leave the theatre just yet. I may have you do something else for us later on. You can find the greenroom? Good. All right. Next!"

We sat through half a dozen ladies who were desirous of joining the Lyceum. I thought they were all good, but what did I know? I was sitting there simply ready to run any errand that might be called for, not to give my input on the auditions. As it happened I was not asked to do anything, so I was able to sit back in the comfortable stall seat and relax.

"I think we are down to Miss Worthington – a very worthy young lady, if I may say so – and Miss Briggs. Would you agree, my dear?" Mr. Irving looked at Miss Terry.

"I would, Henry. I think of the two I would lean towards Miss Worthington, though it appears that Miss Briggs has a little more experience."

"And is that much older," observed the Guv'nor. "What think you, Abraham?"

My boss shrugged his shoulders. "You are the expert, Henry. But I think I see you favoring Miss Worthington and I would agree with you. I think either one could adequately take over from our Miss Grey."

"Excellent!" The Guv'nor looked pleased with himself. "If you have no objection, my dear, I think we will settle on Miss Mary Worthington. I'll leave it to you, Abraham, to work out the financial arrangements." He got to his feet, "Come, Ellen. I think we need to go looking for sustenance. It has been a long and somewhat tedious morning."

Margery Connelly, the wardrobe mistress, gave me some of the background on Meg Grey's move. I happened to seat myself at the same table as Miss Connelly when we were both taking a quick lunch in the Druid's Head, just before the matinee performance that day.

"Newcastle," she said. "That's where Meg says she's going."

"I knew she was going somewhere in the north but I wasn't certain just where," I said. "Quite a sudden move, isn't it?"

She nodded and sipped a glass of cider. "She's a bit close about it, I must say. Normally

Meg'll talk your head off, but she doesn't seem too sharing about this."

"What's the theatre?" I asked.

"There's a funny thing too." She took a bite from a ham sandwich on the plate in front of her, chewed thoughtfully for a few moments, and then continued. "One time she mentioned it and said she'd be at the Theatre Royal, Newcastle, but another time I'm sure she said it was going to be the Princess' Palace, Leeds. Of course, I may have misheard her. Or perhaps she misspoke."

"I thought I'd heard Edwina Price mention the Theatre Royal, Newcastle," I said. "Though perhaps there was a change of plan."

"But if she got an offer then she got an offer, didn't she? I mean, there wouldn't be a change of theatre, would there? And not in a different town."

I agreed. It was most unusual. "What I'm wondering," I said, "is why she is going there in the first place. I mean, nothing – in my opinion – is as good as the Lyceum. A London theatre! I mean, most actors and actresses would give their first year salary to be a part of the Lyceum. With Henry Irving! I mean, who is at the Theatre Royal Newcastle?"

Miss Connelly shook her head, chewing on her sandwich.

"No one," I said, answering my own question. "I believe E. S. Willard has played there, and Mr. Courtice Pounds, but who are they compared to the Guv'nor? No, I don't understand it."

"She said that she'd have a chance to play roles she'd never get to play here," said Miss Connelly.

"That may be true, but who will be going to see them, I wonder."

Police Constable Jimmy Hathaway came into the inn, crossed, and sat down at the next table. He gave me a cheery wave.

"Time for some grub, eh, 'Arry? 'Ow's it goin' then?"

"Jimmy," I said. "I thought Inspector Bellamy had said that he was taking you and your sergeant off the trail of Mr. Purdy?"

"'S'right!" He looked pleased with himself. "We was to report back to the Yard as slippery as you please. No lollygagging. No shirking."

"So what are you doing here?" I asked.

He affected a shocked expression. "You ain't suggestin' that I go wifout me lunch now are you, 'Arry? Gotta fortify meself before I go running back to Scotland Yard for me next duties."

"I suppose so, " I agreed. I turned to Miss Connelly. "Have you met P.C. Hathaway, Miss Connelly?"

She nodded. "I have seen the constable about; usually within reach of poor Mr. Purdy."

"No more, lady," said Jimmy. "Mr. Purdy is all on 'is lonesome so far as the Metropolitan Police is concerned."

"That is good," she said. "Because Mr. Purdy has been bothered by the likes of you for far too long. What do you think he has done? Murdered poor Mr. Saxon? I don't think so! How ridiculous!"

"Yes, ma'am. I'm sure you're right. But I just do what they tells me to do."

"Really, Miss Connelly," I interjected. "I think we all agree with you but Constable Hathaway is right. It wasn't up to him. He was just following orders."

"Ridiculous orders!" she sniffed.

"Ain't that the truth?" said Jimmy. "As a matter of fact, I got to talkin' to Mr. Purdy, off and on. 'E seems a nice enough mummer. 'E was tellin' me about 'is buddy Mr. Swindon oo's got a brother wot 'e's bothered about."

"Yes." Miss Connolly paused in raising her cider to her mouth, to nod vigorously.

"I know that," I said. "Though I really don't know too much about the brother. He's sick, isn't he? I believe he used to live not far from the theatre. I was trying to check on him some time ago but got side-tracked by John Saxon's murder. What's the latest on Mr. Swindon's brother?"

"All as I 'eard was that 'e was sick and getting' sicker," said Jimmy.

"I really don't have the details either," said Miss Connelly. "I do know that Mr. Swindon was trying to find a place for his brother to live. Mr. Swindon has only a one-room flat himself, apparently, so he can't take him in there, and it seems that the brother was turned out of his last flat simply because the landlady didn't like the look of him! Can you imagine?"

"Yes, that's what I heard," I said.

As I sat there talking it slowly dawned on me that the false wall erected in the box up by the gods might well have been put up by Arthur Swindon – possibly with Guy Purdy's help – to make a room to temporarily house his brother. Was that possible, I wondered? If so it would be temporary indeed. What hope could he have of keeping someone in such a small, cramped space? And how to feed him? The thefts from the commissariat would explain that, I suppose. But again, how could anyone live on a steady diet of pork pies, apples, oranges and ginger beer?

"Penny for 'em, 'Arry."

I looked up at Jimmy's grinning face. "Sorry," I said. "My mind was wandering. It's been a busy time lately."

"I'm sure you'll not be sorry to see that final curtain come down on the twenty-fifth," said Miss Connelly. "I know I won't. Much as I love this life and wouldn't change it for any other, I certainly look forward to those few weeks when we go dark. Helps you get your breath back, as it were."

"It does indeed," I agreed, my mind still on Arthur Swindon's brother. What other mysteries might be explained if he really was being kept hidden in the Lyceum theatre itself?

Chapter Thirty-Three

I had just finished an early light lunch, and then got dressed ready to meet with Jenny, when there came a rap on my living room door. "Living room" might be a bit pretentious. At Mrs. Bell's establishment on Chancery Lane, my flat consists of a kitchen with a tiny bedroom attached. I have bathroom privileges down the hall. A small section of the kitchen could possibly be termed the living room. The food, when I have to eat there, is atrocious and the amenities terrible, but it is conveniently located close to the Lyceum and the rent is not high. These two positives make it tolerable.

"Mr. Rivers?"

It was Mrs. Bell herself. I was surprised since she never knocks at my door except on rent day, and that was yet a fortnight or more away.

"Yes, Mrs. Bell?" I answered as I went to the door and opened it. My ankle felt much better and I had discarded the cane. "What may I do for you?"

"First thing you may do, Mr. Rivers, is advise your caller that I do not run messages for my tenants."

"Yes, Mrs. Bell. Of course. But who is my caller?"

"Constable 'Athaway, 'Arry," said a familiar voice, the figure coming up the stairs behind Mrs. Bell. "'Ere at the insistence of 'is nibs the Hinspector." He beamed at my landlady, who gave him a frigid look in return. "I will make note of your comment, madam. Apologies I'm sure, but Scotland Yard waits for no man, or so I'm told."

"So sorry," I said, as my landlady turned away to go back down the stairs. "I'll make sure it doesn't happen again." I thought I caught a "Hrmph!" in return. "Come in, Jimmy. What brings you here, and on a Sunday of all days?"

"My turn in the barrel, 'Arry. Hinspector Bellamy sent me off post 'aste, as the Froggies say, to get your Mr. Stoker. 'E, in turn, asked me to come around and collect you. You're to meet 'im at Scotland Yard."

I got my coat and we left Mrs. Bell's together. I flagged down a hansom.

"How did you get hold of Mr. Stoker, Jimmy?" I asked, as we settled back in the cab.

"It seems Hinspector Bellamy 'ad 'is address in Chelsea and actually sprung for a cab for me to go over there and get 'im. But Mr. S. insisted I come get you right away, rather than ride back to the Yard wif 'im."

It sounded serious. "Any idea what this is all about, Jimmy?"

He shrugged. "Not a pot o' glue."

I sighed. Cockney rhyming slang again, this time meaning "not a clue." The hansom made good time, since there was little traffic on a Sunday, and we swung off Whitehall and into the Yard.

"Best not keep 'im waitin'," said Jimmy.

I nodded and hurried inside.

"The inspector and 'is visitor is down in the cells," stated the sergeant at the front desk. "You'd better go on down there to 'em. They're expecting you."

He directed me to the plain cement steps descending to the lower levels. I went down, as directed, and turned along a passageway. A constable nodded to me, apparently anticipating my arrival, and unlocked a barred door partway along the passage. I went through and he locked it again behind me. There were individual cell doors beyond.

"Straight on till you see the inspector."

"Thank you," I said and went forward.

I soon came to a cell door standing open. Inside were Inspector Bellamy and Mr. Stoker, studying the cell window. This consisted of a medium-sized opening with two vertical metal bars. I merely glanced at it before addressing my boss.

"Mr. Stoker, sir. What's happening?"

"Isn't it obvious?" snapped the inspector. I took no notice of him and kept my eyes on my boss.

"Ah, Harry. Glad you could make it." He nodded in acknowledgement. "It seems the inspector has a problem."

"A problem?" snorted Bellamy. "Yes, we have a problem!"

"It seems that our two friends, Davey Llewellyn and Lonnie Plimpton, decided that the accommodations here were not to their liking." Stoker pointed to the window.

I looked more closely. I saw that neither of the bars was actually straight but bent, and that one of them had become detached at the bottom, where it had gone into the cement around the window. That substance had been broken apart sufficient to free the base of the bar.

"What happened?" I asked.

"What happened is that your two actors bent our bars apart and went out the window," snarled the inspector, through gritted teeth. "They'll not get away with this. We'll soon have them back under lock and key."

"It seems, Harry," said Mr. Stoker, pointing to the bars and the window as he spoke, "that Davey and Lonnie rethought their situation and decided not to stay after all. These Scotland Yard holding cells do not have the weight of bars found in the cells at Newgate. Our Mr. Plimpton seems to have found that the bars would bend to his efforts, enough to allow Mr. Llewellyn to climb through."

"But Lonnie couldn't have squeezed through," I said.

"No." Mr. Stoker picked up a crowbar that lay on the floor beneath the window. "They obviously thought this through quite carefully. Davey must have squeezed out and gone off to find this crowbar. He then came back and Lonnie attacked the base of one of the bars, where it was attached. He freed it so that he could then twist the bar out of the way, making a big enough hole for his large frame to exit."

"They'll not get far," repeat the inspector. "We'll soon have them back."

"Where do you think they've gone?" I asked.

"What?"

"Mr. Rivers asked – very sensibly, I must say – where you thought they would have gone on leaving here? In other words, inspector, where are you going to go to retrieve them?"

I thought that the inspector's face was extremely red, even in the subdued light of the prison cell. I could make out a vein throbbing in his forehead. He seemed to splutter as he tried to answer.

"Why, where . . . they'd go . . . we'll . . . ! Where do *you* think they'd go then, Mr. clever Stoker?"

"Well, they certainly wouldn't return to their flat in Lambeth, I'm sure. They know that would be the first place you would look."

"We have men on the way there even as we speak," said Bellamy smugly.

"Of course. Well done, inspector. Except that, as I've just said, they won't be there. They are smarter than that, I'm sure."

"So where would they go?"

"Let me see. They are both relatively new to London so I doubt they have much knowledge of safe havens. Mr. Llewellyn, of course, is from Wales."

"You think they'll go to Wales?" The inspector's voice rose. "We don't have the manpower to send men off to Wales!"

"It's none-the-less a possibility," said Stoker. "Otherwise, I suppose they might try to leave England by heading to the coast."

"We will have men at the ports," cried Bellamy. "On the Thames-side docks. Down on the Channel, at Dover and Portsmouth."

"And what about Liverpool, should they decide to make for Ireland? And how about them going up to Scotland? There are many possibilities, it would seem to me."

"We'll catch them1" The inspector's mouth was a tight thin line. "They won't make a fool of us. We'll get them, and then they'll be sorry!"

I never got to see my Jenny that day. I did manage to send a street Arab around with a message for her, explaining my dilemma. I could see that Mr. Stoker was in no hurry to return to his home and family, so we both went back to the Lyceum.

"It's a shame Bill Thomas doesn't come in on a Sunday," said Stoker. "I could use a cup of tea after that."

"Would you like me to make one, sir?" I said. "I'm sure I can dig out Bill's fixings and boil up a pot."

He waved a hand. "Don't worry, Harry. Perhaps we'll go over to the Druid's Head later, if you'd like? For the moment I'll just sit here in my office and think over this latest development."

"Of course, sir."

I took my usual seat and stretched out my legs. Since it was a Sunday I felt I could be a little at ease.

"You really think they might have made for Wales?" I asked.

He shook his head. "I would doubt it, Harry. Though I suppose it is a possibility that Scotland Yard should consider. If they are serious in wanting to recapture the two, of course."

I was surprised. "You don't think the inspector is serious?"

"As we both know, Harry, he does not always operate logically. It did occur to me that if he was unable to get his hands on Mr. Plimpton, then he would be able to pin the murder of John Saxon on him and then sit back and not have to bother with that problem any longer."

"But you don't think Lonnie did it, do you?"

"No, of course I don't, Harry. But Bellamy does, and that would be a nice tidy way for him to put that murder away as resolved."

"But we would know that there's a murderer still running around."

"Exactly, Harry. And that's why we must find him . . . or her." He got to his feet. "Come. My thirst is now joined by hunger pangs. What say we go over to the Druid's Head?"

Since it was now late afternoon, on a Sunday, it was quiet in the tavern. We took a table close to John Martin, who was at his usual station carving meat from a huge joint. I was constantly amazed that he always had the very best food in the city. There was always plenty of it and it was always served hot. Since I had had an early lunch, I decided to have my dinner early also and ordered a full meal: roast beef, Yorkshire pudding, roast potatoes, peas and carrots, smothered in thick gravy, and followed by gooseberry tart and clotted cream. I needed a large porter to wash it all down, of course. Mr. Stoker followed suit and soon we were both tucking-in to the point where there was no conversation.

It must have been a good half hour after we had entered the Druid's Head that we were joined by Police Constable Jimmy Hathaway.

"Might I join you gents?" he asked.

Mr. Stoker indicated the spare chair. "Help yourself, constable. What brings you here? I thought the inspector had you under his thumb for the day?"

"Lor' bless you, sir, no. 'Is nibs would like that, I'm sure. Would like it very much. But 'e's sent me off on a errand wot I find most salubrious."

"What's that, Jimmy?" I asked.

"Why to watch your theatre, 'Arry. 'E's thinking as 'ow them two murderers just might come skulking back to 'ang around their 'ome turf, as it were." He waved to the waitress and indicated the roast beef.

"Well first of all, Jimmy," said Mr. Stoker, "they are not – I repeat not – murderers. Regardless of what either of them may or may not have done, they have been neither tried nor convicted of any crime so far."

"Didn't that big 'un kill a man right 'ere in this very inn, beggin' your pardon, sir?"

"All indications are that he acted in self defense, or in defense of his companion Mr. Llewellyn," said my boss. "You might do well to remember that, constable."

"Yes, sir! Very definitely." Jimmy nodded his head vigorously. "You understand that the picture that is given us by our – you will pardon the expression – 'igher-ups, ain't necessarily the right picture, as it were."

"Yes. I can most certainly believe that."

"So what are you to do, should they appear?" I asked. "Not that I think they are likely to."

"Why, arrest, em!"

"You really think that a big man like Lonnie Plimpton would stand by and meekly let you arrest him?" I said. "Don't forget that, according to the inspector, Mr. Plimpton has already killed a man with nothing but one of these benches."

Constable Hathaway pursed his lips, thinking hard as he thoughtfully rubbed his chin. "Hmm. You 'ave a point there, 'Arry. Though that's what I'm supposed to be 'ere for." He was silent a moment. "You don't think they're going to come back 'ere then?"

"No, we don't," said my boss. "Not if they have any sense. And I do believe they have sense."

"Ah!" Constable Hathaway thought a moment longer and then gave a shrug and accepted the pewter platter of food delivered by Penny, the waitress. She accompanied it with a large tankard of ale, which Jimmy lost no time in starting to drink.

"So where do you think they are headin', if I may make so bold?"

I glanced up at Mr. Stoker, who seemed busy with his gooseberry tart. "The thinking is," I said, "that they may make for the Channel and a crossing to France. If they can get out of England they'll have the whole of Europe to themselves."

Jimmy nodded. "That, too, makes sense I suppose. And good luck to 'em, I says, if they are as innocent as you say."

"Innocent of the charge of murdering Mr. John Saxon," said Mr. Stoker, wiping a smidgen of cream from his mustache. "What transpired here in the Druid's Head is another matter, regarding which I believe they would not be fairly tried. All in all, I would be satisfied to see them able to start afresh in another environment."

"So 'oo do you think murdered your Mr. Saxon then, sir?"

"Ah! That is the burning question, Constable. Who, indeed?"

"The hinspector won't be lookin' for no one now, I'm thinking."

"You are correct, I'm sure." My boss sat back in his seat and pushed his now empty plate away. "So now it is up to us – and I include you in that, Constable Hathaway – it is up to us to find the true murderer."

"Yes, sir!" Jimmy nodded his head, and I felt he was sincerely interested in helping.

Chapter Thirty-Four

It had been some time since I had talked with Arthur Swindon about his younger brother. On Monday afternoon I got the chance to do just that. I was making my way backstage, knowing that I had plenty of time before that evening's performance, when I met Arthur coming the other way. At the time I didn't think to wonder where he was going nor where he had been.

"Good afternoon, Arthur," I said.

"Harry," he acknowledged, and moved to pass me in the passageway.

I stopped. "I've been meaning to ask you, Arthur, how is your younger brother doing? Did you ever find further accommodations for him?" I was aware that all indications were that Arthur had constructed the false room up in the gods and installed his brother there, but I had never actually faced him with that. "I know you were somewhat concerned about finding a place for him. How did that work out?"

He looked slightly uncomfortable and didn't look at me directly. "We are managing," he said.

I didn't want to let it go at that so I thought I'd simply come right out with it. "Arthur, I'm sure you are aware by now that Mr. Stoker and I discovered the secret room in the upper box. That *was* being used for your brother, was it not?"

He had the grace then to look me straight in the eyes. I think he seemed slightly relieved. "Yes. Yes, Harry. I – I'm sorry. It was a desperate move and one, in retrospect, I very much regret."

"Tell me about it, Arthur. If you're comfortable doing that. Why don't you come back to my office?"

He gave a sigh, nodded, and followed me to my main place of work. When we were sitting comfortably around my desk he launched into the story.

"As you know, Harry, my brother – his name is Wallace, by the way – he had been turned out of his rooms because the landlady was uncomfortable having him there."

I raise my eyebrows but said nothing.

"When you meet him, as I'm sure you will, you'll understand. Anyway, I was at my wits' end. My own rooms were insufficient for two of us. I should, in fact, say 'room' rather than 'rooms'. Like many impecunious actors, I have one room which is half bedroom and half living room."

I nodded. "Mine is not much better than that," I said.

"Anyway, Harry, I couldn't take Wallace in with me so I had to find somewhere else for him. Being unable to, I hit upon the idea of hiding him here at the theatre, at least until I could find something more stable, and it was somewhere

where I could keep an eye on him. I didn't intend for it to be long term."

Again I nodded. "I understand, Arthur. So what is the situation now that we have undermined your clever scheme?"

"I'll be honest, Harry. You and Mr. Stoker have always been fair and treated me well. I realize that I should have come to you right from the start. I just hope that you 'll bear with me through a difficult time."

"You know we will. Arthur. I know I can speak for Mr. Stoker on this. Tell me everything and perhaps together we can arrive at a more permanent solution."

The conversation led to Arthur telling me that he had now installed his brother in a room of some sort down below stage level. It could not have been a comfortable place. I knew of the existence of the "catacombs", as I felt them to be, below stage but I was far from comfortable in such spaces myself. I would break out in a sweat and feel an immediate need to return to the surface. But on occasion I had gone down there on some errand or other, usually accompanied by Mr. Stoker or Sam Green.

A thought struck me. "Arthur, when Wallace was in his little room up in the box, did he leave that at all during the night?"

"Oh, I'm sure he must have done from time to time. It was very cramped in that room we made. I only expected him to have to use it when there were people about. But I had told him only to come out at night, after the theatre was closed up. Why do you ask?"

"I was remembering Miss Terry. About a fortnight ago she had complained about hearing noises; moaning, I think she said. Could that have been Wallace, do you think?"

Arthur thought for a moment and then nodded. "Probably, yes. He is ill, you see. The doctors don't seem to know exactly what's wrong with him but he gets these terrible headaches. It's very sad."

"Yes, it must be. Well, we can't have him wandering about all over the place. Especially not down under the stage. Apart from anything else, I'm sure it's not healthy for him."

"He doesn't need sunlight, they say. Or rather, he can't stand the light. Hurts his skin and his eyes, he says. That's one of the reasons his last landlady threw him out. She thought he might be a vampire, or something! Can you imagine? There seems to be a whole lot of talk about vampires these days."

"Yes, I know," I said. "Far too much nonsense, I'm sure." I had another thought. "With no sunlight, I imagine Wallace is very pale."

He nodded. "More than that, Harry. You see, Wallace is what they call an albino."

"An albino? You mean, he doesn't have any color, isn't that the way it works?"

"That's right. His skin is almost white, his eyes are pale and red-rimmed, and his hair is snowy white. From a distance he looks like an old man."

"No wonder!" I slapped the side of my leg. "The vampire up in the gods!"

"What?"

I was excited and couldn't wait to go and tell Mr. Stoker. "Yes, Arthur. This explains a lot. We had reports of a vampire being seen up in the gods . . . a white face with red eyes! It must have been your brother. He must have peeped out from the upper box from time to time and been spotted by someone. No wonder our attendance dropped off!"

"I told him to keep in his little room whenever the play is on. I told him to stay away from people." Arthur looked distraught. "I was afraid he'd be seen and found out."

"An albino?" Mr. Stoker looked surprised. "Of course! Why hadn't I thought of that? That makes perfect sense, Harry. No wonder the poor man was chased away from normal accommodation. With the lack of color pigmentation he would almost certainly frighten many people. And I can see how he would be considered if not a vampire, at the very least the victim of such. People would believe his blood had been drained away."

"Can we help him, sir?" I asked.

"As regards accommodation, you mean?"

"Yes, sir."

Mr. Stoker looked thoughtful, raising his eyes to study the ceiling. "*Othello* has only a matter of a few days to run. If Mr. Swindon can keep his brother tucked away safely below stage for that length of time, I see no reason to disturb him. I would as soon not bring the Guv'nor into this, if possible. Arthur Swindon has done a creditable job so far; let us hope he can continue. That will at least give him another week or more to find a more permanent solution."

"Wonderful." I found myself smiling broadly.

"He must – and I emphasize the word, Harry – he *must* ensue that this Wallace remains out of sight not only of the audience but I think also of the cast and crew."

"Guy Purdy is familiar with the situation," I said.

Stoker nodded. "Yes, and that will be a help for Arthur Swindon. But we cannot judge how others might react. I'll leave it to you to keep on top of this situation, Harry."

"Yes, sir. You can count on me."

"Good man."

Keeping on top of the situation would entail my having to visit the below-stage area at least once, probably more than that. I determined to make sure that it would always be in the company of Arthur Swindon. Once or twice I started to venture down there alone but every time I found myself recalling some other "important" undertaking I had to turn my attention to right away, and that necessitated my staying at stage level.

After Tuesday evening's performance I could put it off no more and finally lingered longer than I would normally after the final curtain in order to go below, with Arthur, to actually meet his brother. We believed that most of the cast and crew had left the theatre and, taking a lamp, we ventured down to a passageway that wound off somewhere below the greenroom and dressing room areas. Arthur led the way; he seemed to have become familiar with the route. We made a couple of turns before arriving in front of an ancient door that, to my eyes, looked as though it had not been opened in a century or more. Apparently Arthur had at the very least oiled the hinges because it opened easily when he turned the handle and pushed on the door.

"It's only me, Wallace," he called out. "I've brought a friend to meet you."

I peered around Arthur and tried to see what was in the room. There was an oil lamp, with its wick turned very low, standing on the floor in a corner. It provided scarcely any light but I could make out a figure sitting huddled on the side of a makeshift bed. It looked up and I saw red-rimmed eyes reflected in the light from Arthur's lamp. Long white hair fell about the face, which was devoid of color. The figure raised a hand to shield its eyes from the fresh light and came unsteadily to its feet.

Wallace was tall and thin. He seemed to tower over me and I took a step backwards. From behind me I heard a gasp and then there came a scream. I spun around to find Sam Green standing open-mouthed, his eyes wide. He turned away and ran screaming from the little room. I cursed. He must have silently followed us down from the stage level. I had thought him to be long gone. Sam was always interested to know what was going on around the theatre – as the stagehands' foreman it was his job to keep on top of things – and I knew only too well of his fascination with vampires. He was the last person I would have wanted to encounter Wallace Swindon.

"Aagh!"

I turned back. Wallace was swaying where he stood, clutching at his chest.

"Oh, no!" Arthur thrust the lamp into my hands and moved towards his brother. The tall, white-haired figure swayed some more, moaned, and collapsed on the floor. Arthur reached his side and knelt.

"Wallace! Wallace!" he cried.

"What's happening?" I asked.

"It was the shock, I think. Suddenly to see us, and then the surprise of Sam and his screaming. Wallace is not well as it is. He's very frail. I should never have brought you!"

"I'm sorry." I didn't know what to say. "What can I do?"

"The doctor; Doctor Cochran. He hasn't actually seen Wallace but he knows my brother is very ill. If you could get him here? Hurry!"

I turned and made for the door, then stopped and half turned back. "The lamp. . ?"
I started to say.

"Take it. I've got the little one."

I ran from the room, glad to have some illumination in those depths.

I was approaching the steps up to stage level when a figure came hurtling at me, knocking me aside. I almost dropped the lamp but managed to hold onto it. The figure was Sam Green. He held his own small lamp in one hand and something else I couldn't make out in the other.

"Out of the way, 'Arry!"

He disappeared back the way I had come. I shouted after him but he either didn't hear me or ignored me. I was in a quandary: whether to go on and get Doctor Cochran or to follow Sam. I opted to follow Sam. Who knew what mischief he might be up to and Arthur's brother didn't need any more upsets? I could run for the doctor as soon as I made sure Arthur and Wallace were all right.

I managed to almost catch up with Sam by the time he reached the ancient door. I followed on his heels as he burst in. Arthur was still kneeling cradling his brother's head. Sam quickly set down his lamp and then almost jumped forward to be beside the recumbent form of Wallace. I could not imagine what was going on until I saw Sam raise his right hand high above his head.

"No! No, Sam!"

I cried out and rushed forward but I was too late. Sam brought down the hammer and drove a wooden stake into Wallace's chest.

Chapter Thirty-Five

On Tuesday morning Mr. Stoker and I prepared to visit Sam Green in jail. Inspector Bellamy had arrested him for killing Wallace Swindon. Arthur was distraught and had collapsed shortly after his brother's body had been removed. The Guv'nor, of course, had been notified and now stood silent and stern-faced while my boss explained the details.

"So you see, Henry, it seemed the best course to allow Mr. Swindon to keep his brother in seclusion, as it were, for the few days that *Othello* has to run. I didn't want to trouble you with it at the time."

Mr. Irving remained silent for a long time before finally nodding, slowly and thoughtfully. "Yes. Yes, Abraham, I can see your line of thought and who am I to naysay it. None of us, I am sure, could have foreseen the actions of . . . of our stagehand."

"Sam Green, sir," I offered.

"First the death – murder, I suppose I must say – of one of our dedicated actors, and now this murder also, of someone living beneath our very stage. This is not a pattern that I would like to see continue at the Lyceum."

"Of course not, Henry."

"You say you are away now to speak with this Mr. Green?"

"Yes, Henry. The very least we can do is to get a fuller understanding of Sam's thinking at the time. I will, of course, keep you cognizant of the situation."

"Of course. Thank you, Abraham, I will leave the matter in your hands then." He walked away, his head bowed and his brow furrowed.

Mr. Stoker and I took a cab to Scotland Yard where we spoke with Inspector Bellamy. The inspector seemed pleased with himself.

"Come in, gentlemen."

This boded well, I thought. He was at least acknowledging my presence.

"I will cut to the heart of the matter," said Mr. Stoker. "We are here to speak with Mr. Samuel Green, since he is a Lyceum employee. I am sure you have no objection?"

The inspector spread the fingers of his hands like two fans, as though to show how open his hands were.

"Please feel free, gentlemen. We are very happy to have brought Mr. Green into custody so quickly after this heinous act. He will surely hang, if only on our own evidence."

"But you weren't actually present at the time of the act, inspector."

He shrugged. "Close enough, sir. Close enough. You know the way down to the cells, we believe. We will allow you half an hour with the prisoner."

We didn't waste any more words but hurried on down the very stairs we had recently descended when viewing the broken bars left by Lonnie Plimpton and Davey Llewellyn. I noted that the door to that particular cell was now closed.

"In here, sir." The constable down at the cell level opened a door and showed us into the presence of Sam Green.

"Oh, Lor'! I'm right glad to see you, Mr. Stoker, sir," Sam cried, coming to his feet from where he had been sitting on the side of the metal cot that comprised the bed, and only seat, in the small cell. "Right glad, sir. More than I can say."

"Yes, Sam. Well . . . there is much we must discuss, I think."

"Yes, sir. Yes. Here, won't you sit down, sir?"

"Thank you no, Sam. I'll remain standing, I think."

"As will I," I said.

"Now then, Sam," said my boss, fixing him with a hard look. "From the beginning, if you would be so good? How did you come to be in that room below stage?"

Sam looked as sad as I have ever seen him. "This is dodgy, an' no mistake. I mean, I was just watchin' out for the Lyceum, as I allus does."

I noticed that Mr. Stoker raised his eyebrows questioningly but said nothing, leaving it all to Sam.

"Yes, sir. I likes to see 'oo is doin' what, if you catch my drift? Know what's going on all over, kind of thing. Anyway, I sees young 'Arry, 'ere, and Mr. Swindon 'urrying along to go below stage, and 'ere it was after midnight. Leastwise, the performance was long over and I thought as 'ow most of everyone 'ad gone 'ome."

"But you hadn't?" said Mr. Stoker.

"No, sir. Old Bill Thomas prides 'isself in making sure the place is empty afore 'e locks up and 'e relies on me to check out backstage for 'im. So I 'ad done that and was about to give the wink to Bill when I sees you, 'Arry, and Mr. Swindon, like I says, ducking down below stage. I says to myself, 'Ello,' I says. 'What are them two up to?'"

"It didn't occur to you that it had nothing to do with you but was something I was engaged upon?" I said. I felt a little annoyed to learn that my movements were being watched so closely by backstage staff. After all, my movements were no business of theirs.

"All right, Harry." Mr. Stoker nodded at me. "Carry on, Sam."

"Yes, sir. Well, I thought it was a good idea – an idea in the interest of the Lyceum, like I says – that I should see what you was up to."

"Up to?" I echoed.

"To see just what it was you was doin'," he provided. "So I follows you. I might say it was a bit tricky since I 'ad to rely on the light what you was carrying. Anyhow, I saw you go into that room. I never knew that was there, I swear. I've buzzed around down there a bit, off and on, but never got to know the 'ole layout, as it were."

"Go on," said Stoker.

"Yes, sir. Well, blow me! 'Oo do I see stand up in there but a vampire! I real, honest-to-goodness vampire!"

"What made you think it was a vampire?" my boss asked, beating me to the question.

"Well, it were obvious, weren't it? If you recall, 'Arry, I 'ad been reading *Varney*."

How could I forget? I thought. The wretched book seemed to have affected half of London. I still had thoughts of the old lady being consumed by the flames in the Old Nichol row of houses. It haunted my nights and kept me awake many a time.

Sam continued. "White skin, from 'aving 'ad his blood sucked out of 'im. Red eyes and white 'air, from lack of sunlight. Just the very look of 'im; the feel of 'im, standing there! Oh, I knew all right. I knew!"

"Except that you didn't now, Sam," said Mr. Stoker. "You had no idea."

There was a long silence before Sam again spoke.

"I don't know what you mean by that, sir. I thought as 'ow I was, in a way, protecting you. I 'ad to destroy 'im afore 'e did for you."

"And you did it by pounding a wooden stake through his heart?" I said.

"That's what you do! It's in the book. I'd got one or two sharpened stakes ready and tucked away, just in case. You just never know, I thought. If you ask me, it's a good job I 'ad 'em. I just rushed back upstairs and grabbed one, and a mallet, and came right back to put paid to 'im."

"Well you certainly did that all right." I glanced at Mr. Stoker before I went on. "In fact, Sam, it was . . ."

My boss interrupted me. "I think we might leave the full explanation for the moment, Harry. Until we have all of the facts. Then we can give Sam the details."

"Am I going' to 'ang, sir?" Sam looked pleadingly to Mr. Stoker.

"That will be up to the judge and jury, I imagine."

"Don't seem fair, in a way, now does it?" He looked to me for support but I couldn't help him.

"The coroner will decide. We will visit whoever is doing the autopsy to try to discover his findings," said my boss. "Harry and I will go along there to get the facts. We will know more after that."

"Yes, sir. Thank you, sir."

The medical examiner was our old friend Dr. Cochran. He was performing the autopsy in the morgue there at the Yard. I had once before had to visit a morgue and did not relish repeating the experience. On entering the below-pavement-level facility I felt the chill of the low temperature at which the white-tiled room was kept, and my nostrils were immediately assailed by the smell of carbolic soap. It did a relatively good job of overcoming the deeper odors of urine and human excrement, yet did not completely eliminate them. It was no wonder, I thought, that the good doctor smoked large and obnoxious cigars while he worked.

"Good afternoon, doctor," said Mr. Stoker, who seemed completely unaware of the effluvium. "We are here enquiring about Mr. Wallace Swindon."

Dr. Cochran had been bent over a naked female figure and now straightened up to look at us. He rolled his cigar from one side of his mouth to the other. I noticed a clump of ash drop from its end onto the corpse. He didn't seem to notice.

"Ah! Mr. Stoker." He spoke without removing the cigar from his mouth. Since both of his hands held gleaming metal instruments I could understand that. I looked away from the actions he was performing on the dead body in front of him.

"Have you yet had time to examine that gentleman?" my boss asked.

Dr. Cochran laid down the instruments on the body and had the grace to wipe his hands on a none-too-clean cloth slung over his shoulder.

"The albino? Most interesting. Do come in, gentlemen."

He had the grace to pull up a stained sheet over the female corpse and then crossed to the wall where large drawers could be pulled out to present further corpses. He selected one such. As the drawer slid open I saw a white arm visible from under its sheet. It was Wallace.

"We don't get many albinos in here," said the doctor. "To be frank, we don't get *any* albinos in

336

here. This is the first and, indeed, the first such that I have encountered anywhere."

"It is certainly most interesting," said Stoker. "Even to a layman such as myself."

Dr. Cochran threw off the sheet revealing dark stitches on incisions that had been made across the chest and stomach areas. Similar cuts had been made about the head, where most of the long white hair had been shaved away. Thankfully the wooden stake had been removed from the chest and the skin around the hole drawn back into place and sewn shut. My boss moved forward to look more closely though I hung back, quite content to merely listen to their observations.

"The assailant either knew what he was doing or had a good sense of where to place the pointed shaft. It entered the heart with great accuracy."

"I think it was more luck than any specific knowledge."

"His thinking was that this man was a vampire, is that right?" To me, Dr. Cochran sounded surprised.

"Oh, yes." Mr. Stoker sadly shook his head. "Regrettably there is a veritable epidemic of fear spreading across London regarding the possibility of vampires running loose and attacking the citizens." He paused. "All nonsense, of course, but you can't educate the masses overnight."

"How true."

"The person who did this was heavily influenced by a book on the subject – a fictional work, I might add – which originally appeared many years ago as tracts, or 'penny dreadfuls', as they were termed."

"I'm aware of them." Dr. Cochran nodded. "To titillate the masses. And they could certainly do that! You say they have been put together in book form?"

"Yes. It would seem that there is a fair amount of money to be made from such. But tell me, doctor, about the victim's death. Would it have been instantaneous?"

"Oh, yes," said Doctor Cochran. "But it wasn't the stake through the heart that killed him. By then he was already dead."

Chapter Thirty-Six

I didn't think I had ever seen Inspector Bellamy speechless, but that is what he was when Mr. Stoker and I returned to the inspector's office and told him what Dr. Cochran had said.

"I – I don't understand," was what the inspector finally managed to say. I think it was also the first time I had ever heard him refer to himself as "I" rather than "we". But he quickly corrected himself. "How can the doctor say that the victim was already dead when we saw the stake driven through his heart?"

"Again, inspector," said Mr. Stoker. "You yourself did not see the stake being driven into poor Mr. Swindon. Harry, myself, and Mr. Arthur Swindon were the only ones present, together with the perpetrator Sam Green, of course."

"Nonetheless, we were the first on the scene. It was we who arrested Mr. Green."

"Wrongfully, as it now turns out," I said.

"What do you mean?" The inspector swung around to look me in the eyes; another first. His face was slowly turning a deeper and darker shade of red. He was, to my eyes, angry, perplexed, desperate . . .

"Wallace Swindon had suffered a massive heat attack, according to Dr. Cochran," said Stoker. "He was dead before Sam Green had even entered the room. So what Mr. Rivers means," he spoke as quietly and calmly as he could, "is that since Mr. Swindon had already passed away when Sam drove the stake into him, then Sam could not have killed him and is therefore not guilty of murder."

"What!" The inspector's mouth hung open. His eyes were wide, as he looked first at Mr. Stoker, then at me, and then back at my boss. "But – but . . ."

"Oh, I'm sure there is some technicality that you can lay upon Sam," Stoker continued, in a consoling tone. "Attempted murder, perhaps? No, I don't think that would stand up either. Hmm! Conspiracy of some sort? No. No, that wouldn't work."

"But – but . . ."

"This is one we must leave to the lawyers, I think, inspector. Meanwhile, I presume that Mr. Green will be allowed to return to his duties at the Lyceum, at least for the present?"

The inspector was still incapable of speech but he nodded vacantly, waved a lifeless hand, and allowed us to return to the cell. There we retrieved Sam and the three of us went back to the theatre.

The events of Tuesday took the rest of that day to digest. It was a subdued, silent group of actors and stagehands that presented the performance that evening. Word had spread rapidly, of course, and

340

although neither myself nor Sam Green contributed to the gossip, the truth of the matter somehow came out. At the Guv'nor's insistence, a stand-in was quickly found to play Gratiano and Arthur Swindon retired to his solitary room to grieve the loss of his brother alone.

The next morning, leading up to the Wednesday matinee, promised to be much the same low-key affair. However, I reflected that the atmosphere was quite different from that at the time of John Saxon's demise. That had been a sudden occurrence right here in the theatre, affecting one of our own. Although Wallace Swindon was the brother of one of the Lyceum family, he was still quite unknown to virtually everyone here. Even Hugh Purdy, who knew of Wallace's existence and had been such a support for Arthur, had not known Wallace intimately. And yet there was still that connection, through his brother, enough to subdue us all.

It was therefore something of a relief – if that is the right word – when Meg Grey disappeared.

Mr. Stoker called me into his office as soon as I arrived at the theatre Wednesday morning.

"Harry, we have a problem."

"Sir?"

"I don't yet know the full story – the whys and the wherefores – but I can tell you that we are suddenly missing Emilia."

"Emilia?" I felt stupid simply repeating the name, but for the moment I couldn't place anyone of that identity.

"Emilia, wife to Iago," said Stoker. "Miss Grey's part in *Othello*."

I nodded my head, as though I had understood that all along. "What has happened to her?" I asked. "Or rather, to Miss Grey."

"That, Harry, is the question. What has happened to Miss Grey?"

I must have looked perplexed. I admit I am often not the fastest to appreciate my boss's allusions. His mind works at a far greater speed than does my own. He is, of course, juggling figures, personnel, big decisions, all day long.

"It would appear," he continued, "that after the curtain fell on last night's performance, Miss Grey quickly changed out of her costume and left the theatre. Her close friends assumed she had gone back to her lodging house but then someone later observed that all of her personal effects had been cleared from her dressing room area. Even her make-up case has gone. Miss Connelly had arranged to breakfast with Miss Grey this morning but Meg did not turn up. Miss Connelly walked around to her lodgings but the landlady advised her that Meg had left her rooms with a packed valise late last evening, stating that she would not be returning. Miss Connelly was most put out. "

I was surprised. Meg Grey had been with Mr. Irving's company for years . . . from before I joined it. It was true that she had advised the Guv'nor that she was about to move up north and continue her career there, although many of us felt this to be a wrong move for her at this time in her career. But who were we to nay-say her? To suddenly leave before the play had finished its run, and to disappear like this was unconscionable. She had, after all, agreed to stay till the end of the season, which was only a matter of a few days. What could be behind this, I wondered? Why the hurry?

"What should I do, sir?"

"I have already sent word, post-haste, to Miss Worthington. There is a chance – though I think it a slim one – that Miss Grey has not entirely left us and will appear in time for her entrance this afternoon. Yet I wonder? At her audition Miss Worthington demonstrated a familiarity with the part of Emilia. Pray that she knows more than just the major speeches. She will have to fill in at least for today's performances. Beyond that will depend on what you find out about Miss Grey."

"What I find out . . . ?" I didn't even finish the sentence. I knew the routine. I was to go off – post haste for myself too – and track down Miss Grey, or at least find out where and why she had left in such a hurry. I sighed, as it seemed I always did at this juncture, and gave my boss my best smile. "Of course, sir. I'll get on it right away and see what I can uncover."

The first stop was obviously Miss Grey's late lodgings. It was but a short walk from the Lyceum and I hurried there, enjoying the morning sunshine and feeling that things could not be all bad. I had opted to wear my straw boater in lieu of my bowler and wished I had a striped blazer, as was so popular at this time. Arriving at the address Mr.

Stoker had given me, I rapped on the door and waited.

"Miss Grey was a proper young lady, even though she was a theatrical," said Mrs. Appleyard, seated across from me in her heavily chintz-decorated sitting room. In short order she gave me her whole life history, emphasizing the fact that she had never married but had never given up hope for such a situation.

"Excuse me," I said, "but I thought you had introduced yourself as *Mrs*. Appleyard?"

She gave a slight nod and smiled as though sharing a great secret; not that I considered her capable of keeping any secrets.

"That is simply for trade, Mr. Rivers, you understand? The tradespeople are notorious for taking advantage of unmarried ladies, so I have to call myself Mrs. in order to keep them at bay, as it were."

She was old enough to be my mother yet that did not seem to dissuade her from frequently leaning towards me and smiling broadly while batting her eyelashes at me over the teapot, as she insisted upon pouring me a cup of tea.

"Miss Grey, did not entertain any young men. Not that I would have permitted it unless it took place here in this very room, with myself present."

"Of course," I said, feeling sorry for Miss Grey and any other young lady lodgers who might have hoped for privacy. "So she didn't, then, have any young men to your knowledge?"

"As I've said, none that she entertained here. Of course, what she might have got up to elsewhere is not for me to say, nor to imagine."

I could almost see her imagination running riot even as she spoke.

"Did she give any indication of where she was going when she left?" I asked, breaking into her fantasies. "We understood that she might be going to join another theatrical company up north. Possibly Newcastle?"

"Newcastle?" she cried, as though I had mentioned some dark and dangerous section of the East End. "Oh, I don't think so."

"You don't?"

"Goodness to heavens, no! Miss Grey may have had her faults but she was, deep down, a young lady of talent and of adventure."

I had never thought of Miss Grey in that light exactly, not even as a "young" lady, so I tried to get more information from Mrs. Appleyard.

"So you do know where she was going?"

She leaned forward again and spoke in a conspiratorial whisper. "Have you ever been to France, Mr. Rivers?"

"Er, no. No, I haven't."

"Nor I. I'm not one for foreign parts, I can tell you. But our Miss Grey was, as I think I mentioned, up for adventure. She told me not to tell anyone but she took off for Paris, France."

"Paris?"

"Yes." She poured herself another cup of tea, after ascertaining that my cup was still full.

"But – but did she have a job there to go to? Was it a French theatre?" This was quite a shock for me. I had never in my wildest dreams imagined that Miss Grey would leave England, especially after having made some sort of a name for herself at the Lyceum.

"I imagine it is one of those wicked theatres in Montymart, or whatever they call it. But I don't think she has gone to be a chorus girl. Oh, no! That would not be our Miss Grey. No, I imagine she has gone to put some British backbone into the plays of those foreign actors." She nodded her head as though confirming her suspicions to herself.

"Ah, yes," I said. "I'm sure you are right. Now, you are quite sure she has gone to France, Mrs. Appleyard?"

"Like I told you, gone off to Paris. She confided in me about it, of course. Asked me to keep it to myself."

"Of course," I said.

Mr. Stoker was as surprised as I had been when I told him of Mrs. Appleyard's news.

"This makes it even more of a mystery, Harry. I could see that she might, for whatever reason, decide to move on ahead of the time she had planned, to get established in the Newcastle theatre. But to go to Paris? No, surely she would have taken all the time she could in order to adjust to the country let alone the theatre. Did she speak French, do you know?"

"I really don't know, sir. I have certainly never heard her speak any foreign language. Miss

Grey didn't seem to me to be the sort of person who indulged in that sort of thing."

"No, of course not." Mr. Stoker sat thinking for a while.

"Please don't ask me to go to Paris, sir," I said.

He gave a slight smile. "Have no fear, Harry. I will not send you off to France. No, I'm afraid Miss Grey is now out of our jurisdiction."

"Mrs. Appleyard claimed that Miss Grey did not have a young man," I volunteered. "But I was wondering if such a move might not be spurred by some sort of romantic intrigue."

"Good reasoning, Harry, and my mind had been travelling the same route. Yet, on reflection, I do believe that Mrs. Appleyard is right. I can't imagine our Meg Grey being swept off her feet and into a foreign country, even by a Gallic lover. Or any sort of lover, for that matter. No, there must be more to this than meets the eye."

Chapter Thirty-Seven

Miss Mary Worthington slipped into the role of
Emilia as though she had been playing it throughout
the run. Mr. Booth had taken over the role of
Othello for that week and he seemed well pleased,
as did the Guv'nor. Her evening performance was a
duplicate of the matinee one, which showed it not to
have been a fluke. Suddenly everyone was beaming.

On Thursday morning I did a quick run
through the set, to make sure all properties had been
returned to their rightful places ready for that
evening, and then I retired to my office to start work
on what I always thought of as "the big clean-up".
This occurs at the end of every season and involves
me trying to organize and catalog what props have
been used since the start of the year . . . quite an
undertaking but necessary to keep on top of things. I
was just starting to think about lunch when Mr.
Stoker came in.

"Harry, I have a job for you, if you are not
too busy?"

"Of course, sir." What could I say?

"I'd like you to make another trip over to
Bishopsgate and the National Provincial Bank."

"Where John Saxon's strongbox resides?"

"Exactly. Cast your mind back, Harry. Did you not say that resting therein is an old theatre program showing Mr. Saxon in the role of Romeo?"

"Yes," I said. "With the Charles Kean Company. It was old. Early 1860s, if I remember rightly."

"1861." Sometimes my boss could be maddeningly precise.

"How – how do you know that, sir?"

He looked smug, closed one eye and laid a forefinger alongside his nose. "You shall see, Harry. You shall see. Here is the key. No. 37, if you recall. Now get along if you would, and bring back that treasure. Oh, and you also mentioned an envelope with Mr. Saxon's birth certificate? Bring that too. Time may be of the essence." He turned and walked away.

I looked down at my desk and the floor around it, at the countless papers and memos strewn about. I shook my head. Tomorrow will be another day, I told myself, and hurried away. Time may have been of the essence but I did determine to slip into the Druid's Head for a very hasty sandwich before hailing a hansom.

At the National Provincial Bank I faced a different clerk from the one I had first encountered. This one was not as smartly turned out as his fellow had been, nor as efficient. He seemed to be most interested in starting a conversation with a young lady typewriter operator in the office space close by. Consequently he gave my signature and request a very cursory look before bouncing off to get the strong box. When he returned with it he handed it to me, indicated the private cubicle I was to use, and hurried back to the young lady.

I was quite relieved to go through the procedure so quickly and lost no time inserting the key and opening the box. It was as I remembered it, with the old betting slips, the Charles Kean Company program, more of the cancelled checks, and the envelope with the birth certificate in it. I thought of all the work waiting for me back at the theatre and so I lost no time in picking out the theatre program and the envelope. I closed up the box, pocketed the key, and then spent several minutes trying to catch the attention of the young clerk.

Once back at the Lyceum I went straight to Mr. Stoker's office and placed my treasures on his desk.

"Ah! Well done, Harry," he said, as he picked up the program. "Now look here."

He opened the top drawer of his desk and brought out an object, which he laid down beside the program. I caught my breath. It was a second program that, to my eyes, looked identical to the one I had just brought back.

"Is that the same, sir?"

"The exact same, Harry."

"But I don't understand. If you already had the one then why did you need the other?"

"Here is where it gets interesting," he said, sliding the two programs around so that I could see them fully. "Both are for a Charles Kean production of Romeo and Juliet, both from Thursday June 27, 1861. One of these, as you know, was kept by John

Saxon as a memento, since he played the part of Romeo."

"And the other?"

"The other was in the detritus left behind in her dressing room by Miss Meg Grey."

"Don't tell me she played Juliet," I said. I knew that she was fifteen years John Saxon's senior so I would have been surprised if such had been the case.

Mr. Stoker shook his head. "No, Harry. But she was in the production. She played the part of the Nurse to Juliet. Her name is much lower down so I'm not surprised we didn't notice it especially."

"I am certainly surprised to see that they were both with Mr. Charles Kean and both in the same play, back then," I said. "But . . . ?" I knew there had to be more to this than just that coincidence.

Mr. Stoker picked up the envelope I had also brought back. "I'm glad you remembered to bring this, Harry." He dipped into it and pulled out the large folded form that was a birth certificate. I was surprised to see that there was more than one such document there. I leaned forward as my boss opened them out.

"Ah, yes. Mr. Saxon's birth certificate, as we suspected. And also, see Harry, a marriage certificate."

"His parents'?" I asked.

"No." His finger traced the names. "It is for the marriage of Mr. John Saxon and Miss Margaret Grey."

"Margaret Grey? Our Meg Grey?" I was stunned.

"Indeed. I think it all now falls into place, Harry."

Not for me it didn't, so I kept my mouth shut.

"You recall the envelope from the solicitor that you originally retrieved from the strong box? And you discovered that John's business with that gentleman was for a divorce?"

I nodded.

"And do you further recall the Christmas card on the wall of John's lodging; the one of the cottage, which you so ably traced to Devon?"

"Of course, sir. How could I forget Paignton and Tor Bay?"

"The card was inscribed and signed by a Margaret."

A glimmer of light came into my head. "Margaret! Our Miss Grey!"

"We always call her Meg rather than Margaret, do we not?" said Stoker. "No wonder we didn't connect the two immediately. I blame myself for that."

"So Orchard Cottage was probably their honeymoon cottage," I said.

Mr. Stoker tapped the marriage certificate. "That ties with the date of their marriage. Then there is the fact that the lady you spoke with in Devon did say that the young wife's name was a color, if I recall? Brown or Green . . . Not Green, but Grey!"

"It was all there, sir," I said.

"Indeed it was, Harry. We were blind not to see it."

"So again, sir, what does this tell us?"

Mr. Stoker looked serious. "There is even more to this story, Harry. What was the name of the young lady who played Juliet?"

I looked down at the program. "Jane Summerfield," I said, and then stopped and looked up at him. "Summerfield? Isn't that the name on the checks that Mr. Saxon was paying out so regularly?"

He nodded. "It is." He sat back in his chair and steepled his fingers. "Here is my conjecture, Harry. Listen carefully. Hear me out. Then tell me if I am wrong."

Me tell Mr. Stoker that he was wrong? I doubted that would happen but I sat down in the chair in front of his desk and listened.

"The married couple of John Saxon and Margaret Grey are engaged in Mr. Charles Kean's admirable Shakespearean company and are cast in *Romeo and Juliet*. However, much as they might have liked to play the leads together, it is John who is cast as Romeo and Margaret who is passed over and given the minor role of the Nurse. In the role of Juliet a young, and we may presume attractive, young lady named Jane Summerfield is cast. As rehearsals proceed and then the production blossoms, John and Jane are – as the play demands – required to act out various love scenes. Now bear with me, Harry, this is just what my mind sees as a possibility, albeit a very strong possibility."

"Yes, sir. Of course." I now sat on the edge of my seat, caught up in the story.

"John and Jane are of an age, while we know that Miss Grey - or Mrs. Saxon, as she actually was – is older by more than a few years. John and Jane fall in love . . . or perhaps just lust. These things happen, there is no denying. We do know that shortly after this, the Saxons divorced."

"And the checks?"

"All in good time, Harry." He sat forward and again perused the programs, then continued. "I am no storyteller, Harry. This is probably all nonsense. But supposing things did go as I've just suggested and that, as a result of this 'attraction' between our Romeo and Juliet that Juliet, or Jane, conceived a child? The world of the theatre being what it is, they may or may not have decided to marry, after John got his divorce. Either way, I think I knew John Saxon well enough to say that he would most certainly have done the right thing and contributed to the upkeep of mother and child."

"The checks!" I cried.

"Exactly. The checks, made regularly over many years, were John Saxon's payments to his child and the child's mother." He again sat back, this time looking very pleased with himself. "What do you think, Harry?"

"I think you have hit the nail on the proverbial head," I said. "What I don't understand is how Mr. Saxon and Miss Grey were able to both be a part of the Guv'nor's company here at the Lyceum. And for several years."

"I agree," my boss said. "It's hard to understand. But it is many years since the Charles Keane Company was a force. I think that after the years that have passed, John and Meg both made peace with the cards that Life had dealt them. It is just for the past three or four years that they have come to meet again and both become members of the Lyceum family. I think they came to tolerate one another here. In retrospect it seems there was never any particular interaction between the two here, other than what was called for in any particular roles they were playing."

"Well, sir, that was a most interesting story. But where does it leave us?"

Mr. Stoker again opened the top drawer of his desk and brought out a sheet of paper. "Back in May, in the early weeks of *Othello*, a young lady applied for employment but I had to turn her away. I've since learned, from Bill Thomas of course, that she tried to get one of our regular actors to exercise some sort of influence on her behalf."

"John Saxon?" I hazarded.

He nodded. "The young lady was Miss Jane Sommerfield. Whether she had been pursuing her acting career after having her child or whether she has only just decided to return to the stage, I do not know. However, she applied to the Lyceum and hoped that John Saxon, through their past relationship, would be able to bring her into the Lyceum family."

"And did Miss Grey know of this, sir?"

"That is what I don't know for certain, Harry, but it is my suspicion that Meg Grey did find out about this reappearance of her rival and old feelings erupted to where she felt she could not tolerate Miss Sommerfield's intrusion."

"And . . . ?" I knew there had to be an "and".

"John Saxon's death occurred just two days after Miss Sommerfield applied to come here."

There was a long silence.

"You – you think that there is some sort of connection between the attempted intrusion of Miss Sommerfield and the murder of John Saxon." It was more a statement than a question. "You think Miss Sommerfield killed John?"

"Or Meg Grey did."

Chapter Thirty-Eight

It was Friday, 17 June, 1881, the penultimate day of the Lyceum's *Othello*. Mr. Irving, the Guv'nor, was playing Iago with anticipated bravura performances for both today and tomorrow. The entire theatre seats were sold out for both days, including all of the gods.

At ten of the clock in the morning I stood at the rear of Mr. Stoker's office and looked on as Inspector Bellamy blustered and shouted at my boss, as though Mr. Stoker was one of his long-suffering constables.

"Do you not realize, *sir*, that another few minutes and your Miss Grey could have been on her way to the Continent and freedom and there would have been nothing we could have done about it?"

"Only too well, inspector," said my boss, unfazed by the remonstrations of the policeman. "Why do you think I advised you to send men to Dover and Calais, to look for her and apprehend her?"

"Ten more minutes . . . no! Five more minutes and she would have been on that boat and pulling away into the English Channel."

"If you had sent your men promptly, instead of spending time arguing with me, you would have had plenty of opportunity to apprehend her."

"She could have been on her way to Paris, thumbing her nose at Scotland Yard and the Metropolitan Police Force."

"And at its inspector. Yes, we know. But the bottom line is that she did not board the boat, it did not leave these waters, and she is now in your custody. Am I not correct?"

The inspector mumbled something I did not catch and threw himself down into the chair in front of Mr. Stoker's desk. I was happy to remain standing as a spectator.

"We gave out instruction that the woman is to be brought directly to us here, in your office. It seems fitting that we should hear her confession in this very theatre where the murder took place," he finally said, in a quieter tone.

"You think she will confess then?"

"What? Why . . . from what you told us . . ." He was again agitated.

"I gave you my thoughts on what might have taken place, inspector, but I think you will need more than that for a conviction."

"Miss Grey is the one who murdered Mr. Saxon."

"You are, then, crossing Mr. Lonnie Plimpton off your list? Along with Mr. Guy Purdy, whom you were so convinced was your man. Then, wasn't there some doubt in your mind about the innocence of Mr. Bidwell, our front-of-house manager?"

The inspector remained silent. I must admit, there was not a great deal he could have said. No one said anything for a while, before the inspector pulled out his pocket watch, studied it, and then thrust it back into his waistcoat.

"Sergeant Fairview and Constable Hathaway should be here any minute now, with the prisoner."

"Yes. Well you will pardon me if I get on with my work, which at the moment is more important, in my mind." Mr. Stoker pulled a ledger in front of him and proceeded to busy himself checking entries.

I relaxed a little as the tension in the room eased, but I remained standing at the back of the office, hoping not to catch the eye of the inspector.

There came a knock at the door and, almost before Mr. Stoker could answer, it opened to reveal the red face of Sergeant Fairview peering in. He looked happy to see the inspector there.

"We came as fast as we could, sir."

Bellamy got to his feet. "You have the prisoner?"

"Oh yes, sir. She's given us no trouble."

The sergeant pushed the door wide open and, uninvited, came in with Miss Grey behind him and Constable Hathaway bringing up the rear. The room started to feel crowded.

"Please take a seat, Miss Grey," said my boss, coming to his feet. "Inspector, if you would please allow the lady to sit?"

With a twirl of her skirt, and compressing the crinoline, Miss Grey squeezed past the policeman and sat on the seat in front of Mr. Stoker's desk.

"All right; I'm here," she said. "Now what is it you want? Why was I forcibly removed from the cross-channel steamer?"

"We think you know why," said Bellamy.

"Miss Grey," said Mr. Stoker. "I wonder if you would be kind enough to correct, if necessary, some thoughts that I have had. For example, we know that you and John Saxon were married at one time. Did the separation and divorce come about because of Miss Jane Sommerfield?"

The mention of that name brought a very noticeable change to Miss Grey's face. She pressed her lips together, narrowed her eyes, and to my ears her voice had hardened when she replied.

"Jane Sommerfield is a scheming woman. She stole John from me. I despise her."

"Here!" cried Inspector Bellamy. "Who's this Jane Sommerfield?"

Mr. Stoker ignored him. "She played Juliet opposite John's Romeo, did she not?" he asked of Miss Grey.

"That's something else she stole. That part should have been mine."

I was surprised. Even back in 1861 I think she would have been too old to play the young lead.

"Who's this Juliet?" demanded Bellamy.

"And now she has come sneaking around again. I wasn't going to stand for that. Once was enough."

I couldn't help myself. I had to ask.

"Was it you up in the gods with Mr. Saxon the night he fell from the balcony?" I asked.

"I was leading up to that very question, Harry," said Mr. Stoker, "but it is as well to cut to the chase. Miss Grey?"

She had turned to look at me. I don't think she had realized I was even in the room. She gave me brief acknowledgement with the slightest of inclination of her head.

"Mr. Rivers. So you are part of this team of inquisitors also, are you?"

"Would you answer the question?" said Bellamy, who had apparently decided to join the "team", if that was what we were.

"I was up in the gods with John, yes." She did not elaborate.

"You were arguing," said Stoker. "Your loud voices were heard, as it happens, though not what was said."

"Yes, we were arguing! John had told me about their child. I hadn't known before. And would you believe what they named her?"

No one ventured a guess, so she continued.

"Juliet," she said, spitting out the name. "Juliet, of all names. I couldn't have children, did you know that?" Again, no one answered. "But she could! Oh, yes. I'm sure that made John happy. He always wanted to be a father."

"What happened, up there in the gods?" asked Mr. Stoker, softly.

After a long silence she shrugged her shoulders resignedly. "It was as I said, we argued. We blamed each other."

"Did it become physical?" asked Stoker.

"Eventually, though I hadn't wanted it to go that way. As you know, I am bigger than John; taller. He was always a gentle soul, that's what I liked about him. But he got very angry, shouting in my face. Then I have to admit that I lost my temper. I pushed his shoulder and tried to slap his face, though it was only a glancing blow."

"Go on," urged the inspector.

"We were down at the front of the gods, face to face at the foot of the aisle. When I struck out at John he jumped up onto the front row bench. I think he was planning on getting around me. He didn't even try to defend himself. But I again struck out at him."

"And?"

"And it caught John off balance. He fell backwards, striking his back across the retaining rail. For a moment – it seems like a long moment; an eternity now – he hung on the rail and then toppled over the side."

"He fell," put in the inspector.

"Yes. He disappeared from view. I spun around and leaned over to see him. He bounced off the balconies below before landing on the stall seats far below. I was sick; almost physically so. I think for a moment I might have fainted."

Her face was chalk white. Her eyes were unfocused as she relived the moment in her memory. I felt for her. With the love-hate relationship that had developed between them, I couldn't imagine what John Saxon's death must have meant to her.

"And then you recovered enough to run from the building," said Bellamy.

"Yes."

"Margaret Grey I must arrest you for the murder . . ."

"It was an accident," she protested.

"You hit him!"

"Yes, but – but . . ."

"Self defense?" I offered.

"John did not strike back, according to what Miss Grey says," observed Stoker. "No, I'm afraid this is something that will have to go to a judge and jury."

"Then so be it." Miss Grey stood up and extended her wrists.

"I don't think there is any call for that, is there, inspector?" Mr. Stoker looked pointedly at the policeman.

"Er – er, no. No, we don't suppose there is. Sergeant, please take Miss Gray back to the Yard. We will return shortly . . . after we have had a few words with Mr. Stoker here."

A group of Lyceum principles gathered upstairs at Romano's Vaudeville Restaurant, on the Strand, after the final curtain on Saturday. I was happy to be among them, though it entailed having to borrow a dinner jacket from the wardrobe department. It was the first time I had actually dined at Romano's, which was a legendary eatery. It was owned by a small, dark, Russian gentleman with a large mustache and a big smile. It was rumored that many theatrical deals were made over a table at Romano's. It was a favorite place for Mr. Irving.

The Guv'nor sat at the head table, with Mr. Edwin Booth, Miss Ellen Terry and my boss, Mr. Abraham Stoker. I was some way down; "below the salt" as they used to say. Bill Thomas was on my one side and Timothy Bidwell on the other. We all sat back with our coffee and liqueurs and digested the excellent meal we had just devoured. My memory is a little hazy but I seem to recall Julienne soup, soles à la Normandie, mutton cutlets with mashed potatoes, haunch of venison, pigeon pie, Brussel sprouts, peas, carrots, parsnips, ragoût of lobster, boiled fowls and bacon, plum pudding, apple tart, fondue à la Brillat Savarin, apricot jam tartlets, and much, much more.

"You would think that, after all this time, one would get used to dining at midnight, would you not?" asked Mr. Bidwell.

I nodded. "Indeed, though I don't know if one ever truly does get used to it. But I must say that by the time we started eating I had worked up quite an appetite."

He chuckled in agreement.

"*Othello* was a good run and no mistake," said Bill.

"One of the best," I agreed. "I think it made quite a stir in the theatre world for us to have Mr. Booth here."

"The Guv'nor is always at his best as Iago," said Bidwell. "Though I have to admit that I do like his Shylock. I really look forward to next season."

We were interrupted by Mr. Irving standing and tapping the table with the handle of a knife. All conversation died and all heads turned to face him.

"Miss Terry, Mr. Booth, my friends. Once more we have come to the end of a successful run. I do not hesitate to label it as successful. We do not measure our success by house seats sold nor by praise garnered in the press. No. We measure success purely by our own satisfaction. And I would like to go on record as being extremely satisfied with this production."

There was an enthusiastic round of applause with certain gentlemen, who had indulged more than adequately, banging their tankards on the table or raising their glasses for one more swallow.

"This has been a remarkable time," continued the Guv'nor. "We have had the honor and the pleasure of hosting our American cousin as he delighted our friends and neighbors, showing this Sceptered Isle that the genius of the Bard is not restricted to our shores."

"What?" whispered Bill.

"Ssh!" said Mr. Bidwell.

"Oh, we have had our adventures," continued Mr. Irving. "Yes, indeed. And we have had our casualties along the way. Most recently – and here I must admit to a personal feeling of loss – there was the murder of one of our finest actors . . ."

"Mr. Saxon would never have heard the Guv'nor call him that while he was alive," commented Mr. Bidwell. I nodded.

". . . and then the discovery that the perpetrator was one of our own finest actresses."

Miss Terry chose that moment to take a long drink from her wine glass rather, perhaps, than acknowledge Miss Grey to have been of that caliber.

The Guv'nor went on to praise various members of the Lyceum family, though not surprisingly I did not hear myself mentioned. He then spoke enthusiastically about the coming season and urged us all to get some rest and relaxation while we might so that we could come back to make *The Merchant of Venice* yet another great success for the theatre. By the time he sat down I found myself repeatedly nodding off and jerking awake again. I was glad when the speech-making was over and we were allowed to stand up and move around a little, for a last chance to socialize.

I found myself standing next to Mr. Stoker, as though I hadn't not seen enough of my boss over the past several months. Not that I was complaining, for I truly respected Mr. Stoker and had great regard for all that he said and did.

"So it's all over for now, Harry," he said, smiling as he looked about him. "Do you have plans for the break?"

"My big plan is to go and see Miss Jenny Cartwright tomorrow, sir," I said. "I missed seeing her last Sunday. And I do hope to see something of her while the theatre is dark."

"Well said, Harry."

I paused a moment and then asked something I had been wondering. "What do you think will happen with Miss Grey, sir? Did she really murder John Saxon or was it an accident?"

"Ah! Did he fall or was he pushed? That is the question that has been asked ever since Humpty Dumpty fell off the wall. From Miss Grey's own account of what happened – and let us not forget that she is the only living person who actually knows – it was an accidental result of her striking out at John Saxon, yet without the intention of truly harming him. As I told the unfortunate lady, I think that blame may only be placed by a judge and jury, after due deliberation."

"Yes, but what do you think, sir"

He paused for a long time, so that I began to think that he wasn't going to answer me. Then he did reply.

"I believe that for murder to be committed there needs to be intent in the mind of the person committing it. I do not believe, for one moment, that Miss Grey had that intent. I do believe, and can understand, that she was greatly agitated at the thought of John and this younger Jane Sommerfield casting her aside, as it were. No woman likes to be told, if only by implication, that she has become old. In this case the matter of child-bearing obviously enters into it. No, Harry. I do not believe that she murdered John Saxon in the legal meaning of the word. I just hope that the jury will take the long view and put her actions in perspective."

I very much agreed with him. "And what is going to happen with Davey Llewellyn and Lonnie Plimpton?"

He sighed. "They have made off to the relative safety of the Continent, yet other than having escaped from what was actually wrongful imprisonment, they are not guilty of anything. It is a shame that the impetuous action of our Inspector Bellamy should have deprived us of two very useful stagehands. Who knows, Harry? Perhaps one day they will find their way back to us. We will just have to wait and see."

"And have we seen the last of vampires, sir?" It was a slightly more lighthearted question, I felt.

Mr. Bram Stoker smiled. "You will never hear another word about vampires from me," he said.

So I finally left the celebrations and made my way back to my lonely rooms at Mrs. Bell's establishment on Chancery Lane. It was relieved to finally sink down into my bed, such as it was, knowing that on the morrow I would see Jenny.

49316428R00209

Made in the USA
Middletown, DE
12 October 2017